TR

&
THE
SEARCH FOR
KAUNN

BY

J E STIRZAKER

To John
With best wishes
J E Stirz

BOOK 2

Published by New Generation Publishing in 2015

Copyright © John E Stirzaker 2015

First Edition

The author asserts the moral right under the Copyright, Designs and Patents Act 1988 to be identified as the author of this work.

All Rights reserved. No part of this publication may be reproduced, stored in a retrieval system or transmitted, in any form or by any means without the prior consent of the author, nor be otherwise circulated in any form of binding or cover other than that which it is published and without a similar condition being imposed on the subsequent purchaser.

www.newgeneration-publishing.com

 New Generation Publishing

Chapter One

The days turned into weeks. Every day was the same. We were up at 7 o clock for our walk before breakfast; weather it was hail, rain or snow. They did not mind what the weather was like, all you heard from Mrs. Pickersgill, (the Matron of the home through her loud domineering voice) that it was good for you. She was not bothered if you froze or not. The only thing to look forward to was school days with Mr Trinity. How he taught us how to read people's minds and their thoughts, also their body language and the way they moved. All this would stand us in good stead if we ever came across any danger. However he was insistent that what he taught us we only used against evil people whom we may come across on our travels through life.

Mr Trinity's lessons were not about magic wands and turning people into frogs or toads or other inexplicable creatures. As mentioned before it was mind games, Mr Trinity could stop people in their tracks if they tried to run away, he could bring them under control with just his thoughts and bend them to his will. Of course we had to do the boring lessons as well, maths and history, English and geography, just like normal school but the special lessons were the best of all. As Mr Trinity informed everyone in the school classroom, it would take a long time to learn everything and to be ready to go out into the big wide world.

One morning as we all sat at our desks, Mr Trinity said "Boys I have something to tell you", in a calm soothing voice he spoke "I have to go away on a short trip, don't worry I will be back to carry on with your lessons when I return".

"Right", "take out your books and we will take the first lessons maths" he said. Everyone started groaning at the thought of doing the most boring lessons of all. The day seemed to drag by ever so slowly. I could not concentrate all that day and I think Mr Trinity noticed that I was not paying much attention. He was giving me a piercing stare with those deep blue eyes which looked like two pieces of ice. They reflected in the sunlight that came through the schoolroom window. Suddenly the school bell rang for the end of the days lessons. Everyone began to put away the books in their desks and then slamming the desktop lids down in unison. The noise was like thunder, you could sense Mr Trinity was not at all pleased by the show of our displeasure at him leaving us in the care of another teacher who would just give us the same boring everyday lessons that other schools received.

"Boys, Boys", Mr Trinity said, "be patient with me, I cannot put off this trip" he said". "It is really very important that I go, I will tell you all about it when I get back". That seemed to cheer everybody up and we all began to smile. "Right now" he said, "time for tea and I will see you all when I get back". With those final words he walked past us and out of the schoolroom door to his small cottage that he occupied at the edge of the trees just beyond the school grounds. We all shuffled along to the dining hall for our tea where everyone sat in complete silence. All you could hear was everybody's teeth chomping away, and then looking to one side at Mr Trinity's empty chair.

    I decided I was going to find out where Mr Trinity was going I was not going to wait till he came back. I was curious as to what was going on and where he was going to and whom he would meet. I took a chance last time and everything turned out fine.

    I decided this time I would not take Sutherland with me. Sutherland could not remember our last adventure so what would be the point in taking him with me this time, I would wait until it got dark and then make my way to Mr Trinity's cottage and hopefully follow him if I could without him noticing me, which would be difficult knowing of his extraordinary perception and how uncannily he knew every move you made and all your thoughts before you made them. I would just have to brave it out and try not to get caught. I lay on my bed for a while until Mrs. Pickersgill came in ringing the bell up and down in her huge left hand and shouting in her booming voice "Bed time, come on, into your pyjamas and into bed with you", "hurry, hurry" she said. She was walking up and down the floor past everybody's bed. I had put my pyjamas on over my school uniform and buttoned them up to my neck and jumped between the sheets. The top blanket tucked under my chin so all you could see was my head sticking out of the sheet. I just hope she had not noticed anything untoward. Mrs Pickersgill headed for the dormitory door, turned round and said "Goodnight boys". She then switched off the light and left the room closing the door behind her.

The room was now plunged into complete darkness, all you could hear was the wind in the trees as it moved through the branches. The leaves casting eerie shadows on the dormitory walls as the moon peeped through the passing clouds. I lay there for what must have been about two hours, daring not to move and pretending to be asleep. I was finding it very difficult to keep awake but I had to, I had to find out what Mr Trinity was up to and where he was going. Curiosity was getting the better of me. I lifted my head up from my pillow and looked around the dormitory, everyone was fast asleep. No one was moving, there was just the odd snore, and muttered word as they slept on. It was probably Sutherland, he had a tendency to snore and mutter in his sleep the most indescribable words which made no sense at all. I did not want to wake him; I was going alone this time.

There was no point in taking Sutherland as I knew he would not remember anything, just like last time. I did not have time to explain everything to him. I looked around once more just to make sure everyone was sleeping. Slowly I removed my pyjamas from over my school uniform, took my hat from out of my bedside cabinet along with a short length overcoat, this was in case it became cold as I did not know where Mr Trinity was going. I also had my school satchel with a few sandwiches I had smuggled out of the kitchen that night. I had managed to sneak away the food only because I had volunteered to help Mrs Meek, the cook, to wash up. She did not suspect anything; she thought I was a good boy and did not know I was only using her to get what I wanted for my journey that night. I was ready now, I looked around once more then slowly eased open the large sliding door of the dormitory just enough so I could squeeze through. I stepped into the dark night and slowly closed the door behind me. I stood there for a couple of minutes to get accustomed to the darkness all around me. My heart was beating fast, thump, thump, thump, like the sound of a train as it sped along over the tracks. Clickity clack, clickity clack, no going back, no going back. I took a few deep breaths and set out across the field towards Mr Trinity's cottage at the edge of the trees just in the distance.

You could just see the light in the distance emitting its glow from the small window at the front of the house. I knew that by being there before the door was round at the side of the house between two large oak trees whose branches hung low over the roof. It looked as if the tree was holding the cottage in some form of embrace. I slowly crossed the field stopping now and then and looked all around me to make sure I was not being followed by anyone my heart thumping in my chest. I crept nearer and nearer towards the small cottage window.

As I reached my destination I could see Mr Trinity's shadow moving across the wall, back and forth it went. He was pacing up and down. As I neared the window I got down on my hands and knees and crept slowly until I was under the window. I slowly raised myself up until my eyes could just see into the room. Sure enough Mr Trinity was pacing up and down in front of the fire. He had his long thin bony left hand under his chin, his long thin fingers stroked the right side of his cheek and his blue eyes just kept staring at the floor as he paced up and down deep in thought. I just watched, not daring to move in case he heard or saw me. What was he thinking I wondered, when he would make his move and remove the carpet that covered the glass mirror to the entrance of his world. Surely soon he would go then I could follow him just like before when Sutherland and I had followed him. Mr Trinity just paced up and down, back and forth, and every time he walked past the fire that was burning brightly in the hearth he cast an eerie shadow on the cottage walls, like some mysterious ghostly apparition.

As he paced back and forth he just kept muttering to himself, the only word I could hear through his muttering was the word Kaunn. That name made my blood curdle and Kaunn's words kept coming back to me, the words he had said to Mr Trinity as he disappeared into the distance after the bloody battle with Dr Zaker. "We will meet again Mr Trinity, we will meet again". I could still hear them in my thoughts and every time I thought about them it sent shivers down my spine. I could understand now why Mr Trinity was so perplexed Kaunn would do anything to try and regain control of Mr Trinity's world Sofala. I could not quite hear what he was saying so I decided to move round to the side of the cottage towards the front door. I slowly crept through the bushes and through the trees towards the door, the night was darkand the trees made an eerie noise as the leaves brushed back and forth over the roof tiles of the small cottage.

The clouds cleared in front of the moon and I could see the small door in front of me. A faint beam of light shone through the small diamond shaped window that was in the centre of the wooden door, the light in the window would disappear now and then as Mr Trinity's shadow went past the window as he continued to pace up and down. The closer I got my shoulders began to brush past the overgrown brambles that lay either side of the small crazy paved path that I was walking down very slowly, stopping now and then to take a deep breath. My heart was pounding so I decided to stop for a couple of minutes to calm myself down.

Chapter Two

I was only a couple of feet from the door, I could make out the white paint on the door which was now a dull grey, it was cracked and flaking off in places leaving the wood underneath a dark grey. I slowly put one front in front of the other and got closer to the door, I took a deep breath and put my hand on the cold round brass doorknob that was now a dull green from lack of polishing. As my hand gripped the doorknob, it flew open and a long hand reached out, grabbed me by the front of my school blazer, and pulled me through the open door. I was pushed to the floor in front of the fire. I slowly looked up and there in front of me stood Mr Trinity, his arms folded across his chest and looking down at me. His blue eyes piercing into mine, "what do you want?" he asked in a deep angry voice, "well" he said again, "what do you want", this time it was louder than the first. I plucked up the courage and stammered in a small squeaky voice my whole body was shaking with fright, I had never seen Mr Trinity this bad tempered, he always seemed so calm. "I was curious" I replied. "Curious" he shouted, "you were curious", "yes" I said back. "I am sorry Mr Trinity" I said, "I really am very sorry."

That is not good enough at All" "please, please don't send me back to school" I begged, let me come with you "Please", I said in my best grovelling voice which I could turn on when I wanted to which usually made people change their mind. I had learnt a lot at the home and I was trying to get by the best I could because it was not easy in a home of forty boys. Mr Trinity picked me up with his thin bony hand and sat me down on a small stool by the fire. He stared at me with his deep blue eyes and I could tell he was reading my thoughts. I turned away from his stare and began to look around the room; it was just the same as it was the last time I had been here. The sideboard underneath the small window the cupboard where Sutherland and I had watched Mr Trinity disappear through the glass mirror in the middle of the floor and there was the carpet, the same carpet with bits missing leaving bare patches in the carpet. A single bed lay in the corner of the room covered by a grey wool blanket. At the other side of the room stood a sink with a cupboard underneath and a small cooker with pans on top and a small black kettle. Above this was a wall cupboard that I surmised Mr Trinity kept his tea and sugar and other utensils. A door was at the other side of the fireplace with a sign on it saying 'bathroom'. It was very sparse but I suppose it suited Mr Trinity. He was not a person for material wealth of any kind; he just lived a simple life. The only enjoyment he received was his books that lay on top of the sideboard. They were piled up in rows next to each other and they looked really old. I sat looking at the books and wondering which one was the magic book I had read from and which had sent Sutherland and me through the glass mirror in the floor. "Ahh" Mr Trinity said, his voice beginning to mellow "I see you are admiring my books, John he said! 'Those books are centuries old" he said. "They have been passed down for hundreds of years for the scholars in my world of Sofala to learn from and they have now been past to me and when I am no longer here they will be, passed on to someone else whom I think will be worthy to carry on with my teaching to other people, and that person will pass them on to someone else and so on he said.

Besides we all cannot live forever can we. Mr Trinity took a book from the pile of books that lay on top of the sideboard. 'Here he said take a look, he had calmed down now; I held the book in my hand and ran my fingers over the cover. It was beautiful the leather was covered in a strange pattern all the letters were etched in gold I ran my fingers over the gold letters and as I touched them my fingers began to tingle; Mr Trinity told me that what I was feeling was the magic power of the book. Mr Trinity told me that it was centuries old. I slowly opened the book it was exquisite it looked like the ancient books that I had seen in museum of ancient history which we had visited on one of our day trips from school, but this was much better. The colours and pictures' jumped out at you from each page you turned. All the writing was in gold leaf and the coloured drawings on each page was of Mr Trinity's world of Sofala, the most beautiful scenery and buildings I had ever seen. Mr Trinity reached out and took the book from my lap closed it and put it back on the sideboard! 'You will have to go back now John you cannot come I have to go and meet master Remlin he said, and I do not think he would be very pleased if he saw you, again Mr Trinity said." Please let me come I pleaded! Mr trinity pointed to the door, which as if by magic slowly opened by itself, I shuffled slowly towards the door my head bent down upon my chest my shoulders hunched forward as if I was very sad at leaving, but I was not going to give up that easily. I passed through the open door I turned around slowly and took one more look at Mr Trinity he stood there his arm outstretched pointing his long bony finger at me. As I looked the door started to close slowly towards me and then slammed with a bang, making the whole doorframe shake. I waited for a few seconds, and then I looked through the small round window in the centre of the door. Mr Trinity had removed the carpet and he was standing in the centre of the glass mirror": he snapped his fingers and one of the books that lay on the sideboard slowly moved through the air its pages slowly turning over and over as it moved towards Mr Trinity who stood in the centre of the mirror.

Mr Trinity grabbed the book and began to recite air earth fire and water send me on my journey, and with those words, he began to spin through the mirror. This was the time now, I turned the handle of the door it would not open, so I ran back a few feet and charged the door, just as I was about to hit the door with my shoulder, it flew open I fell in and landed face down on the floor with a thud. I turned my head to one side I could just see Mr Trinity's head and shoulders sticking out of the mirror, he was starting to disappear bit by bit, no time to lose I thought? I jumped up and ran towards the mirror" I leapt feet first into the mirror just as Mr Trinity's head began disappear, I felt two arms grab me by the ankles and pull me down. I had just cleared the mirror when it became a solid piece of glass once more I knew that carpet and table would go back to their original positions, so no one would suspect anything untoward had happened. Mr Trinity had hold of me as we fell and tumbled on our way down through the darkness, in my mind I was thinking if I would be missed by Sutherland but then again on our last adventure, when we got back it seemed as if we had never been away I always thought in the back of my mind if time had stood still when we had been away. Because no one had questioned us where we had been I just hoped that it would be the same when I got back, It seemed like an eternity as we fell repeatedly through the blackness, when suddenly I hit the ground, I lay for a few minutes not daring to open my eyes. My chest was thumping up and down like a steam hammer; all of a sudden, I was yanked to my feet by the collar of my coat. "What are you doing boy Mr Trinity said" in a very angry voice, and shaking me as if I was some rag doll. He threw me down on the ground again and started to walk away from me, panic began to set in me my whole body shaking with fear I did not know how to get back to where we had come from. I jumped to my feet "PLEASE Mr Trinity I shouted do not leave me my voice piercing the night air. "Please I shouted once more, Mr Trinity turned around his blue eyes piercing into my frightened eyes, he raised his right arm and with his long bony finger beckoned me towards him. I walked towards him not knowing what to expect, I just kept looking into his deep blue eyes as I walked slowly towards him. When I reached Mr Trinity my whole body was shaking from head to toe with fear, I knew deep down that he would not hurt me, but that did not stop me from being afraid for I had seen the wrath of Mr Trinity before on our last adventure.

So I was rather surprised when he put his arm around my shoulders and told me not to worry, I felt much more at ease now knowing that he was not angry with me anymore. "See that light over by the edge of the forest Mr Trinity said! "Yes I replied feeling much better, there is a horse waiting there for me to take me on to meet Master Remlin who will waiting for me, I shudder to think what he will say when he sees you "he said. "Come let us be on our way as time is short! We walked across the open field towards the light at the edge of the forest; there was no sound except our feet walking through the grass and the odd hoot of an owl in the distance. It was a full moonlit night that made everything around us seem like daylight, apart from when the clouds past across in front of the moon plunging us into total darkness and just leaving the light shining at the edge of the forest. As we neared, I could just make out the shadow of a horse tied to a small branch from a tree by the cottage. Nearer and nearer we got and much to my surprise, it was the same cottage, where I had encountered Master Remlin, who had threatened to send Sutherland, and I to the forest of no return., still the same old rickety, building nothing had changed, I was beginning to get excited, thinking of the adventure that lay ahead, and would I meet any old friends from our last adventure. Mr Trinity stopped me in my tracks, put his bony finger to his lips as if to say be quiet. He beckoned me to kneel down in the long grass, we knelt down and looked at the cottage which was a few yards away...Mr Trinity whispered in my ear we will wait here for a few minutes we cannot be too careful, you never know what or who could be lingering in those trees. Mr Trinity looked all around and listened for a few minutes, and said I think we can carry on now.

The horse by this time was getting more nervous; we stood still not moving when all of a sudden two big yellow eyes started to come towards us. And in a flash it was there in front of us, my heart was beating so fast I thought it was going to jump out of my chest, but Mr Trinity did not look too concerned. "Young John he said? I want you to meet Jemima." My throat went dry and I tried to speak, the words came out in a stammer,"pl..eas..ed to Meet you I said." and you the creature said! You gave us quite a fright Mr Trinity replied, while they were talking, I looked Jemima up and down, it was a bird like creature big round face and a small beak just like an owls, thin. Body and scrawny legs, with webbed feet just like a duck, she had wings, but at the end of her wings were two tiny hands. She did not have too many feathers, mostly on her wings, to cover her modesty, she wore a pair of skin tight trousers that came just down to her knobbly knees' I thought to myself I had seen some, strange creatures, in this world of Sofala and now another one, "why have you come along?" said Mr Trinity. "Why your journey, thinking you would be alone, but I guess not she said?" Ah that is another story Mr Trinity replied not to worry I will tell you all about it later he said! Come now said Jemima follow me to the cottage I have prepared some food for you before we start on our journey to the lands of Anuti, where Master Remlin awaits you. Jemima turned on her webbed feet and in a flash she was gone. "Come said Mr Trinity you can share some of my food as it's quite a journey to where we are going." He put his arm around my shoulder and we headed for the cottage, as I neared the door the aroma of the food reached my nostrils and my mouth began to water, I could taste it already .Mr Trinity pushed open the small cottage door and then the wonderful aroma hit me I just hoped it tasted as good as it smelt." sit sit Jemima said! Mr Trinity and I sat down at the old rickety table to await our food, "it's a good job that I have made plenty of stew or somebody would have had to do without said Jemima" looking at me through her big yellow eyes. She took the pan off the fire that was burning in the hearth, and brought it to the table, ah smells good really good", "said Mr Trinity just what we need for a long journey nice full belly. Jemima began to serve the stew onto our plates which I started to devour it greedily." take your time Mr

Trinity said do you want to make yourself sick boy. I began to slow down but it was too good, we finished our meals and Jemima brought us a large flagon of water to drink." Come now said Mr Trinity we will rest for a while before we start on our journey. I moved away from the table and sat on the chair beside the fire, the heat of the fire quickly sent me into a deep peaceful sleep. The next thing I knew was Mr Trinity shaking me buy the shoulders, "come on John, we have to go, I rubbed the sleep from my eyes, and looked around me. Jemima was dousing the fire in the grate. Mr Trinity and I, headed for the door and stepped out into the cool night air. The rush of air woke me up and brought me to my senses Mr Trinity took the horse from the small branch it was tied too. He mounted the horse held out his arm and grabbed mine and pulled me up beside him. Hold on tight I put my arms round his waist, he dug his heels into the flanks of the horse and reared up it gave out a large neigh and galloped off into the night. I held on tight to Mr Trinity's waist as the horse picked up speed, on we travelled into the night not, speaking to each other as the horse galloped on. When we reached the edge of the forest, we came into a large open field, in the distance I could just make out a fire, the flames, flickering into the night air. Mr Trinity turned to me and said we will dismount and walk from here, to give the horse time to cool down. I dismounted into the cool grass which came to just below my knees and we started to walk towards the inviting firelight. Mr Trinity spoke to me "that will be Jemima she will have come on ahead of us to prepare a meal! "She really is a great cook we will have to thank Master Remlin when we see him again! "I'm sorry Mr Trinity if I have caused any trouble, I did not mean to really. It's okay he said, I know you are a very impulsive young man, and that is something you will have to learn to control as you get older. He looked down at me and smiled that's when I knew that everything would be fine all I had do now was face the wrath of Master Remlin, which I was not looking forward to at all. Maybe he had mellowed slightly after our last encounter; he was not a bad person really, just a bit bad tempered when he wanted to be, I think that was just for show.

Once again I was so deep in my thoughts, before I knew it we were at the campfire, it felt so warm and comforting, Jemima had some sort of animal turning on a spit over the fire, the juices dripping into the flames, making them sizzle. I Asked Jemima what sort of animal, was cooking over the open fire, she looked at Mr Trinity for reassurance has to what to say. "Mr Trinity said it is a Manx in your world what you might call a rabbit "he said, go on and taste it, it's really good, I pulled a leg from the carcass of the Manx sniffed it for a while, closed my eyes and took a bite, mmm I thought! This is really, good. Mr Trinity and Jemima just smiled at me as I stuffed my face the juices running down my chin, and onto my shirt, leaving grease stains. "Come said Mr Trinity I think it is about time we settled down, for the night...Jemima took a blanket from a bedroll that was attached to the horse's back, and gave it to me. I settled down at the edge of the fire, wrapped the blanket around me, and looked up at the moon, I thought to myself was it the same moon that we had in our world. I watched as the clouds drifted slowly past the moon, until I fell into a deep, sleep

Chapter Three

The next thing I knew was someone, shaking me buy the shoulder, I slowly opened my eyes and there in front of me, was Jemima with her big yellow eye's staring at me. I jumped back with a bit of a shock; Mr Trinity let out aloud laugh and said! That's woke you up, young John frighten you did she, Come time for breakfast before we set out for my home of Uteve. I sat up and removed the blanket from around my shoulders. I looked at the campfire and there in a frying pan cooking over the open fire was six large eggs with bright red yolks' Mr Trinity had brought some bacon along with him, and that was also frying in the pan alongside the eggs. Jemima gave Mr Trinity and me a plate each with a knife and fork "help yourself Mr Trinity said eat well as we have a long day in front of us! 'You never know when we will stop again! I took two large eggs from the pan along with some bacon; Mr Trinity removed a large loaf of bread from his saddlebag, tore off a large chunk, and threw it to me. As I ate my breakfast the sun started to come over the horizon, 'looks like it is going to be a nice sunny day said "Mr Trinity, I just nodded my head up and down as my mouth was too full to speak. As the sun rose in the morning sky, I began to look around at my surroundings we were in a field, on three sides of us were some small bushes; I had not really noticed them the night before. There was small entrance, at the front and through that in the distance, you could see, a large mountain range! Through those mountains" said Mr Trinity is the lands of Anitu where Master Remlin awaits us" he will know you are with me! Master Remlin knows everything" I gulped. "Do not worry I do not think he will hurt you", besides he, like's anyone with a bit of bravado? That seemed to ease my fears a little bit. While we talked, Jemima began to saddle the horse ready for our journey. The sun was now over the horizon and it was going to be a beautiful day...Mr Trinity mounted the horse, and I jumped up behind him. Jemima took to the air and we set off, towards the Mountains of Anuti.1 felt as if I did not have a care in the world I felt safe with Mr Trinity he would look after me. On we travelled over the flat plain, the morning past into afternoon by this time I was getting rather thirsty my throat was quite dry," we will stop in an hour. There is a small type oasis's ahead where we can shelter, and drink before we carry on the rest of our journey he said." the sun in the sky was really quite hot now, no clouds to give us shelter, from the heat. And there it was. I could just see it in the distance, it was small just a couple of small palm tree's but it would at least give us some shelter from the midday sun. We arrived at last I fell from the horse and crawled to the small, pond that lay between the two trees. I buried my head into the water and drank until I could drink no more, the heat did not seem to bother Mr Trinity. Then again, nothing bothered him; he led the horse to the pond to drink.

He had a drink himself, and then sat down underneath one of the palm trees to rest... Jemima was splashing about in the pond enjoying herself, so I joined her after all, I may as well make the most of it, before I had to face Master Remlin. Mr Trinity shouted at us to come over to where he was sitting. "Look, look" over there in distance, I could see a cloud of dust beginning to get near. We did not have any weapons of any kind, to protect ourselves with... 'We have visitors and they are not very friendly' 'get behind the palm tree out of sight! How did he know? However, like Master Remlin he knew. The dust cloud got nearer and nearer until it was upon us. The dust settled and much to my surprise. There in front of me sitting on their horses was Poppy one and two, they were covered from head to foot in dust they had picked up from the dry sandy ground. They dismounted together and began to shake the dust from their clothes. They were still dressed in the same old clothes' they wore from the last time that I had seen them. The same baggy trousers tucked into knee length red boots, they still wore that large black coat held together around there waist with a large red belt, with a jewelled buckle at the front. Mr Trinity did not get up from his sitting position from underneath the tree, he just looked at them his deep blue eyes watching them as they started to walk towards us both of them limping on their crippled left legs. I began to rise up from my sitting position, when Mr Trinity put a bony hand on my shoulders to stop me. The two Poppy's began to get closer and closer and Mr Trinity still did not move, I was beginning to get frightened by now; after all, they were our friends. In a flash Mr Trinity jumped up, it all happened so quick there in front of me lay Poppy one and two, lying lifeless in front of me on the ground, blood was pumping from a small wound just below their left ear, I ran towards Mr trinity crying and shouting at the top of my voice Why? Why? Did you do that, they were our friends why, I dropped down onto the ground my knees digging into the soft sand, and I began to sob, uncontrollably. I felt a hand touch me on the shoulder, and a soft voice said to me get up, John and look at me.

I lifted my head and looked Mr Trinity I stared into his blue eyes, I cannot understand why you did that, I said, I then buried my face into his long black cloak and began to cry again. Mr Trinity held me for a while till I stopped crying. Turn round and take a look I turned round and there on the ground was two of the most horrible creatures that I had the misfortune to set eyes on. What are those I stammered, it certainly wasn't Poppy one and two. What are they I asked? "Those, young John," Mr Trinity said "are troglodytes, cave dwellers, but not your usual troglodytes they can take on the form of different people, hence the two Poppys." I looked down at the creatures lying on the ground there faces were like a monkeys big black eyes each mouth was pulled back in a snarl their black razor sharp teeth protruding over their lips their bodies were covered in long shaggy fur they had hands and feet just like a humans except they had six toes and six fingers on each hand and foot.

I looked down at them I ran my eyes up and down their

torsos then I realised where I had seen these creatures before. They were early cavemen exactly like the ones I had seen in my history books at school, I could not believe it but then again this was Mr Trinity's world, and anything could happen in his world. How did you know I stammered, Mr Trinity took me to one side and put his arm round my shoulders, you know that I have great powers but this is simple enough", those troglodytes can take on any form of human or creature that they want to, but one thing they cannot change is their hands or feet. That is their Achilles heel you might say six toes and six fingers that is how I knew replied Mr Trinity". "Come Jemima said Mr Trinity we will cover these two body's with sand we do not want anyone to find them, Kaunn has something to do with this I do believe" " We cannot be too careful there may be more in the area Mr Trinity said". You fill the water bags young John said Mr Trinity while Jemima and I bury these creatures. I collected the two water bags and began to fill them from the small pond that was sheltered from the sun by the two palm trees.

In the distance I could just make out a small cave surrounded by a few bushes dotted around the entrance of the cave I thought to myself I just wish we had Alcoyneaus with us and his two giant dogs", because if anything or anyone was in that cave they would not stand much of a chance against Alcoyneaus and his two giant dogs, but they were not here so we just had to hope that there was no one or any kind of creature in that cave. Don't worry said Mr Trinity it's quite safe I was reassured after all Mr Trinity knew it was safe because he had that sixth sense which made him a rather special person, I had never seen his magical powers yet, he was quite a modest man deep down, maybe I would see them one day. I don't think he would use a magic wand more mind over matter but what I had seen was quite awe inspiring to say the least. We approached the cave and dismounted our horse's Jemima began to cut a few small branches from the bushes that surrounded the cave to make a small fire just inside the entrance of the cave. Mr Trinity told her to wait a moment while we entered the cave to look around inside. As we entered to my surprise, it was quite large there was a beam of light shining down through a small opening in the roof of the cave making a circle of light on the cave floor.

Mr Trinity told Jemima to bring the horses into the cave through the narrow opening. 'We will cut some bushes to seal the entrance so no one can see the fire from outside, this way we will be safe no one will know we are here "said Mr Trinity." Jemima took the horses to the back of the cave and settled them down for the night, while I began to make up the fire for Jemima to cook our evening meal, Mr Trinity began to seal up the entrance to the cave, so nobody would know we were there.

We settled down on the cave's sandy floor and watched as Jemima began to cook that wonderful stew that I had ate the night before I could not wait it smelt so wonderful my mouth was watering with the thought of that succulent meat passing across my taste buds. We sat in silence just eating our stew all you could hear was the chewing of food and the licking of lips and fingers to savour every last drop of meat juice. After everyone had eaten their fill Mr Trinity spoke "well young John? What am I going to tell Master Remlin of how you came to be here he said in a not to confident voice, "he will not be very pleased to see you and he will not be pleased with me either for letting you come. I'm sorry I said" I just wanted to come with you please forgive me" Master Remlin won't send me to the forest of no return will he, Mr Trinity smiled no he won't it's too far away to send you there. Come Mr Trinity said I think we should get some rest now as we have a long day ahead of us tomorrow, I smiled at him and turned over and snuggled into the bed that Jemima, had made me with the soft grass that she had gathered from outside the cave. I watched the shadows on the cave wall that came from the fire burning in the centre of the cave making strange shapes as the flames flickered up into the darkness above me. After a while I drifted off into a deep sleep I dreamt of my friend Sutherland and wished that he had remembered our last adventure together. The next morning I awoke to Jemima shaking me by my shoulder I slowly opened my eyes and there she was staring at me with those big round yellow eye's, 'breakfast is ready she said in her squeaky voice, sorry but it is the same stew that I made last night. "Come Mr Trinity is up and having his breakfast. I looked over to where he was sitting eating his breakfast and staring into the fire deep in thought. I brushed the bits of grass from my hair and clothes and joined Mr Trinity at the fire with Jemima. I sat down on the ground Jemima passed me a plate and a spoon Mr Trinity told me to tuck in as we had a long journey ahead of us that day.

I eagerly tucked into the stew that Jemima had made the night before I know it was leftovers but it still tasted really good, after I had eaten my fill I sat there for a couple of minutes compensating my situation and wondering if I had been missed but then again on my last adventure with Mr Trinity no one had missed Sutherland and I. Mr Trinity brought me back to reality out of my daydream come John it Is time to go and get your horse ready for the journey? I arose from the hard stony ground and went to where my horse was tethered in the corner of the cave, the horse which I had gained from one of the dead troglodytes. Jemima helped me to saddle the horse, when I was ready Jemima removed the branches from the cave entrance and the sunlight flooded into the cave, we all mounted and galloped out into the bright sunlight which was just coming up over the horizon onto the large desert plain. All you could see around us was the flat desert plain that disappeared into the distance on all sides. I looked back at the cave entrance and the two solitary palm trees that stood tall beside the water's edge of the oasis. I kept on looking until they disappeared into the distance leaving nothing but desert all around us.

We travelled on not saying a word everyone deep in

their own thoughts; I kept thinking to myself what Master Remlin would say to me when I arrived at the lands of Anuti where we were going to meet Master Remlin. As we rode on the heat was beginning to become unbearable I was feeling rather weak with the sun beating down and burning into my back making my clothes soaking wet with perspiration, I just wished it would rain to give me some respite Mr Trinity and Jemima did not seem to be too concerned as they were used to this heat, just when I thought it would not get any better it did suddenly the heavens opened and down came the rain I looked up into the sky there was not a cloud in sight. I could not understand why there was no clouds up above me, the rain came down in torrents soaking and flooding the ground all around me the water beginning to come over the horses hooves, I was beginning to get a bit apprehensive by this time everywhere was water no ground just water for miles around me.

Mr Trinity I shouted in a voice that was quaking with fear HELP HELP ME? Mr Trinity turned towards me don't worry it will stop soon it rains this time every day; no sooner had he said those words the rain stopped. Jemima jumped from her horse and began to gather the rain water into the water bags that she kept on either side of her saddle no sooner had she filled them the rain water began to disappear into the ground leaving nothing but the soft sand of the dessert I looked into the distance and for miles all you could see was the heat vapours rising up from the ground as it dried out leaving once again the hard sand baking in the sun and cracking with the heat. Mr Trinity how far is it now I am tired and hungry I need to rest, won't be long now he said; we will reach the pass of arika in an hour there we can shelter for the night it's a day's march through the pass to the outskirts of the lands of Anuti where Master Remlin will meet us, and lead us to the city of Uteve, I am looking forward to going home it's been quite a while since I was there! I looked at Mr Trinity and smiled he really was looking forward to seeing his home again, and I was wondering what Master Remlin would say when he saw me. Mr Trinity shouted across to me "look John the pass of arika I looked ahead and there in the heat haze was the pass of arika, Mr Trinity shouted at us to pick up speed I dug my heels into the horses flanks and galloped off towards the pass of arika, as I got nearer I could see that it was long and narrow just wide enough to go through in single file, the walls were sheer and smooth and they disappeared into the now forming clouds above us. Look over there said, Mr Trinity we will shelter underneath that large hanging rock for the night, as we got nearer I could see just below the rock a small opening good said; Mr Trinity that will do us just fine we have some shrubs to the side of us to form a windbreak and a couple of trees to tether the horses to. Jemima dismounted her horse and started to gather a few dead branches that had fallen from the trees to make a fire in the opening below the base of the hanging rock for the night.

Mr Trinity and I unsaddled our horses along with Jemima's we gave them some water and a little horse feed that we had left and settled them down for the night. By this time Jemima had the fire going and what remained of the stew warming over the open fire, it smelt so good I was really hungry I just sat there with my mouth open and licking my lips then Jemima gave me a plateful of stew and a large junk of bread of which I started to devour greedily. Take your time Mr Trinity said don't want to be sick do you for tomorrow you will have as much as you want to eat, the three of us sat round the fire talking between mouthful's of food I kept asking Mr Trinity what the city of Uteve was like one question after another Mr Trinity held up his hand slow down slow down you will find out tomorrow when we arrive at the city so try and rest for we have a good five hours march through the pass before we meet Master Remlin I lay back with my head on my saddle and looked out at the stars shining brightly in the night sky and wondering what Uteve was like till I drifted off into a deep sleep the next thing I remember was Jemima shaking me by the shoulder come John she said breakfast sorry but it is stew again as she looked at me with her big yellow eyes. Time to get up now Mr Trinity is ready and waiting for you we have a long journey ahead, I rubbed the sleep from my eyes and sat up Jemima thrust a plateful of stew into my hands I looked at it for a couple of minutes then began to devour it as if it was the last meal I was going to get. Mr Trinity just sat there watching me with a smile on his face he looked really happy probably with the thoughts of going home.

I never ever asked him if he had any family to speak of I often wondered if he had but I did not think it was any of my business but I would soon find out when we arrived at the city of Uteve, besides I had other troubles of my own i.e. Master Remlin and what he would say when he saw me. Mr Trinity spoke have you had your fill because it's time to go now Jemima has saddled your horse ready for you, 'thank you I replied I arose from the ground and stretched out my arms and legs to get some feeling back into my body having lain on the hard ground all night, right lets go said Mr Trinity just a few more hours and we will meet Master Remlin to take us into the city of Uteve. Jemima doused the fire and we mounted our horses and headed towards the mouth of the pass. as we entered there was just enough room for us to go through in single file you could reach out and touch the sides of the pass with your hands, it was very Erie nothing in front of you but the long narrow winding path through .The walls of the pass were as smooth as glass I looked up above me, they rose up till they disappeared into the clouds above us, it was as silent as the grave as we carried on our journey towards the end where Master Remlin would be waiting for us. We travelled on for hours no one speaking just their own thoughts for company, when in the distance I could see the end of the pass and a figure on a white horse it was Master Remlin my throat began to dry out and my stomach churn seeing him there on his white horse staring into the narrow pass.

Chapter Four

Mr Trinity spoke to me now is the moment of truth not just for you but me also for letting you come with me. I am really sorry Mr Trinity I replied "but I couldn't help myself, it's okay I will take the blame like I did last time, when he said that I felt really bad about what I had done. As we got nearer, I could see Master Remlin his long white beard had been cut so it just rested on his chest, his long white hair tied back in a ponytail. He was dressed in black leather trousers and waistcoat he was bare-chested and in his left hand he held a long spear with the base of it resting on the ground.

I was feeling a bit apprehensive by this time because I had seen him lose his temper once before, the last time we had met in the cottage when I had followed Mr Trinity to his world of Sofala. He could not see me as I was in the middle between Mr Trinity and Jemima. Won't be long now until he sees me with, those piercing blue eyes of his. Nearer and nearer we got until Mr Trinity stepped out into the open then he saw me 'COME HERE he shouted at me. I trotted over with my head bowed down, my chin resting on my chest what are you doing here did you not learn your lesson the last time boy, look at me when I am talking to you boy! I raised my head and looked into his deep blue eye's WELL he shouted speak? I tried to speak but I could not get the words out of my mouth through fear, Master Remlin grabbed me by the collar of my coat put his face close to mine! I could feel his hot breath on my cheek as he whispered to me. I know Mr Trinity is not to blame because you are a spoilt and stubborn child. 'Did you not learn from your last encounter in our world he said?" Just as I was about to speak Mr Trinity rode up I will take care of him he said to Master Remlin. "Master Remlin spoke 'you are a very lucky boy if the forest of no return was not so far away you would definitely be sent there he said in a gruff voice. "Please forgive me I'm sorry really I am, "well it's to late now for you to go back looks like we are stuck with you once again you ignorant boy Master Remlin said "Follow me it's about an hour's ride to the city Mr Trinity rode alongside Master Remlin I could hear them talking to each other in whispers probably so I could not hear what they were saying to each other; just as well I was in Master Remlin's bad books anyway.

I just trotted alongside Jemima who told me that Master Remlin's bark was worse than his bite. On we rode I just sat there in silence with my own thoughts and watched Master Remlin and Mr Trinity deep in conversation with Mr Trinity laughing now and then when Master Remlin said something funny, I was beginning to feel a bit apprehensive about Master Remlin and what plans or punishment he had for me when we reached the city of Uteve.

I raised my head and looked and their it was the city of Uteve it was surrounded on three sides by mountains of which the sides were flat and smooth as we neared I could see a large inland sea in front of me that stretched out on either side of us the sea flowed around the base of the mountains and disappeared into the distance. As we reached the edge of the inland sea a large flat bottomed raft was waiting to take us across to the city, everyone stepped aboard it was just big enough for the three of us and our horses I stood there in awe of my surroundings and then as if by magic the raft began to move across the sea. Master Remlin beckoned me forward towards him, I thought to myself here it comes he is going to take his revenge on me for disobeying Mr Trinity, I shuffled slowly towards him I just hope he was not going to throw me overboard as I could not swim, he looked at me with his deep blue eyes and then a smile came on his thin bony face I knew then that I would be quiet safe and that I would have nothing to fear from Master Remlin I leant on the front rail of the raft and Master Remlin put his left arm around my shoulder Mr Trinity came up and stood alongside us, he looked down at me and gave a very reassuring smile which made me feel quite safe and wanted. Look young John there is the city of Uteve as we got closer I could see that a wall ran all the way round the three sides of the mountains just like the battlements of a castle. In front of us was what looked like a solid wall that stretched across from one side of the mountain to the next, how do we get into the city I asked Master Remlin" "watch he replied" Jemima took a small round like horn from her waist and began to blow giving out deep a noise just like a foghorn that you would hear from a lighthouse when it was foggy at sea to warn ships of dangerous waters. From such a small horn it gave out quite a loud noise which made me cover my ears to shut out the noise. I looked ahead of me and to my astonishment the great wall began to sink down into the sea, and there in front of me was the city of Uteve.

It was beautiful, large pointed golden spires reached up into the morning sky the sun bouncing off their gold tops making different colours as the sun shone down onto them. We passed over the submerged wall which I could see just below the surface through the clear blue water, we entered a wide river I looked up at either side of me and all along the sides of the sheer flat mountain walls was a walkway with the same castle type battlements that went all the way down either side of each mountain. Soldiers marched up and down along the walkway all you could see as they marched along was their silver helmets as they appeared now and then between the battlements I also noticed about every fifty yards large wooden doors which went all the way along the side of each mountain.

As we sailed up the river we past people working in the small fields either side of us planting crops and tilling their piece of land, they looked up and began to wave at Master Remlin and Mr Trinity who waved back at them, I looked back and saw the great wall start to rise from the sea to shut off the city from the outside world. On we sailed down the river past the small fields with more and more people gathering to welcome Mr Trinity back home after all he had been away a long time Jemima had told me, as we sailed up the river, everyone was waving vigorously as we passed them by. As we past the fields I could see people working in what looked like some sort of shipyard, building small boats there was a quay where a boat lay alongside which a few of the Uteve people were fitting out, there was lots of banging and shouting especially from one person giving out the orders to everyone going about their shipbuilding tasks' Mr Trinity told me that the Uteve people were a self-sufficient people and did not rely on anyone for their survival. I could see the city in front of me now the gold spires reaching into the sky we pulled alongside a long jetty where five small ships were tied up alongside each other. People paid no attention to us just the odd glance as we descended down the gangplank onto the quayside.

I looked around at my surroundings, people were milling around some had what looked like market stalls selling the crops they had grown in the fields we had passed by earlier on our journey up river. There were small shops dotted around selling everything from fresh meat to vegetables' clothes and most other things that you would find in a small town. We walked towards two large wooden gates of which one had a small door at the side, Jemima opened the door and we all stepped through into the most beautiful sight I had ever seen, in front of me was a great fountain in the centre of the fountain stood a large stone figure in one hand he held a round shield and in the other he held a spear round his waist hung a sword the statue was wearing a stone helmet which covered his head the face was adorned with a long beard he looked a very fearsome warrior indeed ,around the sides of the fountain were what looked like dolphins their mouths spouting water from them into the pool below the statues feet the sides of the fountain was adorned with figures of soldiers in various modes of dress of which Mr Trinity told me were scenes of battles that their ancestors had fought long ago. I turned to Master Remlin excuse me please who is the stone statue of I said? Master Remlin turned to me with a smile on his face his eyes twinkling in the sunlight, that young John is the founder of the Uteve peoples he was called as you can guess Uteve he was a great warrior and diplomat he replied." I looked at the statue again and said to Master Remlin he must have been a great warrior, Mr Trinity put his arm around my shoulders and said he was a very great man a very great man. I took in the rest of my surroundings it was fantastic the roads and pavements were all made of what looked like marble, the houses were beautiful each one had a porch in front of it which was kept up by two great marble columns each house had a great black wooden door with large brass hinges and a large brass circular handle the windows had black shutters either side of them they too had brass hinges which attached them to the marble walls.

On one side of each house was painted a scene from the history of the Uteve people. We walked along the marble road past house after house everyone that we past lowered their heads as Master Remlin and Mr Trinity past by I was beginning to get quite curious now for the two of them must be very important people in the Uteve tribe, on we walked till we came to a small bend in the road as we turned the bend there in front of me was the palace of Uteve its golden spires reaching up into the morning sun shining and giving off a bright yellow glow that filled the sky as if the whole of the sky was on fire with flame. I looked up at the palace which stretched up the side of the flat mountain wall with its many windows and balcony's which protruded from the side of the mountain the palace's marble walls was painted with different scenes from the history of Uteve the same scenes I had seen on our way to our destination, on one side of the sheer flat mountain wall was a painting of Uteve the founder of the Uteve peoples in all his finery except this time he was not dressed in his soldiers uniform but the clothes of a king a long blue robe with a red belt round his waist a great shield lay at his sandaled feet along with his spear and sword, his white hair hung down over his shoulders mingling with his white beard which hung down onto his chest, around his head was a jewelled headband with red green blue and yellow jewels I stood back and looked for a while at this magnificent man in all his finery and could not help thinking to myself that there was a resemblance of Master Remlin about him." "Come young John!" I turned to Mr Trinity He smiled at me and beckoned me forward come lets enter and partake of some refreshment you must be hungry by now after your journey. I walked towards Mr Trinity and Master Remlin and the great black door opened in front of me of its own accord. We entered a great marbled hall with an arched carved marble ceiling from which hung three great chandeliers, each one had candles as thick as your arm and each chandelier had at least forty candles.

In the centre of the hall stood a long narrow carved wooden table at least thirty feet long, on either side of the table stood thirty chairs each one carved with ornate heads of animals on the arms of the chairs the seats and the backrests were made of bright red silk each one with a gold cushion on it, on the marble walls alongside each other there was painted portraits of different people each one looking out at you their eyes seemed to move with you as you walked by watching every move you made, on the far side of the hallway stood a great marble fireplace with a large chimney breast which was covered with weapons of all different kinds swords crossbow's lances and shields with small daggers protruding from around each shield. At the end of the hallway was a wooden doorway Master Remlin said 'come young man follow me and off he set towards the door which as we got near it seemed to open of its own accord, as I entered it was just a square room with flat walls and a stone floor, Master Remlin clapped his hands he then uttered some nondescript words and the floor we were standing on began to move upwards I began to panic but Mr Trinity took hold of my arm and said there's nothing to be afraid of its quite safe I began to calm down with his reassurance and up we went up and up passing wooden doors on every side of the wall till we finally reached a large black door Master Remlin clapped his hands and the door began to open slowly on its large brass hinges here we are said Master Remlin" my home "come in and take a look around you! I stepped into the room and surveyed my surroundings it was a very large room at least thirty feet square all the walls were made of different coloured marble on one wall there was a tapestry which went the full length of the wall, as I stepped further into the room I turned round and in front of me there was two large open windows with a balcony in front of each one, to my left there was three brown wooden doors at the far end of the room was a marble fireplace and in the hearth a small fire was burning.

The room was furnished very sparingly a large couch like settee and a couple of chairs on either side of the fireplace a large wooden sideboard stood against one wall with a pile of books on one end, then I noticed in the centre of the sideboard there stood the crystal globe the golden heart and the silver shield that we had taken with us on our last adventure to defeat the evil Dr Zaker" but the most important thing on my mind at present was the great table in front of me overflowing with food and drink. Master Remlin beckoned me to be seated and to eat my fill from the table, I sat down and looked at the food that was laid out in front of me apples pears different kinds of vegetables chicken and what looked like beef also other plates of meat which I did not know of and other fruits that I had never seen before but that did not deter me from surveying the different kinds of food on offer it was just which to eat first. I looked at Master Remlin and Mr Trinity who both said in unison 'tuck in help yourself I did not need any more encouragement I started to stuff my face eating from every plate that was on the table, and taking a drink of what looked like some sort of green liquid but it tasted a bit like strawberries funny I thought green strawberries still everything is different in this world of Mr Trinity's I ate my way through everything that was on the table not wanting to miss anything out Mr Trinity and Master Remlin just stared at me in disbelief as I devoured the food. After I had eaten my fill I lay back in the great big comfortable chair at the table belched and said; 'oops sorry I said" to Master Remlin and Mr Trinity, they just looked at each other and smiled at each other they then shook their heads in unison" "come young man sit by the fire with Mr Trinity and I and rest for a while, while Jemima prepares your room for the night, I got down from the table and shuffled over to the fire my stomach was bursting with all the food I had eaten I dropped down into the chair and sank my body deep into the cushions, that was scattered on the chair.

I had just settled down when Jemima came into the room and told Master Remlin that my room was ready for the night. Master Remlin held out his hand and I began to rise from the chair to my feet as if he had control of my entire body he looked at me and smiled and said" go with Jemima now and try to get some sleep for tomorrow is a busy day for all of us. I walked across the room to where Jemima stood next to a brown wooden door with a large brass handle engraved on the front of it was the face of Uteve the founder of the Uteve tribe, Jemima turned the large handle and the door began to swing open on its large brass hinges to reveal a square marble room, nothing hung on the blue marble walls all that stood in the room was a long wooden sideboard on which stood two great candelabra which Jemima lit from a small candle she carried in her left hand. as she lit the candelabra the whole room burst into light I took in my surroundings and looked around the room once more, there was a large window at one end which opened onto a balcony to the left of the room in the corner stood a four-poster bed covered in blankets and cushions with two huge pillows at the head of the bed, at the side of the bed stood a small table I looked at the bed in front of me it looked very inviting indeed with those huge pillows and cushions scattered on the bed. Jemima placed the candle on the bedside table and said try to get some rest as she made the bed ready for me I will snuff out the candles on the side-board as Master Remlin does not like them to burn all night as they are a very expensive, not many people have these they have to do with small oil lamps which doesn't give off much light. As she spoke she began to snuff out the candles one by one just leaving me with a candle flickering now and then as the breeze caught the flame as it came in from the open window. Jemima said goodnight and left me sitting on the edge of the bed the room was in darkness except for the small candle that flickered on the table casting ghostly shadows on the walls around the room.

I did not feel very tired as my mind was going over the events of the day and me being in Mr Trinity's world and his home city of Uteve, I headed for the open window and stood on the balcony and looked out into the cloudless night sky with the stars twinkling above me and the odd shooting star passing overhead, I looked down onto the roof tops below and watched as the odd yellow and orange sparks came out of the chimney's below me along with the grey smoke that disappeared into the night sky like some ghostly apparition, I kept on looking and watched as the oil lamps in the windows of each house began to go out leaving the whole village in total darkness' I looked out into the distance across the rooftops, and I could just make out a small orange flame as it flickered in the evening breeze, of which I later found out was the fire the sentry's had lit to keep them warm as it could get really cold at night in this world of Mr Trinity's and Master Remlin's, I turned around and went back into my room and closed the large sliding window took off my clothes blew out the candle and settled down into the warm blanket's and buried my head into the large fluffy feathered pillows and fell into a deep sleep. The next thing I knew was Jemima whispering in my ear come young

John time to get up and get ready for breakfast I have brought you a bowl of warm water for you to wash in so don't be too long as Master Remlin does not like to be kept waiting. With those words I jumped out of bed got myself a quick wash down put on my clean clothes which Jemima had washed and dried little to my knowledge she must have come into my room while I was asleep and taken them, they had a wonderful perfumed aroma about them which smelt like roses after I was ready I made up my bed and headed for the door.

Chapter Five

I reached the door and turned the handle and slowly opened the door to reveal Master Remlin and Mr Trinity sitting down at the table eating their breakfast. "Come young man sit down beside me and eat said" Master Remlin between mouthfuls of food Mr Trinity just smiled at me with a twinkle in his ice blue eyes's. I sat down Jemima walked over and placed a metal plate in front of me much to my surprise it was overloaded with eggs and ham and with what looked like beans, except they were a funny purple colour, 'don't worry said Mr Trinity they are just baked beans our baked beans nice colour are they not" I did not reply I just smiled at him and started to shovel my breakfast down my throat in between mouthfuls taking a drink of that green looking liquid I had in front of me which tasted a bit like strawberries'. After I had finished Master Remlin looked at Mr Trinity smiled and said to him does he always eat like that I'm surprised he is not as fat as a pig, Mr Trinity just smiled and nodded his head. I settled back into my chair and looked at the great tapestry that hung the length of the wall opposite me, 'come Master Remlin said take a look and I will explain to you the story. That young man is our founder Uteve a great warrior who had great exceptional magical powers he went on to explain the battle to me and how the great Uteve defeated the armies of Modecica and their king Todec just with a thousand soldiers to set up their homeland of Uteve a great man and a very great warrior, we walked down the length of the tapestry in the room and he kept pointing out the different parts of the battle scenes, explaining in minute detail every gory part of the scene before me. I was beginning to feel a bit queasy as he explained everything to me, as if he was getting some sort of perverse pleasure from talking about it. What happened to King Todec and his people, I asked Master Remlin after the battle," ah he replied they fled to the green Mountains; 'their lands are the plains of Modecica that lye over the Green mountains, which you can see in the background of the battle scene but that is another story he said.

After my brief history lesson on the founder of the Uteve peoples we headed back to the table where Mr Trinity sat lounging back into the soft back of the chair his arms crossed on his chest the long bony fingers protruding from the sleeves of his coat he sat there with a wide grin on his thin skeletal like face. Master Remlin and I sat down at the table they both looked at me for a while then Master Remlin spoke is there anything else you would like to ask me before we get down to the task in hand he said" I looked into his blue eyes and said just one thing it's your magic Ah replied Master Remlin it's not magic in the sense that we can make people disappear or turn them into toads or some horrible creature, we use our minds as you might say mind over matter which is much stronger than some wizard with a so called magic wand" watch he said he looked at the now dead fire in the hearth and in seconds it burst into flames I jumped back in amazement my eyes wide with disbelief the candles on the sideboard also burst into life and as suddenly has it happened they went out, we could be here all day showing you tricks but we have other business to attend to he said? just one question please I replied does everyone in Uteve have this thought magic, alas no replied Master Remlin just the elders of the tribe which much to our regret Kaunn is one of them, you saw the control he had over the evil Dr Zaker, I nodded my head and my mind went back to that final battle where Dr Zaker had been defeated and the loss of all those lives' Mr Trinity brought me back to reality it looks like we have to start all over again he said? We have to find him before he finds someone else's mind to control and start the evil process all over again. I looked at them both and I could see in their deep blue eyes a touch of sadness at the thought of having to repeat the same situation all over again. Master Remlin got up from his chair and walked over to the sideboard and picked up the crystal globe he walked back and set it down in the middle of the table, they both looked at it for a while and then Master Remlin placed his hands over the crystal globe and began to rub them in a circular motion a red mist began to appear in the globe and the lady of the crystal began to rise from out of the mist, she settled down onto the great oak table she could not have been more than a foot tall, she was dressed in a long white dress with long blond hair hanging over her tiny shoulders down to her waist, a silver headband kept her hair in place to stop it from falling over her perfectly formed features she was beautiful I had never seen anyone so beautiful in my short life. "Tell me Master Remlin what can I do for you? Master Remlin bent forward his elbows resting on the table, "we need you to help us find Kaunn replied Master Remlin we would not ask this of you but time is of the essence" 'I understand replied the lady of the globe, she took a small silver wand from the tiny silver belt that hung loosely around her waist and waved it in a circular motion to my astonishment a large circular ball appeared in front of us inside you could see a desert, mountains, blue skies and green fields it was as if we were travelling through these places on we went passing over villages with people working in the fields, you could see warriors hunting on the flat grassy plains. We passed over great lakes and mountains through forests, till everything in the ball became still and their below us you could just make out a small fire burning at the entrance of a small cave, which seemed to be on the side of a small hillside closer and closer we got till you could see Kaunn sitting round the fire his cloak pulled around his shoulders his thin hands was tearing at the flesh of some animal roasting over the open fire the juices running down his chin and onto his cloak, then in the blink of an eye he looked up pulled his cloak over his head and disappeared it was as if he knew he was being watched from afar. The lady of the globe waved her wand and the ball disappeared, "thank you said Master Remlin? The lady bowed and began to disappear once more into the crystal globe the red mist cleared leaving nothing but a solid piece of glass.

I sat there with Mr Trinity and Master Remlin who just looked at each other for a couple of minutes I was dumfounded I had never seen anything like that before this truly was quite a magical kingdom of Master Remlin's. 'Come young man it's time to go now said Master Remlin and prepare you and Mr Trinity for the journey ahead it will be long and fraught with danger along the way, I looked at Mr Trinity who just smiled back at me with a twinkle in his bright blue eyes. We got up from the table and headed once more for the door that we had entered on our way up to Master Remlin's rooms at the top of the palace, we opened the door and stood on the large piece of stone Master Remlin waved his hand in a downward motion and the stone we were standing on began to descend downwards till it suddenly stopped in front of a large iron door. Master Remlin said some nondescript word and the door began to open slowly creaking on its great iron hinges. As it opened I could hear voices coming from the other side, everyone laughing and joking by this time the door had opened fully to reveal much to my surprise a large underground lake at least fifty feet wide, and a thousand feet long, on either side of the lake was a jetty which ran the full length of the underground lake with ships tied up bow to stern along each jetty .One ship which I presumed was our ship had a large mast in the centre and a large beam about ten feet across with what looked like a rolled up sail attached to the masthead, down the sides of the ship were shields attached to the side in one long row either side of the ship, each shield decorated with different drawings of animals some of which I had never seen before, I had seen ships like this before, in my history books at school. Viking ships I thought exactly the same, everyone was busy carrying sacks and boxes up the gangway, which I later found out were the provisions for the long journey ahead of us. I watched in awe as the soldiers busied themselves with their tasks for the forthcoming journey into the unknown...Master Remlin said? 'Come young man time to go and join your ship it's about a two days sail to the painted mountains which you have to cross to reach the plain of Tongees a desolate place but you will be alright you have Mr Trinity with you and a hundred of my best soldiers so you will be fine, "are you not coming I replied" "alas no said Master Remlin I have other tasks to perform here? You will be fine with Mr Trinity. We started to walk along the quayside and as we walked along I noticed we were in a large covered in cave there was no opening for the ships to leave the cave the walls all-around us just looked like solid rock. The whole area of the great cave was lit by great burning torches placed about ten feet apart. As we walked towards two ships that was tied up alongside for our journey we passed by a group of soldiers who stopped what they were doing and bowed to Master Remlin as we walked past. We reached the bottom of the gangway and I looked up at the ship in front of me with its tall mast the sailors walking along the masthead untying the ropes that held the great sail in place and then letting it fall so it hung limply against the mast as there was no wind to make it billow and fill the sail. I lowered my eyes from the top of the mast and looked at the top of the gangway and there in front of me stood a tall man about six feet he was dressed in dark blue knee length trousers and a dark blue jacket round his waist was a thick brown leather belt on his feet he wore calf length boots with a pouch strapped to each one which held a short dagger a short sword hung from the right side of his leather belt which was held together with a large silver buckle, his blonde hair was tied back into a pony tail with a silver broach. Master Remlin Mr Trinity and I started to walk up the gangway as we reached the top and stepped onto the ship's deck the man standing at the top bowed in front of Master Remlin and said welcome aboard, Master Remlin turned to me and said let me introduce you to captain Rogas he will take you to the painted mountains, 'pleased to meet you I said" "and you young man 'Mr Trinity has told me about your last adventure together; ' it must have been an experience for you he said" I just nodded and did not say anything in return he smiled and said" 'would you like to see round my ship Captain Rogas talking and pointing out different aspects of the ship most of it I could not understand but I just nodded my head and looked as if I was interested in what he had to say about his ship, which I gathered from his conversation, he was quite proud of. As we walked I kept looking all-round me at the soldiers storing the food and weapons for the forthcoming journey that lay ahead of us, Captain Rogas took me to the bow of the ship and pointed out the other ship he explained to me in an excited voice that ship is to carry the horses and a couple of wagons that you will need for your journey tomorrow, I just wish I was coming with you all the way it's been a long time since I had been in a good fight, he slammed the flat palm of his hand down onto the ships thick wood rail the noise echoed around the cave he then shouted at a bunch of men standing talking 'you there he shouted get a move on they looked up at Captain Rogas and quickly scurried away to their duties, lazy beggars he said" 'I will deal with those later can't have laziness it might spread to the rest of the crew, I just smiled and nodded. I looked back along the ship's deck there was no cabins just the flat deck except at the stern of the ship some of the sailors were erecting a large tent like awning "that is for you and Mr Trinity some shelter from the sun and rain that's if it does rain always warm this time of year he said" "come young man let us join Master Remlin and Mr Trinity and partake of some refreshment, we walked along the ship's deck as we past the soldiers that was going to accompany us on our journey they were laying out there bedrolls and placing their weapons alongside a large sword crossbow and arrows with a pouch of small throwing knives, as we past not one of the soldiers looked up they just went about their business with great precision. We reached Master Remlin who said to me "did you enjoy your tour he said with a sly grin on his face, he had probably guessed that I been bored with all the technical information that Captain Rogas had been trying to feed my brain with. 'Come Mr Trinity said have some food a large pot hung over a fire which was encased in a large square thick iron casing this will be the last hot meal you will have for the next two days we don't have fires at sea not safe for a wooden ship as you know" Jemima was stirring what looked like some sort of stew Captain Rogas rang a large bell that was attached to a post at the stern of the ship all of the soldiers stopped what they were doing, and proceeded to walk to the stern of the ship each one carrying a metal plate and cup. Each soldier looked fearsome in his thick padded breast plate each one wore a skirt made of leather, and each one also wore leather calf length boots with a dagger, attached to the side of each boot, they also wore thick leather on their arms from the wrist to the top of the shoulder with a break at the elbow so as not to restrict any movement of the arm. Each one also wore a steel helmet with steel straps that covered their cheekbones and each helmet was adorned with a red plume that ran all the way down the centre from the front to the back. they all formed up in single file to receive their meal from Jemima. Each plate was filled with the stew and there mugs with the green strawberry looking liquid, each soldier bowed to Master Remlin turned away and proceeded to their bedroll that they had put out for the night. Right? Said Mr Trinity help yourself the soldiers always eat first then we do so tuck in" Jemima threw me a plate and mug along with a large metal spoon and I eagerly began to fill my plate till it was starting to spill over the edges, I sat down with my back against the ships rail and began to devour it greedily, Master Remlin just shook his head to and fro in disbelief, Jemima threw me what looked like a piece of hard brown bread to mop up the last of the gravy from my plate which I also devoured greedily but I took my time drinking the green strawberry looking liquid as it tasted so nice. After I had eaten I sat there for a while thinking what adventures lay ahead and wondering if I would meet any of my past companions from the last adventure, it was a shame Sutherland could not be here he would have enjoyed every moment of this. Mr Trinity brought me back to reality "come young man it's getting late try and get some rest busy day tomorrow, we set sail for the painted mountains in the early morn. I nodded at Mr Trinity and unfurled my bedroll got between the blanket's and settled down into the soft pillow and fell asleep.

Chapter Six

I awoke the next morning to Captain Rogas ringing the great bell on the stern of the ship. I jumped up and rubbed the sleep out of my eyes everyone was running about doing their duties getting the ships ready to sail. I looked along the deck of the ship towards the gangplank where Master Remlin stood with Mr Trinity. I hurried along to join them all the soldiers stood alongside one side of the ship facing the quay, "ah so glad you could join us said Master Remlin as if it was my fault I had slept in after all nobody had decided to wake me, I just did not want to argue with him he was always right anyway, so I just kept quiet. Well? young John I have to leave you now as I have other things to do but you are in capable hands with Mr Trinity, Master Remlin took Mr Trinity's hand and shook it up and down vigorously good look and a safe journey he then proceeded to take the crystal globe along with the golden heart that hung round his waist in a bright red silk pouch he past the pouch to Mr Trinity 'You will need this on your journey good luck to you all! He then turned and proceeded to walk down the gangplank onto the now empty quayside. Two of the sailors released the mooring ropes from the quayside that held the two ships alongside they ran back up the gangplank pulled it in and laid it along the wooden side of the ship and strapped it down with thick leather straps. I was curious how we were going to get out of the great cave we were in after all I could see no opening. Jemima blew on the horn she carried around her waist giving out a long deep note and to my surprise a great rumbling began to come from the far cave wall and two great steel doors began to open slowly to reveal the river that we had sailed up two days before. The doors had been disguised to look like solid rock. We drifted towards the entrance and as soon as we left the cave entrance, a rush of wind filled the sail and it billowed out making the ropes strain on the cleats that kept the sail tied to the sides of the ship. We were on our way at last sailing into the unknown and a new adventure.

We were on our way sailing into the unknown little did we know what dangers lay ahead of us. The ship by this time had left the sanctuary of the cave, we sailed down the river past people who stood on the riverbank waving and throwing flowers some reached the deck we were standing on while others hit the side of the ship and floated back towards the shore from the wake of the ship as she sailed down the river.

I stood on the stern of the ship with Mr Trinity and Captain Rogas and looked at everyone waving as we slowly sailed by, we past the shipyards no one was working they just stood there waving their arms and shouting safe journey Mr Trinity other people were leaning out of their open windows waving and shouting good luck Mr Trinity come back safe won't you. On we sailed past the green fields with people tending their crops and as we passed by stood up and gave us a wave then turned to tend their crops once more. After we had been sailing for most of the day I could see in front of me the great solid gate that we had come through two days before, Jemima took the horn that was attached to her waist held it to her owl like mouth and blew out a deep sound like a ships foghorn. I could see in the distance the soldiers running along the top of the gate to take up their positions either side of the great gate. Then with a rumble and creaking the great gate started to descend into the river. We passed through the gate it then started to rise once again and shut us out from the city of Uteve.

We were on our own now just the two ships sailing into the unknown, Captain Rogas shouted to the sailors who were busy tidying the deck of the ship, set the foresail we need more speed four sailors ran to the bow of the ship, where two large winches sat either side of a small opening at the bow of the ship. The sailors took two handles that lay alongside of each winch and placed them into a slot on either side of each winch.

Two more sailors ran forward to each winch, they stood side by side and in unison began to turn the handles of each winch. Slowly they turned and out of the opening began to appear what looked like a small round like mast, the sailors kept on turning till it was about six feet out of the opening, then two more sailors ran forward and began to release two round solid pieces of wood which was attached to the mast they fell down on either side of the mast to form a crossbeam, which was then fastened into place by two large pins which went through a large round steel plate attached to the mainmast four more sailors dragged a large bail of canvas and began to tie it to the ringbolts that was attached to the crossbeam. Captain Rogas cupped his hands to his mouth and shouted through cupped hands raise the mast" the sailors began to turn the handles of the winches and the mast began to rise from an opening on the ship's deck, up it rose till it stood at least twenty feet tall. Hanging from the crossbeam and down onto the deck hung four thick ropes two larger ropes hung from each corner of the sail that went through a block attached to the ships rail, "release the sail shouted Captain Rogas and with his orders the four sailors tugged on the ropes and the sail began to fall as it fell the wind caught the sail, making it billow in the breeze. The two sailors that held the ropes on either end of the sail pulled them tight and fastened them to a bollard on either side of the ship's deck. Suddenly a gust of wind caught the sail and the ship picked up speed we were on our way at last.

Captain Rogas gave the helmsman orders to bring the ship about and head east towards the painted mountains. The great ship turned east towards a small river that ran alongside the mountains of Uteve. As we sailed down the river there was nothing but the sheer flat walls of the mountains and on the other side of the ship just a flat desert plain, not a tree or a bush could be seen just sand that stretched into the distance as far as the eye could see. Mr Trinity put his arm on my shoulder, looked at me with his deep blue eyes, smiled and said "no turning back now young John" he said! I just smiled nodded my head and looked out across the ships bow into the distance.

On we sailed past the flat mountains of Uteve and the desert, after about four hours sailing we finally came to the mouth of the river and there in front of me was the open sea. We left the mouth of the river the ship began to pitch and roll slightly as we were now officially at sea. I turned round and looked as the land and mountains of Uteve began to disappear on the horizon leaving nothing but blue rolling waves all around us. Jemima began to prepare some food for Mr Trinity, Captain Rogas and I, but I did not feel like eating as my stomach was churning over and over with the pitch of the ship. Mr Trinity said 'you have to eat something you will be alright in a few hours it will soon wear off when you get your sea legs! I suppose I would have to try and eat something I was actually very hungry indeed and it did smell really wonderful even though we could only have cold food. I sat down with my back against the ships rail feeling really sick and retching now and then as the ship bobbed up and down on the rolling waves. I just wanted this feeling to go away I was feeling rather sorry for myself and thinking I just wanted to be snuggled in my bed back at the home. Jemima brought me a plate of food which looked like cold chicken along with some weird looking green leaves which I later discovered was a dark green lettuce, there was spring onions and a couple of tomatoes which were a purple colour topped off with a white sauce a bit like mayonnaise but it had a sort of sweet taste to it, the whole dish was covered in what looked like herbs it really did smell wonderful, she also gave me that green liquid which tasted a bit like strawberry's to drink which I really did enjoy. Mr Trinity and Captain Rogas sat down beside me along with Jemima and began to tuck into their evening meal, the roll of the ship did not seem to bother them they just sat there and ate while all I could do was pick at my food really not wanting to eat it in case I was sick. Jemima came across to me and put her wing round my shoulder and patted my arm with her hand which protruded from the end of her wing try and eat she said in her soft reassuring voice I looked into her big yellow eyes smiled and said "I will try" she smiled at me and said "good you know it makes sense, eat now for me please."

I sat there putting small mouthfuls of food into my mouth, trying to eat but with every mouthful I could feel my stomach churn I could feel myself retching to so I put my head over the side of the ship and was sick, it felt awful my stomach was hurting me it was as if somebody was squeezing my insides. "Come and lie down said Captain Rogas and rest you will be alright in a couple of hours laughing at me as he spoke! I just smiled at him I could not be bothered to say anything to him at all. Jemima unfurled my bedroll and laid it out onto the ship's deck I crawled into the blanket rested my head onto the soft pillow and drifted off into a deep sleep to the pitching and rolling of the ship.

I awoke the next morning feeling much better than I did the night before, everyone was busy, the sailors were washing down the wooden decks, while the soldiers were busy sharpening their swords and daggers on a round flat stone that lay on the deck at the bow of the ship. Mr Trinity sat with Captain Rogas at the stern deep in conversation. I stood up and leaned on the ships rail and looked out across the open sea it was flat calm just the ripples of the ship as she ploughed through the vast open sea. There was a slight breeze that just filled the sails so the ship was just moving through the sea at a slow leisurely pace. I watched as the ripples from the bow of the ship spread out across the open sea disturbing the flying fish that lay just under the surface as they jumped from the sea two of the sailors with large nets began to gather them up and throw them onto the ship's deck where they wriggled for a short time then lay still under the hot Sun. I walked across to Mr Trinity Captain Rogas and Jemima "good morning Mr Trinity said did you sleep well" "and how do you feel this bright new day? Fine I said," sit down then? Mr Trinity beckoned Jemima towards him "bring some food for young John will you please! "You must be hungry after the rest you had last night you have been asleep for fifteen hours at least. Jemima hurried away to the bow of the ship and hurried back with a plate of food which contained cheese some of those purple tomatoes and bread which by now was beginning to go a bit stale, still it was better than nothing I was after all feeling rather hungry after my nights rest and having not being able to keep my food down the night before.

A shout came from the lookout that in the crow's nest at the top of the mast "ship two points off the starboard bow? Some of the sailors ran to the starboard side of the ship. Mr Trinity rang a large bell that was situated at the stern of the ship the soldiers who had been sitting sharpening their weapons jumped to their feet one of the soldiers ran towards Mr Trinity came to attention and gave a slight bow, "prepare your men sergeant Pedec, Mr Trinity said to him" "yes sir? And with those words, he turned on his heels and ran back towards his men barking out orders as he ran.

Captain Rogas was barking out his orders take in the foresail load the cannon of which there were four two at the bow and two at the stern, all four cannon swivelled in a three hundred and sixty degree arc. Everyone ran about doing their duties each one doing their particular job to make the ship one incredible fighting machine it was a remarkable sight. The second ship that was with us was signalled to keep well away as we could not afford to lose her if it came down to a fight. She held most of the provisions and extra weapons for our journey. We sailed round the ship a couple of times, there did not seem to be any kind of movement coming from the ship that we circled round she just lay there bobbing up and down. Her sails hung limply in the breeze, "Captain Rogas shouted ahoy their where from are you? No reply came from the ship it just lay there in the water bobbing up and down on the slight swell. Once more Captain Rogas shouted ahoy there. Still no reply came from the ship.

Captain Rogas turned to Mr Trinity what do you want us to do? Mr Trinity looked at him for a few moments and said, "We can't leave it there "I know it could be a trap but if it has been deserted there might be spare food and weapons we can use? Mr Trinity beckoned sergeant Pedec to him, "take five of your best men across in the small boat, and board her. Sergeant Pedec saluted Mr Trinity he turned on his heels and shouted to five of his soldiers "come with me? By this time, two of the sailors had lowered the small boat that had lain strapped down in the middle of the ship's deck.

The five soldiers along with sergeant Pedec climbed down the small ladder into the boat and began to row across to the ship. After about ten minutes they reached the side of the ship threw a grappling hook onto the ships rail and began to climb up the rope, one by one they climbed over onto the ship's deck and disappeared. Everyone stood there with bated breath just wondering if anything was wrong the minutes went by slowly and still no sign of sergeant Pedec and his men I think Mr Trinity was becoming quite concerned as to why there was no sign of the sergeant and his men. Mr Trinity summoned Captain Rogas to him "we will wait one hour if they are not back by then we will sink her.

The time went by slowly Mr Trinity paced up and down the ship's deck; he waved Captain Rogas towards him 'turn your cannon onto the ship" "yes? Mr Trinity replied Captain Rogas he turned to his men and told them to wait for the signal to fire the cannon. "Look? Mr Trinity" I shouted tugging at his sleeve "it's Sergeant Pedec" Mr Trinity looked across at the ship lying idle in the water and there was sergeant Pedec waving his hand to and fro in the air beckoning us to come along side. Captain Rogas sounded the ships bell the sailors ran to their stations and lowered the sails we then started to drift slowly towards the other ship that was bobbing up and down on the calm sea.

Closer and closer, we moved towards the stricken ship, when we were about two feet away four of Captain Rogas's sailors came forward with a grappling hook each and threw them towards the ship each one catching onto the ships rail. Captain Rogas shouted to the men take us alongside. The rest of the sailors grabbed the ropes and started to pull us alongside the ship until the two ships came together with a slight bump. One of the sailors put out a piece of wood that had been strapped to the ships side and laid it across the rails of the two ships to form a walkway across to the other ship.

Chapter Seven

I watched as some of sergeant Pedec's soldiers clambered onto the plank and started to walk across to the other ship, after a while Mr Trinity spoke to me 'come young John' 'let's board it's quite safe! I looked at Mr Trinity and I did not say a word I just nodded my head and leapt onto the plank and started to walk across to the other ship. I jumped down onto the ship's deck with the help of sergeant Pedec the ship was deserted not a soul on board. 'Mr Trinity the ship is deserted? Said sergeant Pedec! Mr Trinity nodded his head 'tell your men to search well something must have happened here we have to know!' Sergeant Pedec shouted to his men 'search the ship from bow to stern' 'see if you can find any sign of life? The soldiers began to search the ship while they were searching one of them moved a large piece of canvas that was crumpled up at the bow of the ship to reveal a small hatch about three feet square 'sergeant shouted one of the soldiers 'over here? Sergeant Pedec made his way to where the soldier was standing they both drew their swords then sergeant Pedec beckoned one of the sailors and told him to remove the hatch cover, "hurry hurry? He said to the sailor who by this time was feeling a bit apprehensive. His hands were shaking and beads of sweat ran down his forehead as he took hold of the handle and began to raise the hatch opening, it very slowly until it finally rested on the ship's deck, leaving nothing but a gaping black hole in front of us. Sergeant Pedec climbed down into the hatch followed by the soldier who was standing beside him? It seemed like an eternity when sergeant Pedec appeared his head just sticking out the opening of the small hatch, 'Mr Trinity I need a hand he said! Mr Trinity summoned two of the sailors forward and told them to help sergeant Pedec they climbed down into the hatch I waited anxiously my body quivering with excitement as to what they had found in the lower part of the ship.

After a while one of the sailors came out of the hatch went over to Mr Trinity and whispered into his ear. I could just not quite hear what he was saying; it was so frustrating not knowing what was going on. Besides, I would get to know in a few moments anyway. Mr Trinity beckoned one of the sailors towards him and told him to go and get one of the stretchers that were kept in a small hatchway at the stern of the ship. He ran to the stern of the ship flung open the hatch retrieved one of the stretchers and ran back huffing and puffing as he did so towards Mr Trinity.

The sailor lowered the stretcher down into the opening to sergeant Pedec after about twenty minutes sergeant Pedec appeared once more, 'everything is ready now Mr Trinity! Mr Trinity gave the signal and two of the sailors began to lift the stretcher out of the hatch opening, gently they lifted out the stretcher and placed it down onto the ship's deck. They then began to unfasten the straps which kept whatever or whoever was laid on the stretcher in front of me. After they had removed the straps they then began to remove a small sheet which covered the person who was lying there unconscious on the stretcher not moving, it was a man dressed in long brown pantaloons brown thick leather boots and a thick brown coat over the coat there was a thick black leather belt round his waist, he was dark skinned with a large black beard which was so long it reached practically down to his waist. Mr Trinity told one of the sailors to open his coat and as he did so he revealed a white shirt covered in blood that was starting to congeal and going a dark red colour. Mr Trinity bent forward and removed the man's shirt to reveal a gaping wound on the left hand side of his body, still oozing blood through the blood that was already beginning to congeal over the wound. Mr Trinity spoke to one of the sailors 'bring me some water! 'Quickly now the sailor scurried off and quickly came back with a bucket of water taken from the large barrel which was kept on the stern of the ship.

Mr Trinity began to wash away the congealed blood to

reveal a large gaping wound that went from under his left breast down to his waist. After Mr Trinity had cleaned away the blood he took a small bottle that he kept in his pouch alongside the crystal globe and the red cloth that he had placed over Sutherland's face to bring him back to life after we had been attacked by those evil Angasaurous we had encountered on our last adventure.

After Mr Trinity had cleaned the wound he opened the small bottle and began to sprinkle what looked like some sort of white powder over the wound he then placed the red cloth over the white powder and patted it gently round the wound. I sat and watched as the red cloth began to give off an Erie orange glow the man on the stretcher began to move his head from side to side moaning as he did so. Mr Trinity took a cup of water from one of the sailors and placed it to the man's lips and told him to drink, 'you are in safe hands now' Mr Trinity said? 'Try and rest now we will speak later!' Mr Trinity told one of the sailors to stay with him until the medicine that he had gave him had done its job. 'Come young man time to eat feeling rather peckish after all that excitement! We headed for the stern of the ship and sat down to some food Jemima had prepared earlier for us. As we were sitting eating our food the sailor who had been sitting with the man on the stretcher came running up to Mr Trinity, 'he is beginning to come round Mr Trinity he said, 'and he is asking to see the person in charge of the ship! 'Thank you? Mr Trinity replied. 'I will be with you shortly' 'come young man? 'Let us see what our guest has to say and tell us what happened to him and the rest of the crew!' I jumped up and followed Mr Trinity towards the bow of the ship where the man was now sitting with his back against the foremast; Jemima was sitting next to him mopping the sweat from his brow with a small cloth, which she kept dipping into a bowl of water to keep him cool from the hot morning Sun. We reached the man and Mr Trinity sat down in front of him 'my name is Mr Trinity of the Uteve people 'and who sir is you? The man looked at Mr Trinity and through his thick black beard whispered 'my name is Captain Thor Black and I was the master of the ship Cellum which lies alongside your ship! 'I am in your debt for rescuing me? 'Am I the only one left? Mr Trinity nodded his head. Captain Thor Black looked at Mr Trinity and a tear began to roll down his left cheek, which he wiped away with his huge hand. 'I'm sorry he said to Mr Trinity two of the crew members were my sons. Mr Trinity placed his long bony fingers on Captain Blacks shoulder and said in his soft soothing voice which he used on solemn occasions like this 'we will find whoever did this to you we are truly sorry for your loss!. Mr Trinity summoned Sergeant Pedec to him and told him to take some of the sailors and try to salvage any food and weapons they could find aboard the Cellum. "After you have done that we will have to burn her we do not have enough sailors to sail her said Mr Trinity, 'signal to Captain Raza of the supply ship to come alongside? 'We will transfer the supplies from the Cellum to his ship! One of the sailors picked up a large blue flag and began to wave it to and fro to signal Captain Raza's ship, which lay about six hundred yards off our port side. One of the sailors signalled back, the sails began to unfurl on Captain Raza's ship and it began to move slowly towards us rounding the sterns of the two ships and came alongside the Cellum till she was sandwiched between our ship and Captain Raza's ship.

The two ships were now tied up alongside each other sergeant Pedec beckoned four more of his troops and told them to go and help Captain Raza's men to bring the supplies over from the Cellum onto Captain Raza's ship. In the meantime Mr Trinity had posted lookouts just in case that whatever had attacked Captain Thor Black's ship we would have some warning of the incoming danger. After about a couple of hours Captain Raza approached Mr Trinity and said to him. "Everything is stowed safely aboard? 'And there are definitely no more survivors!' "Thank you replied Mr Trinity? 'We will have to burn the ship we can't take her with us. 'We don't have enough men to sail her? 'It's shameful but it has to be!' Captain Raza summoned two of his men and gave them the orders to burn the ship. Two sailors lit two torches that had been dipped in some of the fat that was kept in a large barrel at the stern of Captain Raza's ship which was going to be used for our cooking. The two sailors leapt aboard the Cellum, and began to ignite the sails, which were hanging loose from the masts just moving back and forth in the breeze like some ghostly apparition. The two sailors then dropped the torches into the hold of the ship and instantly the flames began to take hold of the stricken ship. We had moved a short distance away and watched as the ship started to burn. The two sailors that had set fire to the ship now stood on the bow of the ship that was now burning furiously. They took one look back and then they both jumped together into the sea and began to swim towards us. Captain Rogas lowered a small rope ladder over the ships side for the two sailors to climb aboard. Jemima was waiting with two blanket's which she held out to each sailor as they climbed aboard Mr Trinity told them to go forward with Jemima to dry off and have a hot drink. 'Thank you sir they both replied in unison! 'And off they went to the bow of the ship.

Chapter Eight

I stood on the deck of the ship alongside Mr Trinity and Captain Rogas and watched as the ship burst into flames reaching up into the now darkening night sky. I watched as the ship began to sink slowly down into the ocean depths extinguishing the flames as she sank, leaving clouds of white steam as she sank down into the ocean and then leaving nothing but a flat calm sea where she had once been. The last of the smoke from the ship drifted away on the breeze into the night sky like some ghostly apparition, a few tears began to roll down my cheeks at the loss of such a beautiful ship. At that moment, I began to feel sorry for Captain Thor Black, as his livelihood had just disappeared into the ocean.

"Come young John? 'It's time to rest' 'we have a long day in front of us tomorrow! He put his arm around my shoulders and gave them a gentle squeeze. 'You have seen worse than this on your last adventure 'he said! 'I know I replied but it just seems so unfair? We walked to the stern of our ship where Jemima had been busy preparing our evening meal. Maybe some hot food and drink would make me feel a little bit better and take my mind of the events of the day. I sat down against the ships rail. Jemima gave me a hot bowl of stew and a large cup of steaming tea that after a couple of mouthfuls I did begin to feel a little bit better. I looked across at Captain Thor Black who was now sleeping soundly tucked into a blanket that Jemima had wrapped him in to keep out the cold night air.

I stared at him for a while how peaceful he looked lying there all wrapped up in his blanket like a new born baby, I just wondered what his reaction would be when he awoke in the morning to find he did not have any ship to take command of. I really did feel sorry for him and I began to shed a few more tears without Mr Trinity or Jemima or any of the ship's crew knowing that I had done so I kept that to myself. I finished my hot food and drink I just sat there not saying a word just looking up at the stars in the night sky and wondering to myself if there was any more worlds out there just like my world earth and Mr Trinity's world of Sofala. 'Penny for your thoughts Mr Trinity said smiling as he did so, 'oh I was just thinking if there was any more worlds out there just like mine and your world of Sofala. Mr Trinity smiled and said 'who knows young John who knows? I looked at him and I knew he wasn't telling me everything if he could travel to my world then why not other worlds after all he had the powers to do so and I thought secretly to myself that I think he had a lot more magic then he had shown me since I had known him.

Mr Trinity smiled at me once more reached out with his long bony fingers, took the now empty bowl and teacup from me, and handed them to Jemima 'time to sleep now? I was feeling rather tired after all the excitement that I had endured during the day, Jemima brought me a blanket and pillow I lay down on the ship's deck looked up at the stars twinkling in the night sky and as the ship rolled gently on the sea I drifted off into a deep sleep.

The next morning I awoke to the sound of the ships bell summoning everyone to their duties for the day. I rubbed the sleep out of my eyes and looked around me it was a beautiful sunny day with just a slight breeze and the odd white fluffy cloud in the morning sky, there was nothing around us but clear blue sea our ship along with Captain Raza's sped through the sea making ripples from the bow of each ship that formed small waves and spread out across the sea till they disappeared into the distance. Mr Trinity sat with Captain Thor Black his arm around his shoulders and every now and then he would squeeze his shoulder to reassure him, as he told him what had happened to his ship the day before. Captain Thor Black just sat there his head on his chest and sobbed as Mr Trinity told him the story and that he was the only survivor of that fateful day.

The peaceful calm was shattered by a loud screeching

noise. I looked up at the blue sky and out from the clouds came what looked like a large bird followed by four others. I had seen these creatures before they were the angasaurous those evil half man half bird creatures, Sergeant Pedec ran about giving his men there defensive orders 'man the crossbows he shouted at the top of his voice, "quickly quickly? He shouted," the other soldiers took up a defensive ring all around the side of the ship. 'Wait for my order? The two large harpoon crossbows were loaded and ready each soldier took cover under his shield they were also armed with a small crossbow each. Down came the angasaurous in a line each one with its crossbow loaded with those barbed arrows, they fired there arrows straight at the side of the ship each one them buried deep into the wooden hull, "they are trying to turn the ship over and sink us?" Shouted Captain Rogas to sergeant Pedec. 'Fire your harpoons and don't miss? Sergeant Pedec shouted fire' the two soldiers who operated the crossbows fired at the creatures who by this time were now trying to turn the ship over. We were listing badly to the left the water was starting to come over the ships rail. I hung onto Mr Trinity and watched in fear as the angasaurous strained on the ropes that was attached to their barbed arrows. I watched as the harpoons left the great crossbows that was at the bow of the ship straight and true they went and buried there large iron tips into two of the creatures who let out such an horrible piercing scream that it sent shivers down your spine. "Cut their ropes shouted Captain Rogas!' One of the soldiers leapt onto the side of the now listing ship drew his sword and with one blow severed the ropes from the barbed arrows that were embedded into the ships side; the ship now came back and settled once again on an even keel. The angasaurous flew above us screeching and flapping their great wings they were trying to load their crossbows once again when they were hit by two more harpoons and with one death like noise they fell from the sky plunging into the blue sea which was now beginning to turn a deep red as the blood seeped from the wounds they had suffered in the attack on the two ships. I watched in awe as the last of the angasaurous fell screaming from the sky into the blood red sea around the ships, they lay on the surface struggling and flapping their wings in their final death throes till they sank beneath the waves leaving nothing but their blood on the surface which the sea began to disperse till there was nothing but the calm blue sea. "Mr Trinity turned to Captain Rogas" "that was extremely close? "Yes-replied Captain Rogas wiping the sweat from his brow with a dirty piece of cloth he had pulled out of his tunic 'mighty close indeed mighty close? He turned round on his heels and started to walk along the deck of the ship shouting out orders to his sailors as he walked 'set sail 'and keep a sharp lookout! Mr Trinity bent down to where Captain Thor Black was sitting against the ships rail that by this time was really now beginning to feel a lot better. 'Are those the creatures that attacked your ship? 'Yes he replied those are the creatures! 'Mmm said Mr Trinity I cannot understand why they should be this far west' 'Kaunn has something to do with this I am sure of that?

Mr Trinity beckoned Captain Rogas and Sergeant Pedec towards him; he took the crystal globe from under his cloak and placed it onto the ship's deck in front of us. He rubbed his hands over the globe and the mist in it began to clear, and there was Kaunn sitting astride some large type bird I thought it was a bird until I looked closer, "what is that I stammered? 'Ah, said Mr Trinity that is a Racicon 'you might say in your world a dragon? 'But don't worry they don't breathe fire! 'Actually they are quite a tame creature there are not many of them left you might say a dying breed! I looked into the crystal globe and watched as Kaunn and the Racicon flew on into the distance and out of sight. Mr Trinity picked up the crystal globe and placed it back into his cloak and sat there for a couple of minutes before he began to speak, 'I do believe he is trying to get to the green mountains where the troglodytes dwell they will fight for anyone if he offers them new lands? "We don't have enough men to fight them there are thousands of them Captain Rogas replied' 'looks like we will have to ask our old friends once again to help us on our quest said Mr Trinity? I smiled at Mr Trinity my heart was pounding with the thought of meeting my old friends especially Poppy one and two and fairy Nough also the peoples I had met on our last adventure.

Captain Rogas? " Signal to Captain Raza to bring his ship about we sail for the lands of the Gawen peoples to meet General Dylantos he is a very old friend? "Yes Mr Trinity? "Captain Rogas gave his orders to the signalman for Captain Raza to join our ship so Mr Trinity could tell him the situation and why we were altering course. By this time the sailors had taken in the sails and our ship just bobbed up and down on the slight swell of the sea. Captain Raza's ship sailed slowly up alongside us where four of the sailors from our ship tied Captain Raza's ship alongside ours. Captain Raza stepped aboard Mr Trinity took him to one side and told him what he had seen in the crystal globe and what Kaunn was up to. Captain Raza nodded his head up and down listening intently to what Mr Trinity was saying he stood and looked into Mr Trinity's blue eyes for a couple of minutes smiled and said 'yes sir Mr Trinity? He turned around and jumped back aboard his ship, four of our sailors released the ropes that had kept Captain Raza's ship alongside. Captains Raza's ship began gently to drift away on the swell of the sea. Captain Rogas shouted out his orders to set sail. Every sailor ran about doing his duty. I looked across at Captain Raza's ship and watched his sailors unfurl the sails. Everything was ready the sails were released and suddenly the sea breeze filled the sails. They were now the way to the lands of the Gawen people and General Dylantos soon we would be on our way too following Captain Raza into the unknown.

We were finally on our way "Mr Trinity? 'How long before we reach the lands of the Gawen people? 'About three days sail if the weather holds out, 'Don't worry this is our summer time and we don't get much bad weather in the way of winds just a lot of rain sometimes! I nodded and walked away to the stern of the ship where I stripped down to my undergarments and lay down under the sun to sunbathe. After all, I may as well make the most of the next three days; I might not get the chance again. I must have drifted off when the ships bell awoke me. The sun was beginning to settle down over the horizon like a large red fireball. Something smelt rather well, as the aroma drifted under my nostrils. I sat up and Jemima gave me a bowl of hot stew, and a large chunk of bread with a beaker of the green strawberry tasting liquid. While I had been asleep, the sailors had rigged up a temporary galley so we could have some hot food for the journey, after all it would not be very nice eating cold food for the next three days. I finished my food, sat back against the ships rail, and thought about all the old friends I would meet again. I hoped they would all turn up and help us once again on our quest to find Kaunn. After all he was the one who tried to use Dr Zaker to conquer this world of Sofala. But he escaped and we have to do it all over again and this time make sure there is no one to take his place when he his eventually found. The stars were now high in the sky nothing all around us but the darkness and the odd white tipped wave which gave off a silvery glow as the moon shone down. Everything was calm except the sound of the waves as the ship sailed through the sea making ripples that slowly drifted away and disappeared into the distance. Mr Trinity came up to me and said 'did you enjoy your sunbathe young John? Yes thank you' "Good good but don't overdo it will you? 'I won't I replied but it is nice to relax now and then. 'Try and get some sleep young man you never know what tomorrow may bring. Goodnight Mr Trinity? 'And you he said and with his last words ringing in my ears I lay down and drifted into a deep sleep dreaming of the forth coming adventure and what would happen when we saw Kaunn.

The next morning I awoke, to the wonderful aroma of food cooking over the small oven that Jemima had arranged at the stern of the ship. I brushed myself down and straightened my clothes and walked to where Mr Trinity was sitting with Captain Thor Black and Captain Rogas. The ship was gently rolling making me stagger from side to side as I slowly walked along the ship's deck. I could see Mr Trinity smiling at my predicament as I tried to stay upright on my feet. 'Good morning John he said! 'Sit here beside me he gently grabbed me by my arm and helped me to sit down. I settled next to Mr Trinity Jemima smiled and gave a hot bowl of what looked like porridge. Captain Rogas gave me a spoon and said! "Tuck in its good for you just the food to start the day full of goodness that food is' 'What is it I asked? Mr Trinity spoke up before Captain Rogas could say anything, 'it's porridge what do you think it was! 'We have porridge in our world as well you know' 'sorry, I replied it's a strange world this world of Sofala, 'I know I know Mr Trinity replied smiling at me, 'but don't worry you are safe we won't let anything happen to you. The sun was now beginning to rise higher in the sky like a big yellow ball of fire a slight breeze filled the air filling the sails I strolled forward to the bow of the ship and let the wind blow my hair.

Chapter Nine

I opened my shirt and let the breeze surround my body making my shirt billow out like the sails of the ship. I looked over the ships bow and watched as the fish jumped out of the water as the bow of the ship ploughed through the sea disturbing the fish. You could almost reach out and touch the fish with your hand. Captain Rogas shouted to some of his sailors to bring a net and cast it over the ships side, no sooner had it been cast than it started to fill with fish the sailors started to drag the net in towards the ship where other sailors with nets on long poles began to scoop up the fish, and throw them down onto the deck where they wriggled till other sailors hit them over the head to kill them and lay lifeless on the ship's deck. Mr Trinity said! To me guess what's for supper tonight laughing it was good to see him smile for a change just like his old self.

I was so pleased that Mr Trinity was feeling like his old self again smiling and laughing and telling the odd funny story, but he still kept that sense of mystery I still had the feeling that he did not show us all the powers that he had but maybe one day he would!. It was a lovely sunny day not a cloud in the clear blue sky, I thought to myself that I may as well take the opportunity to make the most of the voyage to relax and enjoy the sunshine till we reached the land of the Gawen people and General Dylantos. I settled down against the ships rail lifted my head and let the rays of the midday sun beam down on me. I felt so comfortable that I fell asleep under the hot sun. I awoke with a start and rubbed the sleep from my eyes it was quite dark. The moon was high in the sky and I could make out Mr Trinity standing at the bow of the ship, looking out across the sea everything so silent except the creaking of the ship and the ropes in the rigging as she ploughed through the sea. I rose up from my sitting position stretched my arms and legs and walked to the bow of the ship towards Mr Trinity I had only gone a few more yards when he said, "good evening John did you sleep well! "Oh yes I replied! he knew it had been me walking up behind him it was that sixth sense again I stood next to him he put his arm round my shoulder his long bony fingers squeezing my upper arm, "such a beautiful night? 'Yes, I replied as I looked out across the dark sea that looked like a sheet of silver as the moon shone across it. We have made good headway Mr Trinity said, 'we will reach the land of the Gawen peoples sometime tomorrow afternoon' 'we have been very fortunate on our journey to have such good weather 'this sea can be very dangerous when the weather changes. I was somehow relieved that it had been such an uneventful sea voyage apart from the angasaurous birds we had encountered on our first day at sea. We both stood their together not saying a word just looking out at the silvery sea, the night breeze gently blowing around me making me feel slightly cold. 'Come young John supper time, we both turned around and headed for the stern of the ship where Jemima was cooking the food. As we got nearer, the aroma of the food was making my mouth water with the thought of eating her delicious food; after all, she was such a good cook. I was just hoping that she would be staying with us till we caught Kaunn. Mr Trinity and I sat down next to Captain Thor Black who by this time was feeling quite chirpy now after his ordeal with those terrible creatures the Angasaurous. Mr Trinity spoke "so good to see you are feeling much better! "Thank you Captain Thor Black replied, 'I have to thank you for that Mr Trinity! Mr Trinity held up his hand to silence him and then spoke 'you don't have to thank me' 'I would do the same for anyone in your predicament he said! Captain Thor Black smiled back at Mr Trinity looked down and then started to eat his food. Captain Rogas along with Sergeant Pedec joined us for the evening meal, Captain Rogas spoke up talking between mouthfuls of food, 'we should reach the mouth of the river tomorrow then it's about an half a day's journey to the inland sea and the domain of General Dylantos and the Gawen people. Everyone sat around talking and telling stories of the adventures, they had encountered. Some were too hard to believe so I thought I would tell them all about my last adventure with Mr Trinity and the great battle that we had with Dr Zaker. As I spoke Mr Trinity just sat there with a slight grin on his face as the others listened intently, their eyes wide and mouths open as I told my story. I knew they might believe me but Mr Trinity knew I was exaggerating because I wanted my story to be better than everyone else's. After I had finished telling my story no one spoke they just sat there dumbfounded looking at Mr Trinity for some reassurance as to if it was true or not. Mr Trinity smiled put his long bony fingers on my shoulder and said 'I think we should all retire now for the evening as we have a long day ahead of us tomorrow! 'after all General Dylantos is not expecting us to arrive so we will have to be vigilant just in case. Mr Trinity and I rose up from our sitting positions and headed for the bow of the ship leaving everyone still thinking that my story had been true or not it was but I had made it seem more exciting and dangerous than it had been.

Mr Trinity and I reached our beds at the bow of the ship which Jemima had prepared for us. I lay down and looked across at Mr Trinity who was smiling he then spoke to me and said 'by you can really tell a good story young man! 'Still never mind no harm done try to sleep now. I lay on my back looking up at the stars in the sky as they seemed to move around in the night sky to the roll of the ship, I stared at the stars in the night sky but I could not sleep as I was thinking of what tomorrow might bring and if I would see any old friends especially Fairy Nough as the island of Siphonos was not far from General Dylantos's village. I tossed and turned for quite some time till I fell into a deep sleep but I dreamt of all the old friends that I hoped to see on this adventure. The next morning I awoke to the sound of one of the sailors shouting from the masthead 'land ahoy 'land ahoy. Everyone jumped up, and ran to either side of the ship, and looked ahead into the horizon. There rising out of the sea was the land of the Gawen people, closer and closer we got and as we did so I could make out the mouth of the river to the inland sea, it was quite wide with rocky out tops either side of the river and below them the whitest sand I had ever seen. We headed for the mouth of the river and entered passing by the rocky out tops either side of the ship, Mr Trinity told everyone to carry on as normal we are being watched he said I knew he was right nothing got past that sixth sense of his. We passed through the rocky out tops which seemed to overhang above the ship as if we were passing through a tunnel. Then all of a sudden there in front of us was the land of the Gawen people, it was a flat desert plain either side of the river as far as the eye could see, nothing like the land I could remember of lush valleys green fields and forests with deer roaming across the land. 'Look pointed Mr Trinity in the distance can you see! I put my hands across my eyes to shield them from the glare of the morning sun. There in the distance I could just make out a few figures on horseback following alongside us keeping their distance. Mr Trinity said to me not to worry they are just watching we will meet a more considerable force of men the nearer we get to General Dylantos village.

As we sailed down the river the banks began to widen out till eventually after sailing for most of the day, we entered the inland sea of the Gawen people. I wondered if General Dylantos would welcome us warmly, or would he tell us to leave, as in the last battle that we had fought with Dr Zaker he had lost a great many warriors more than any other tribe...Mr Trinity stood beside me his arm around my shoulder and said! 'I know what you are thinking' 'but don't worry I know General Dylantos he is a good man he will help us. I looked up at Mr Trinity and smiled but he knew that whatever words he had said to me still left me with that slight apprehension of what might happen when we finally met General Dylantos. A shout from the top of the mast brought me back to reality. "Land ahoy 'land ahoy "everyone started to run about preparing for the worst after all we had not been invited to this land of

Gawen. As I looked closer I could see a mountainous land rising out from the sea, 'look said Mr Trinity it's the island of Siphonos where your friend fairy Nough lives! 'It's not far now to the lands of General Dylantos. I looked into the distance and watched as the island began to get closer and closer when all of a sudden a large black cloud which hung over the mountain began to move towards us at incredible speed as it neared a loud humming noise came from the cloud. 'Don't worry' said Mr Trinity that will be king Ronough! 'We will be fine when he knows who we are. The great black cloud got nearer till it hung above us like a swarm of bees the noise was deafening some of the sailors and soldiers began to take cover under their shields their crossbows at the ready. Mr Trinity walked to the centre of the ship's deck and began to wave his arms from side to side when like a flash out of the cloud came two figures who landed in front of Mr Trinity and me. It was King Ronough and his daughter Fairy Nough who instantly flew towards me and planted a kiss on my cheek I could feel myself start to go red. Mr Trinity and King Ronough started to laugh at my predicament. King Ronough signalled to the black cloud above us, which then began to head back to the island until there was only King Ronough and his daughter Fairy Nough left with Mr Trinity and me.

'So good to see you once again Mr Trinity 'and you young John it's so nice of you to visit but I have a feeling this is not a social call. Mr Trinity nodded his head took King Ronough to one side sat down on the ship's deck removed the crystal globe from his cloak and gently rubbed his hands over the smooth surface of the crystal. Straight away it began to cloud over he rubbed it a couple of more times and the mist in the crystal began to clear to reveal Kaunn, and there he was sitting around an open campfire along with about a dozen of those cave dwelling troglodytes. Kaunn was sitting talking and waving his arms about while he spoke to the troglodytes the crystal began to cloud over once again and then he was gone. King Ronough sat there for a couple of minutes with his thoughts not saying a word "Tell me Mr Trinity is this the same situation we had with Dr Zaker! 'I'm afraid so replied Mr Trinity! 'Kaunn was always the evil one Dr Zaker was just a pawn in his hand to conquer this world of Sofala if he had succeeded he would have rid himself of Dr Zaker, that is why we were on our way to General Dylantos to ask for his help. King Ronough looked at Mr Trinity 'I will send my Daughter Fairy Nough to see General Dylantos and tell him you are coming' and prepare him for your arrival we should be there just before nightfall. King Ronough summoned his daughter to him and told her to go and see General Dylantos and prepare him for our arrival that evening. She patted me on the cheek and said see you later and in an instant, she was gone. "You do know that we are going to need more than General Dylantos's soldiers! 'I know replied Mr Trinity but the longer we wait Kaunn will gather more men and it will be just like the last time. King Ronough nodded 'but I have Portis the bird she can travel along with my daughter John and yourself if you wish to the lands of the other tribes that helped us on our last quest to defeat Dr Zaker where you can ask them for help! 'But will Portis be big enough for John and me? "oh she is big enough twice the size as when you last saw her said King Ronough smiling at Mr Trinity. 'Anyway you can think about it while we sail to the lands of General Dylantos if you wish.

"Come said Mr Trinity I think we should partake of some refreshment before we reach the lands of Gawen and you can tell me all about what has happened these past months while I have been away...Mr Trinity King Ronough and I began to walk to the stern of the ship for our afternoon meal. Mr Trinity was laughing as King Ronough told him everything that had happened while we had been away. We reached the stern of the ship and sat down next to sergeant Pedec and Captains' Rogas and Thor Black, who Mr Trinity introduced to King Ronough. We, must have sat there for hours talking and laughing, when one of the sailors came to us stood to attention and saluted Captain Rogas. 'Excuse me sir the lands of the Gawen people is just off our starboard bow! 'Thank you said Captain Rogas who smiled and looked at Mr Trinity 'well here we are at last, we all stood up and headed towards the bow of the ship.

Chapter Ten

I ran along the ship's deck towards the bow and looked across at the village of General Dylantos; you could make out the island of Siphonos the home of Fairy Nough in the distance. As we got nearer I could see those lush green fields with the deer roaming and feeding on the lush green leaves and fruit that hung from small bushes scattered about the fields. We entered the mouth of a small river that passed below the mountain that was on our port bow with its snow topped peaks high above us, the sunlight shining off the snow making all the colours of the rainbow, a small waterfall tumbled down the side of the mountain into the river below. We headed for a long wooden jetty were two of General Dylantos's men were waiting to take the ropes from our ship to secure us to the jetty. There was General Dylantos standing a big round portly man he still had his large red beard and the same clothes that he always wore. His deep red pantaloons his brown leather jacket with no sleeves red shirt and knee length leather boots. A thick six-inch black belt around his waist, red shoulder length hair, he had four long daggers tucked into his belt and his long broadsword hung down his back between his shoulder blades.

He began to wave his arms back and forth in excitement. By this time, Fairy Nough had joined her father aboard our ship. Captain Rogas ordered two of the sailors to lower the gangplank onto the jetty for us to disembark. I looked out at the village with its perfectly formed round houses with straw roofs and small leaded windows, the smoke rising up into the evening sky each house with its own little garden at the front. I looked across the fields where some of General Dylantos's men were tending the crops, I could see the two small wooden bridges' that crossed the river that ran round the village. In the distance I could see the forest of Parek where Hipictu lived with his pygmy cannibals it was so good to be back. Mr Trinity turned to me and said! "Well shall we go and meet General Dylantos? I nodded and we proceeded to walk down the gangplank followed by everyone else. We reached the jetty where General Dylantos strode forward and flung his arms around Mr Trinity 'ah so good to see once again he said! 'Likewise also Mr Trinity replied General Dylantos stepped back "AH young John pleased to see you also as he gave me a hug nearly squeezing all my breath from me, 'tell me? 'Where is young Sutherland I began to explain to him the reason why he could not come and why, 'never mind' 'you are hear now young John. General Dylantos turned to Mr Trinity and asked to be introduced to the other people that were with us, "oh forgive my manners he said! And he then began to introduce everyone to General Dylantos, after the introductions had been made everyone shook hands with the General he then spoke to one of his soldiers! 'Take everyone to our large guesthouse at the edge of the village and make them welcome "Come with me said General Dylantos we will stay in my house tonight! 'We will eat and talk and you can tell me why you have come! Mr Trinity nodded his head; we began to walk towards his house along with Captains Rogas Raza, and Thor Black with Sergeant Pedec and King Ronough bringing up the rear. Fairy Nough was sitting on General Dylantos shoulders. After a few minutes' walk, we reached the guesthouse I looked at the front door, which hung on its large black hinges. I thought of the last time I was here with Sutherland and the rest of the leaders of the other tribes. I was deep in thought when General Dylantos's voice brought me back to reality. 'I have a surprise for you and Mr Trinity young man! "Come follow me the General said! I began to get rather excited at the thought of what it might be. I stood outside the door 'open it the general said with a grin on his face. I pushed open the door its hinges making a creaking noise and I stepped into the room but all I could see was the great fire in front of me with a large animal roasting over the open fire and a table full of fruit bread and flagons of drink. I could not see anything that would surprise me. General Dylantos along with Mr Trinity and the others entered behind me. The great door began to close slowly when all of a sudden it slammed shut making me jump and turn round suddenly, and there to my surprise stood poppies one and two with a large smile on their faces from ear to ear. I ran towards them and they both hugged me together their huge arms squeezing me gently. I stood back with tears of happiness running down my cheeks Mr Trinity just stood there and smiled showing no signs of emotion just his usual calm self he then spoke in that soft voice of his that he would use on special occasions. 'This is quite a nice surprise boys been here long have you he then held out his hand and shook their hands vigorously. General Dylantos interrupted and said "come let's eat and talk about old times tonight and tomorrow we can discuss Kaunn in the morning we don't want it to spoil our reunion everyone nodded in agreement and head for the table full of food and drink. We all sat at the table General Dylantos at one end and Mr Trinity at the other facing him everyone else sat down on either side of the table. General Dylantos clapped his hands and two of his warriors crossed to the large open fire where a large animal was roasting on a spit. They removed the animal and placed it in the centre of the table on a large metal oblong plate. It looked like a pig at least I hope it was a pig because I was quite partial to a nice bit of roast pork.

Tuck in now don't want it to get cold do we. It really did smell so good everyone picked up the large carving knife that was beside everyone's plate. I watched as Fairy Nough tried to pick up the knife with her two tiny hands but it was too big for her to handle after all she was such a tiny person. She flew towards me with her small plate sat down in front of me on the table and whispered cut me a piece of that lovely smelling meat for me please will you John. Not a problem I replied how much do you want! "Just a small piece; please! I began to cut a small piece of meat from the carcass in the centre of the table and placed it on her tiny plate, 'thank you she said and in a flash she flew to the other end of the table where her father was sitting picking at the carcass with his tiny fingers. Everyone just sat there not saying a word, just eating and drinking and with their own thoughts. General Dylantos's beard along with the beards of Poppy one and two were covered in grease from the animal making them glisten in the light from the candles that were placed at intervals along the table. General Dylantos let out a loud belch and rubbed his large stomach, then in unison the two poppy's let out a loud noise from down below of which the smell was quite nauseating well they had never changed still done everything together. Two of the Generals men ran forward and began to sprinkle the air with a sweet smelling liquid to take away the horrible stench, that had come from the nether regions of their trousers. Mr Trinity did not look very amused after all, he was a well-mannered person, but when everyone started to laugh, then he saw the funny side and joined in the laughter. After everyone had ate their fill the two soldiers began to clear away the table until all that was left were the flagons of drink and the candles burning in the centre of the table. General Dylantos lit up his pipe and sat there puffing away looking around the table at everyone. No one said a word we just sat there each one of us with our own thoughts I was thinking what Sutherland was doing now back at the home I just wished he were here with me now after all he was my best friend the only one person who had made feel welcome when I arrived at the home, but still if his mind had been stronger, he would have remembered our last adventure together and would be here now.

General Dylantos spoke up 'it's getting rather late now' 'I think we should rest, and tomorrow we will discuss what needs to be done as regards Kaunn. Everyone nodded in agreement "good that's settled then said the General who tapped his pipe on the table to put it out. He lifted his portly frame from the chair and headed for the great bed that lay in the corner of the room.

We all had to share the bed I remembered it from the

last time I was here a great big bed with large fluffy pillows and an extremely soft mattress the only thing I did not enjoy was the two poppies flatulence that they seemed to do at regular intervals during the night making the whole room stink. "Come young John time for bed I will sit here for a while and think about tomorrow and try and make some plans I don't think I can sleep at present I arose from my seat and headed for the bed in the corner of the room and lay down on the soft mattress, I could not sleep I just lay there between the poppy brothers and watched Mr Trinity sitting at the table deep in thought, it must have been quite a while before I drifted off to sleep. I awoke the next morning to the most unearthly stench I jumped out of bed and ran to the door flung it wide open and started to take in deep breaths to fill my lungs with fresh morning air. Everyone was sitting on the balcony apart from Fairy Nough. King Ronough explained that she had gone to get her pet bird Portis, for our journey to the lands of the other peoples, who inhabited this world of Sofala. General Dylantos summoned two of his warriors and told them to bring some scent sticks and place them in his house to get rid of the smell that Poppy one and two had left behind. They must have thought it funny as they just sat on the balcony smiling at everyone, still you had to see the funny side something to cheer us up on such a gloomy day.

We sat there for a while till the smell had cleared from the room then we all entered and sat at the table to have some breakfast, which looked like porridge and a drink of what looked like dirty dish water. General Dylantos told me it was made from some root that grew in the forest of Parek. We have an agreement with Hipictu the cannibal leader we give him some of our deer in return for the root! 'That is if he cannot find any fresh meat that strays into the forest if you get my meaning young man, besides its good for you gives you strength flexing his thick muscular arms. I smiled at the General as if I was impressed but it still tasted like dirty dishwater to me.

After everyone had finished their meal, the General took out a large map from a cupboard on the wall, and placed it on the table in front of everyone; he unrolled it to reveal the lands of the different tribes of Sofala. I looked at the map the General pointed out the flatlands of Sondron where Christinos lived, the lands of Scordisi where Alcoyneaus lived with his giants, and other lands where we had not been. The land of General Giedroyc of the Tyrocdils, that was called Tyrocdils the lands of the ice people, who had helped us in the last battle to defeat Dr Zaker. We are here in the land of Gawen! "This is the inland sea you came on. As you can see from the map its about four days sail back to where you came from to the plains of Tongees, across that plain lies Modecica and the armies of King Todec! And I know they will fight for Kaunn as there is a long history of conflict between yourselves the Uteve people and the people of Modecica! "Then we have the Troglodytes to contend with whom you know can take on any human form they wish... Mr Trinity nodded and replied! "We have already encountered those creatures they tried to fool me by taking on the forms of the poppy brothers, but I dealt with that situation didn't I young John? 'Yes, I replied! General Dylantos nodded his head and smiled at Mr Trinity, he knew what Mr Trinity had meant. The problem is how do we get from here to the plains of Tongees as we do not have any great ships. Just a few small boats for fishing and they will not stand any storms at sea, that is our dilemma, suppose we could take about seventy men on each ship and that is going to be a tight squeeze said the general. Will Kaunn not come to us the general said. King Ronough spoke up "how many warriors can you get on your two ships! Mr Trinity turned to Captain Rogas and asked him how many warriors we could take, 'One hundred and forty' replied Captain Rogas! Mm said Mr Trinity one hundred and forty and I already have a hundred sailors and soldiers with me which makes two hundred and forty still not enough I'm afraid. "Look replied General Dylantos King

Gandelin of the Volsci people has those huge birds "oh what do you call them! Poppy one interrupted 'they are called Synisaurous huge things ugly as well! "But can they fly all that distance the General said, everyone just stood there in silence looking at each other not knowing the answer to the question.

After a few minutes, Mr Trinity spoke "we will only find out when we consult King Gandelin and if they can't we will have to find some other way round the problem! Everyone nodded their heads in unison and General Dylantos had the last word you are right Mr Trinity lets worry about that, later our main priority is to try to get the tribal leaders here with their warriors. At that moment, everyone's attention was to a loud screeching sound coming from outside, we all headed outside to the balcony and looked up and there she was Fairy Nough on her pet bird Portis, by how she had grown to at least twice the size since the last time that I had seen her. Portis circled around the village a couple of times to get her bearings then down she came her wings spread out like an aeroplane she landed in a clearing in one of the fields. Some of General Dylantos's people ran out to greet Fairy Nough and her pet bird Portis. By this time Portis had flopped down on her belly and buried her head into her large feathered wings so she just looked like a large boulder in the field. Fairy Nough flew to her father and greeted him with a kiss on both cheeks, 'what about me?' Poppy one said smiling! even though she was an eighteen inch fairy she was very beautiful, she flew towards Poppy one and kissed him he then started to dance in a circular motion singing 'she likes me 'she likes me smiling as he danced.

Everyone began to laugh aloud even Mr Trinity was laughing along with everybody. General Dylantos beckoned two of his warriors to him and told them to set a table of food on the balcony for us to have some lunch, it was a beautiful day not a cloud in the sky just clear blue sky as far as the eye could see.

After a few minutes we all sat down to an early morning

lunch before Mr Trinity and I along with Fairy Nough would set out on our journey to contact the other tribes. After we had sat for a few minutes to digest our food General Dylantos took out a small map from his waistcoat pocket and laid it out on the table. "I drew this for you last night' 'it will help you to find your way to where you are going! 'Thank you said Mr Trinity! 'That will be a great help he told the General! However, I knew Mr Trinity did not need any map he knew how to get to wherever we were going, but he took the map from the General anyway, and placed it in his cloak and thanked him. Mr Trinity did not want to upset the General at this moment in time.

I was really beginning to get rather excited at this moment thinking of all the people I would meet again on this journey we were about to take. "Come young John time to leave we have a long journey ahead of us the quicker we start the quicker we get back say your goodbyes. I stood up, hugged Poppy one and two, and shook hands with everyone, and then Mr Trinity and me descended the steps of the balcony and walked to where Portis was lying with her head still tucked into her feathered wings. Fairy Nough flew towards Portis and woke her up she took her head from underneath her wings and looked around with her big yellow eyes. That is when she saw me, she rose to her feet and waddled towards me her great head moving back and forth, she reached me and nestled her head in the small of my neck and began to coo. "She recognizes you John 'she never forgets a friend. 'well shall we leave now, Fairy Nough placed a leather harness on Portis which had three small seats just big enough to sit on at the front of each seat was a small T shaped handle Fairy Nough mounted, then me with Mr Trinity behind me "are you ready?" said Fairy Nough "then off we go." She tapped Portis on the top of her head, and she started to run along the ground picking up speed and flapping her great wings, until all of a sudden we were in the air. Portis circled around a couple of times over the village to get her bearings. I looked down below me I could see everyone waving their arms saying goodbye, then out of the corner of my eye I saw Jemima flying alongside us. "Mr Trinity she shouted your bag she flew alongside and handed Mr Trinity a small bag some food for your journey she said, and then flew away into the distance back to where everyone was still waving goodbye. I looked back and watched as everyone started to disappear into the distance until there was nothing around us but the earth below and blue sky above.

I turned my head round and asked Mr Trinity where are we going first please? "Well I think we should go and see Alyconeus first; 'and ask him for his help first as they are the furthest away! 'Then on to see General Giedroyc, 'King Gandelin and then double back to Christinos of the Sondron people! 'That will give the others time to reach the flatlands of Sondron to meet us when we arrive. "How long before we reach the Scordisi giants, Fairy Nough? "We should be there sometime tomorrow if all goes well John, "but first we have to stop for the night! "can you remember that island that we stopped at on the way to see King Gandelin we will rest there for the evening then carry on with our journey tomorrow. Mr Trinity took some bread and a piece of meat from the bag that Jemima had given him and passed it to me "eat this it will be a while before we reach the island! I took the bread and meat from him and began to eat till my belly was quite full, "feeling better now John Mr Trinity said! "Yes I replied and settled back against Mr Trinity's chest and watched as we flew over the flat earth below us. After a while Mr Trinity tapped me on the shoulder, 'look down there can you see the quaking grounds below! I looked down at the quaking grounds the earth moving up and down in a wave like motion I just hope that Portis did not get to tired and decide to land in the middle of the quaking grounds.

But I need not have worried we passed over with no difficultly at all. On we travelled enjoying the scenery below and the hot sun on my face nothing around apart from the odd bird that flew alongside, looking at us with curiosity then flew on their way leaving us all alone again in the clear blue sky. Portis turned and began to head west I knew we were travelling west as the sun was behind us now. On we travelled till the sun began to settle down on the horizon in front of me. "Look Mr Trinity there is the island! Mr Trinity and I looked down in unison and there it was the island surrounded by a large lake, Portis began to circle around the island a couple of times and then began to descend into the sandy clearing that was surrounded by tall trees all around the clearing.

We landed just as the sun went down over the horizon leaving nothing but darkness and the eerie creaking of the branches of the trees as they swayed in the breeze. Fairy Nough gave Portis some food and drink which she had brought with her and settled her down for the night...Portis ate her food and she then tucked her head under her great wings and fell into a deep sleep...Mr Trinity said 'follow me John. I followed him to the edge of the trees where we gathered a few small branches to make a fire. After we had piled the branches I was wondering how we were going to light it, when Mr Trinity looked at the branches for a few seconds which suddenly burst into flames. I just smiled because I knew he had done that with his mind he had that strange power to do things like that, but I could never fathom out why he did not use them more often. As we sat beside the fire, a strange looking rabbit like creature came out from the trees looked at Mr Trinity and before it could turn round, it lay dead on the ground in front of me. I did not see Mr Trinity's hand move it happened so fast, he quickly skinned the creature placed a stick through its body and began to roast it over the open fire. It did smell good; my mouth began to water with the thought of a hot meal inside me. I knew Fairy Nough would not eat much due to her size even more for me, but I should not be selfish she was after all my friend so I put my selfish thoughts to the back of my mind. And waited for my meal. The creature did smell good I awaited with anticipation my mouth watering with the thought of that lovely meat waiting to touch my lips. When the creature was cooked Mr Trinity tore off one of the creatures legs and passed it to me, I started to devour it greedily till nothing was left but the dry bone, I then started to lick my fingers till there was no meat juices left on my fingers. I was still feeling quite hungry but Mr Trinity said we should keep some meat for our journey tomorrow just in case we have to stop for a rest sometime during the day. "Well time to sleep now another long day tomorrow! I looked at Mr Trinity, Fairy Nough said goodnight and lay back on the soft grass, and leaves that I had gathered from underneath the base of the trees. I looked up at the stars above me as they moved around in the heavens and drifted off into a deep sleep. The next thing I remember was Mr Trinity shaking me by the shoulder and saying time to rise young man we have to leave, I rubbed the sleep out of my eyes and opened them wide to find Fairy Nough sitting on my chest with her arms folded! "Good morning John? "Good morning I replied as my eyes began to get accustomed to the daylight, the sun was beaming down into the clearing making the sand lovely and warm next to my body I was so comfortable I did not want to move but I knew I did not have any choice in the matter. I arose from my bed brushed myself down and headed to where Portis was waiting along with Mr Trinity and Fairy Nough, Mr Trinity lifted me up onto Portis he then climbed in behind me. Fairy Nough whispered something to Portis and with one bound and the flap of her great wings, we began to rise into the air just missing the tops of the trees as we left the clearing below us.

Portis circled around the island to get her bearings, once more and headed west again across the great expanse of open water, which lay below us towards the land of Alcoyneaus and the Scordisi tribe. On we travelled across the great inland sea nothing above us but blue skies and the clear blue sea below. All you could see on the water below us was shadow of Portis's great wings as we moved over the open sea.

Chapter Eleven

We travelled on most of the day underneath the hot sun no clouds in the sky the breeze from Portis's wings kept me cool as they flapped up and down as we travelled along over the sea below us. I was beginning to feel rather tired by now as we had been travelling most of the day when Mr Trinity tapped me on the shoulder 'look John over there in the distance! 'There are the mountains of Thodulf, below them is the flatlands of Sondron where Christinos lives and over those mountains is the lands of the Scordisi people, 'we will head for their village first and meet Alcoyneaus I just hope he is pleased to see us. I nodded my head and then spoke up, "why can't we just fly over them I asked Fairy Nough! 'it's too cold once you get above their cloud rim you will begin to freeze also Portis's wings will begin to form ice on them and we will fall from the sky; 'that is why we have to fly round the mountains! A lump came into my throat I did not fancy falling of Portis into the ice and snow of those mountains. Portis began to veer away until we reached the base of the first, mountain she kept close to the side of the mountain its sheer walls going straight down into the sea below. All you could hear was the thunderous noise of the waves as they crashed against the base of the mountain spouting water into the air. The spray that soaked our clothes was quite cold, I was feeling a bit apprehensive I did not want to fall into those waves and be dashed against the side of the mountain, so I hung on tight to Mr Trinity with all my strength.

When all of a sudden Portis veered sharply to the left taking me by surprise. Mr Trinity held me tight his arm around my waist to keep me from falling into the sea below, my heart was beating like a drum, 'sorry said Fairy Nough 'falling rocks hope she did not frighten you, I just smiled but she could probably tell I was shaking from head to toe with fear. After what seemed like a lifetime Portis slowly began to veer to the right around the base of the mountain, as we came round the side of the mountain the sea disappeared and there below us was a green flat grassy plain with a small river running through it. I could not believe my eyes for there below me were these large what looked like antelopes but they were at least three times bigger. Fish jumped out of the river they were massive at least four feet long, I just hoped we had not gone back in time to some strange dinosaur world but after all this world of Sofala was a strange place. We flew along the river following the turns and bends until we came across a forest which stood either side of the river, we travelled through the trees Portis's wings just missing the branches as we travelled along. I looked and then looked again they were fruit trees apples pears plums all different kinds of fruit, some I had never seen before they were Hugh twice the size of my head and Mrs Jones said I had a big head but I did not believe her. We flew through the trees, when all of a sudden we were in a large open field where different kinds of crops were growing. Every kind of vegetable you could think of, except these were big really big my eyes were probably popping out of my head with the sight that lay below me. Mr Trinity tapped me on the shoulder look there in the distance there is the village of Alcoyneaus won't be long now as we got nearer the village I could see some of the giant Scordisi tribe working in the fields, tending their crops not one of them looking up with curiosity to see who was coming to their village.

Fairy Nough pointed to a flat large field that lay at the end of the village 'we will land there she said! Mr Trinity nodded his head and Fairy Nough headed Portis to a field that lay a few hundred yards from the village. She landed with a bump and fell down on her belly puffing and panting with exhaustion, no one was taking any notice of us it was as if we did not exist, after a few minutes wait while Portis began to recover from our long journey. Fairy Nough got back on Portis and we all began to walk towards the village. Still no one took any notice when all of a sudden Alcoyneaus stepped out from behind one of the houses at the edge of the village, there he stood dressed just the way I remembered him from the last time, standing in front of me his bald head shining in the sun his black cloak slung over his shoulder and dressed in red trousers and red waistcoat top. Down by his side hung a huge sword and tucked into a thick leather belt round his waist was a row of knives, also strapped to his left boot was pouch which held another knife. "Good day to you Mr Trinity! Said Alyconeus 'Why have you come? 'You are always welcome at my village! 'And you as well Fairy Nough and young John! "Come walk with me and tell me why you are here! Mr Trinity shook Alyconeus's large hand Alyconeus then lifted me up and sat me on his left shoulder. Fairy Nough sat on his right shoulder, we began to walk slowly towards the village, with Mr Trinity telling Alyconeus about Kaunn. But this time he was going to be the one who would try to take over the world of Sofala. Alyconeus just kept on nodding his head as Mr Trinity spoke 'that is why me and young John along with Fairy Nough are travelling once again to summon all the peoples of Sofala. 'To try and defeat or capture Kaunn so we can all live in peace once again. We reached the village and began to walk towards Alyconeus's round house. Everybody stopped for a second to look and wave at Mr Trinity then got back to whatever job that they were doing.

We reached the roundhouse and Alyconeus lowered me to the ground, from out of nowhere came one of the giant dogs bounding towards me, all at once the hairs on the back of my neck began to stand up with fear, but as it reached me it stopped in front of me and began to sniff around my legs. All of a sudden, it knocked me to the ground and started to lick my face with its large tongue leaving saliva all over my face. Alyconeus and Mr Trinity just stood there laughing. Alyconeus's booming laugh echoing all around the village like thunder. Suddenly he snapped his fingers and the dog went and stood by his side. Mr Trinity gave me a cloth to wipe away the dog's saliva from my face. He recognizes you Alyconeus said still laughing under his breath he never forgets.

Come Said Alyconeus 'we shall partake of some food you must be hungry after your long journey. With those words, he pushed open the Hugh door creaking on its hinges to reveal the big open fire that was smouldering in the grate; it was just as I remembered. The big bed in the corner,; the great table in front of me over flowing with food. Alyconeus picked me up and sat me on one of the great chairs that stood alongside the table. I looked at all the food the huge chickens and fruit that sat beside each other in the centre of the table. Alyconeus cut some of the chicken and placed it in front of me on a plate about twice the size of my head; he also cut some fruit into tiny pieces just big enough for me to eat. "Tuck in he said and enjoy' in front of me was a large flagon of drink Mr Trinity took a cup from the bag that we had used for our food for the journey and passed it to me. I dipped it into the large flagon filled the cup with what looked like a green liquid, but tasted a bit like strawberry's. It seemed to be the most popular drink in this world of Sofala. All the time that I had drank it I had never once asked what it was made from, but then again best not ask, just in case it was made from something horrible.

After we had eaten our fill, we all sat there not saying a word Alyconeus arose from the table and walked towards the door opened it and shouted in his booming voice! "Encaladeus. Encaladeus! He turned round and came back and sat at the table. After a short while, I could hear the sound of footsteps coming towards the great house, the door opened and silhouetted in the doorway his Hugh frame blocking out the sunlight stood Encaladeus. 'You summoned me Alyconeus! Yes, Alyconeus replied you remember Mr Trinity and Fairy Nough and John don't you! "of course of course he acknowledged Fairy Nough and shook Mr Trinity's hand and patted me on the head as if I was some small puppy. "Sit down Mr Trinity has something to ask of us, he will tell you the story much better coming from him. Mr Trinity began to tell the story about Kaunn and why we had come all this way. Encaladeus nodded his head and said 'I understand! 'I will go and ask the men on Alyconeus's behalf if they will help you but you can rely on me! And with those final words he rose up from the table and disappeared through the open door. Will you stay the night? "yes replied Mr Trinity 'we have to travel to the lands of General Giedroyc and try to enlist his help once again I'm afraid. 'I understand said Alyconeus where will you go after that. "Oh then it's off to see King Gandelin and then double back to see Christinos 'we have already seen King Ronough and General Dylantos and they have promised to help our cause. "Good Good said Alyconeus! "I can take my men with me and cross the mountains of Thoudulf and by pass the flatlands of Sondron to the lands of the Gawen it will not take us long, and we can meet you at the village of General Dylantos, "and I know that Christinos will help you! Mr Trinity sat for moment thinking and then spoke up "okay do that but we will have a problem when we reach General Dylantos's village we have a three days journey across the sea to the plains of Tongees and we do not have any ships big enough for you? It could be a wasted journey!" Alyconeus sat their stroking his chin deep in thought he then snapped his fingers we will build some. "But how?" said Mr Trinity! "I have carpenters" said Alyconeus all we need are the trees and you have sailors, Fairy Nough spoke up we can ask Hipictu of the cannibals to use some from the forest of Parek no harm like trying she said! "Good said Alyconeus that's what we will do, just at that moment Encaladeus came back into the house and explained that the men were prepared to fight again for Mr Trinity. 'Thank you Encaladeus replied Alyconeus 'tell the men to get ready for the journey tomorrow we will leave at dawn. Mr Trinity took Alyconeus's hand and shook it thank you he said thank you. "Come let's rest for you have a long journey ahead of you tomorrow. Alyconeus lifted me down from the table and carried me to the great bed in the corner of the room, and dropped me down onto the big fluffy pillows I snuggled into them and fell asleep.

I did not sleep very well I kept on waking up now and then at the sound of Mr Trinity's and Alyconeus voices talking about the coming journey, and how they had wished they had went after Kaunn when they had defeated Dr Zaker but it was too late now. After a while I felt somebody lie down next to me on the bed "sleep now John long day in the morning it was Mr Trinity I closed my eyes and fell asleep wondering what the next day might bring. I awoke the next morning to something scratching the end of my nose I slowly opened my eyes expecting to see one of those large fly's that I had seen flying around the day before with this being a giant world they were bigger than our fly's. However, it was Fairy Nough hovering in front of me smiling. "Come on John time to get up! I rubbed the sleep out of my eyes sat up and looked around me; Mr Trinity was sitting at the table with Alyconeus and Encaladeus talking. I jumped off the bed and walked to the table where Alyconeus lifted me up and sat me down on the chair. In front, of me was the biggest egg I had ever seen. It was about the size of my head, Mrs Jones back at school said I had a big head. Encaladeus took a knife that was lying on the table and with one clean swipe took off the top of the egg, the red yolk began to run down the side of the eggcup. Mr Trinity cut some bread up into small pieces and I eagerly tucked into the large egg on the table in front of me. Everyone just sat there looking at me devouring the egg the spoons were to big for me to pick up so I just dug my hand into the egg and scooped out the rest of the egg till there was nothing left but the empty shell. I sat back in the chair and rubbed my belly contented now that it was full. "Come we have to leave now time is short it's about a day's travel to General Giedroyc's domain. Alyconeus lifted me down from the chair and we all headed for the door I went through and stepped into the bright morning sun light. 'I think it is going to be another nice day said Mr Trinity, 'it's going to be a good day for a bird ride! Alyconeus picked me up and put me on his large shoulders, Fairy Nough sat on Encaladeus's shoulders and off we set to where Portis was waiting to carry us to our next rendezvous to meet General Giedroyc. We reached the edge of the village where Portis was waiting for us to carry us on to our next destination. We climbed aboard Portis and everyone said their goodbyes and wished us luck on our journey. Portis began to run along the flat plain which was at the edge of the village to pick up speed faster and faster she ran till all of a sudden we were in the air, she circled around a couple of times and headed into the bright morning sun. I looked down and saw everyone waving at us from below; from up here in the sky you could not tell that they were giants. We travelled over the treetops and I could just make out Alyconeus, s voice shouting far below "we won't let you down Mr Trinity 'we won't let you down 'good luck till we meet again! On we travelled most of the day, the sun high in the sky and not a cloud in sight. I just sat against Mr Trinity and enjoyed the view as we travelled along. Far down below you could see lush green fields, forests and small streams where deer were drinking from the water's edge. Everything looked so tranquil such a strange fantastic world Sofala but it could be fraught with danger as some strange creatures roamed this world. Mr Trinity pointed up ahead to a large black cloud that appeared on the horizon 'looks like rain he said, "Look down there! I pointed to a small stretch of land that ran beside a stream; we travelled down for a closer look and found a small cave at the side of some trees.

'We will land there and shelter in the cave from the rain Mr Trinity said; Fairy Nough headed Portis for the small landing strip at the edge of the stream. Portis circled and landed just a few feet away from the cave. "Hurry hurry to the cave I did not know what all the fuss was about the rain cloud was quite some distance away but I did as I was told as Mr Trinity always knew best. Fairy Nough led Portis into the cave followed by myself and Mr Trinity everyone be quiet Portis had already lain down on the cave floor a sleep, I was beginning to become rather puzzled and agitated at why Mr Trinity should be concerned in this manner, it was rather frightening.

Mr Trinity took the piece of red cloth from his cloak, and placed it over the entrance of the cave it stretched and changed colour to the colour of the cave walls, it looked like we were sealed inside the cave. I walked over to the entrance and placed my hand onto the cloth it was like a solid wall, but the strange thing was I could see right through to the outside. I could see the stream and the small clump of trees, but I could not put my hand through the silk cloth. A cloth that Mr Trinity had with him certainly had some strange powers or was it Mr Trinity, I still did not know the strength of the strange powers he had control over. 'Sit down John that is not a rain cloud! "Then what is it I asked' Beginning to become quite afraid by this time. 'Don't be afraid I will not let any harm come to you. 'Stand and watch and you will see, I stood there for a few minutes and watched the sky above became darker, and a strange squawking noise and beating of wings got nearer and nearer the noise was unbearable. Mr Trinity waved his hand over the cloth and everything became silent you could hear no noise from the outside. I jumped back as one of the creatures landed just outside the entrance of the cave, 'don't worry Mr Trinity said they cannot see you' 'it just looks like a solid piece of rock to them. I moved closer to the entrance and looked out it was the Angasaurous those bird like creatures half man half bird with their half man and half bird head those big bloodshot red eyes looking all-around. I could see under their wings they carried those horrible crossbows in the four arms that protruded from under their wings. They also carried those vicious barbed arrows that looked like fish hooks. I looked on in amazement they had all landed there must have been about a hundred of them squawking and beating their wings back and forth. All of a sudden falling out of the sky above were the carcasses of the deer we had seen earlier drinking at the water's edge. One after the other they fell onto the ground, some were still alive as they tried to rise up off the ground they were pinned down by those Hugh clawed feet the talons ripping into the flesh. The Angasaurous then began to rip the deer to pieces by those sharp beaks. I watched as they ate their victims' right in front of our eyes, I was just glad that they could not see into the cave that we were hiding in. The three of us just stood and watched as the Angasaurous tore into the flesh of the deer till there was nothing left but bits of bloody carcass lying on the ground in front of the cave. We must have sat there for a couple of hours when those horrible creatures began to take to the sky again to carry on with their journey. Mr Trinity turned to me 'they must be on their way to meet Kaunn! He took the crystal globe from his cloak and placed it on the ground he rubbed his hands over the globe and the mist in the crystal began to clear to reveal Kaunn sitting at a table alongside an evil looking man. I looked closer into the crystal, he was a large thickset man with long straggly hair he had a scar running from the top of his head all the way down the front of his face that ended at the base of his chin. He wore a thick fur waistcoat; on the table in front of him lay a long sword its hilt encrusted with jewels. Mr Trinity spoke that is the grandson of king Todec the founder of the Modecica tribe an evil man! 'What is his name I stammered' 'Todec replied Mr Trinity 'the name is handed down through the generations to the next leader of the Modecica? he will help Kaunn there is no love lost between the Uteve and the tribe of Modecica, 'Kaunn will promise him anything for his help just as he did Dr Zaker' 'then he will rid himself of that evil man when he has no further use for him.

Mr Trinity rubbed his hands once more over the crystal and everything in the globe disappeared he picked it up from the ground and placed it back into his cloak. I think it is safe to leave now! Mr Trinity waved his hand across the silk cloth over the cave opening and it fell to the cave floor when he picked it up it shrunk to about the size of a pocket handkerchief he then placed it back into his cloak. I looked on dumbfounded that strange piece of cloth could really do some wonderful things as I had witnessed in the past...Mr Trinity just smiled at me and said "Come we have to leave now we have been longer than we should have! "However, that's no fault of our own we have lost time to make up to get to General Giedroyc before nightfall. Fairy Nough woke up Portis who had been oblivious to everything that had gone on outside the cave. Mr Trinity said I think it will be all right for us to leave now, and with the wave of his hand across the silk clothe it dropped to the ground. He picked it up and has he did so it shrunk to about the size of a pocket hanker chief which he put back into his cloak. Mr Trinity spoke we will leave now as time is short 'we have quite a bit of time to make up. Fairy Nough led Portis outside into the bright sunlight Mr Trinity and I followed behind. Portis began to struggle as she could smell the unearthly stench that was coming from what was left of the deer that lay on the ground all around us the blood making the sand a deep red as it sank into the sand. Mr Trinity ran his hand over Portis's neck and she instantly began to calm down. We mounted Portis she ran along the water's edge and took off into the blue sky; she circled a couple of times to get her bearings and headed into the sun. Over the tree tops we flew climbing higher and higher till we were just below the clouds, Portis then began to glide on the wind which was coming from behind pushing us along at an incredible speed...Mr Trinity began to explain to me that this was the wind stream that circled the world of Sofala but sometimes could be very dangerous if the weather got really bad, it could cause a vortex just like a whirlpool on your earth, if that happened we would be thrown into the atmosphere but that happens very rarely. We travelled on the sun was by this time starting to go down on the horizon like a big red fireball it looked as if the whole of the sky was on fire. Suddenly it was dark then from behind a cloud, a full moon appeared lighting up the sky. By this time, Portis had descended until we were just above the treetops. I looked down and watched as the shadow of Portis flew over the trees. "Look Mr Trinity pointed! I looked to where he was pointing and could just make out the lights in the distance of General Giedroyc's village. As I looked into the distance, I saw a shadow starting to move towards us. I felt a bit apprehensive but Mr Trinity calmed my fears "don't worry its General Giedroyc and his men 'we will be fine now just as Mr Trinity had said those words General Giedroyc flew alongside smiled and waved at Mr Trinity, I was pleased to see the General and his men; we would be safe now those evil Angasaurous would not bother us now. The lights of the village got closer and closer General Giedroyc signalled to Mr Trinity to follow him he also signalled to his men to descend back down to the village and in a flash they were gone. General Giedroyc took the lead and down we descended into a small field near the village, we dismounted from Portis, the General strode forward to Mr Trinity held out his arm and took Mr Trinity's hand in his and said "So we meet again it's been quite a while! "Walk with me and tell me why you have come? As we walked towards the village, Mr Trinity began to tell the General the story of Kaunn and what he was trying to do. "Ah yes I remember him the one that got away! "Anyway forget about him now you must be hungry after your journey let's eat and after dinner we can discuss what to do with Kaunn. We neared the village I looked at the houses all around me each one shaped in a hexagon with six sides with a gothic shaped door at the front, on each side of the house were gothic shaped windows. As we walked towards the Generals house which was in the centre of the village we passed by the houses each one with a small garden at the front some with verandas. The people did not take much notice as we passed by as if seeing a fairy leading a large bird was just an everyday occurrence, the odd person just said good evening as we passed by.

Chapter Twelve

We reached the Generals house, Fairy Nough lay Portis down on a bed of straw that one of the Generals soldiers had laid down for her in front of the house. Two other soldiers came forward with some food and water for Portis, which she began to devour throwing the bits of food into the air and catching them in her beak, she was quite contented now. Fairy Nough hovered in front of the General and said 'she will settle down for the night now. The General waved his hand in the air and said let's eat now and with those words he opened the front door to reveal a really cosy room a small fire was burning in the hearth there was a carpet on the floor made of what looked like woven straw, in the centre of the room stood a table with six chairs two either side and one at each end. In addition, either side of the fire were two armchairs with cushions. Underneath one of the windows was long sideboard with two candlesticks at each end. From the ceiling hung a six-sided chandelier with candles burning brightly; at either side of the fire were two small doors, which later on, I would find out that one led to two bedrooms at the back of the house and the other to a small kitchen. "Come sit by the fire? The General said to Mr Trinity, 'young John can sit down by your chair Fairy Nough can sit beside me on the arm of the chair, while the table is laid for us for our evening meal. General Giedroyc picked up a small bell that lay on the hearth beside the fire and rang it. The door opened and in stepped a tall slim woman, she was different from the General she did not have those bat like wings that the General and his soldiers had. She was really quite beautiful long dark hair hanging over her shoulders and eyes as black as coal, her skin as white as snow she wore a long blue dress and as the candlelight caught it you could see her whole body through the shimmering silk. Mr Trinity and you of course young John and you Fairy Nough I would like you to meet my wife Indasa! 'Good evening we all said in unison likewise she replied in a soft low voice, "please sit at the table and I will bring you some food! "We all rose up from the chairs and headed for the table! Mr Trinity sat at one side and me the other, the General took one of the chairs at the end of the table and Fairy Nough sat beside me on the edge of the table. The door opened and the Generals wife entered with a large bowl, of what looked like some kind of stew and placed it in the centre of the table. She went back into the kitchen and returned with some plates and utensils' to eat our food. Soon the table was full with bread, fruit, different meats and large flagons of the green drink that tasted like strawberries. The drink seemed to very popular in the world of Sofala. Will you join me dear the General said to Indasa, she replied in her low soft voice that I found to be rather sexy, 'no dear you enjoy your meal you must have lots to talk about! 'I will only be in the kitchen if you need me! General Giedroyc smiled at his wife who then turned away and headed for the kitchen door after our meal. We rose up from the table and sat beside the fire which was burning in the hearth, the General picked up the poker which was leaning against the wall at the side of the fire and poked the now dying embers till they burst into a small flame. He then proceeded to throw two large logs onto the fire which suddenly burst into life making bright yellow and red flames. We all sat there not saying a word each one with their own thoughts, I just watched as the flames of the fire flickered in the hearth thinking of home and the school and wondering what Sutherland was doing now, it was a shame he was missing this adventure.

We must have sat there for quite a while when the General spoke up 'you must be tired from your journey? 'I think you should rest now and we can discuss things in the morning. Mr Trinity nodded his head and said 'I am feeling rather tired' 'after all it has been quite a long and eventful day. General Giedroyc rose up from his chair and said 'follow me! We walked to one of the doors at the side of the fireplace; the general opened it to reveal a small corridor. At one end was a door, the General opened the door to a small but cosy bedroom. A double bed lay alongside the wall, in the corner at the side of the bed underneath the window was a small bedside cabinet on which stood a candle. At the other side of the room was a small fire that was just flickering in the hearth. The General spoke up 'I would leave the fire burning if I was you? 'It gets quite cold at night this time of the year' 'its cold nights and hot days never a happy medium. Mr Trinity smiled and said 'I know what you mean! The General spoke 'I'm sorry there is only one bed but I hope you will be comfortable! Mr Trinity raised his hand and said 'not to worry it's nice to have something soft to sleep on' 'after the hard ground that we had to sleep on during our journey here. The General smiled! "Good well have a peaceful night' 'and good night to you all; 'I will see you in the morning and with those final words he turned round left the room and closed the door behind him.

Chapter Thirteen

The following morning I awoke to a knock on the bedroom door, 'come on John time to get up a busy day for us today! It was Mr Trinity I rubbed the sleep from my eyes and opened them; the sunlight was streaming through the small window shining a beam of light into my eyes. 'We have to leave in an hour not much time to get organised! 'I'm coming I replied as I struggled to get my clothes on, the bed had been so comfortable I could have lain there all day, but Mr Trinity would not have been very pleased as time was short and we had a long journey ahead of us. I opened the door and took one last look at that comfortable bed and wondered when I would sleep in a bed like that again. I ran along the corridor and opened the door to the most wonderful aroma the General and Mr Trinity were sitting at the table along with Fairy Nough tucking into what looked like a full English breakfast, everything was there bacon eggs even something that looked like mushrooms. I sat at the table and the General told me to tuck in I did not need asking a second time. I started to devour the breakfast mopping up the egg yolk with the bread that was on the table. The General and Mr Trinity just looked at me in disbelief as they watched me devour every single morsel, 'would you like some more the General said 'you seem to be quite hungry this morning I just nodded my head! 'Well help yourself plenty more where that came from." Mr Trinity just shook his head and said 'he's rather an expensive boy to keep; 'well in the food department anyway, General Giedroyc just laughed and said I can quite imagine that; 'still best to have a good appetite shows he's a healthy boy! After I had finished my breakfast, Indasa the Generals wife came and cleared away the table the General told her any food that was left to parcel it up, as we might need it on our journey to the domain of the Volsci people and King Gandelin. "How long do think it will take you General Giedroyc said 'maybe a day or a day and a half Mr

Trinity said! 'Take twenty of my men with you as protection General Giedroyc replied they can fly long distances and will be of help to you to hunt for food

"Oh I think we will be fine Mr Trinity said 'but you can do me a favour? 'Anything the General said! You can travel to Christinos and meet Alyconeus there and explain to her why you have come' 'I should be there in four days' time if everything goes according to plan. The General nodded well have a safe journey! "I will take my army to Christinos and meet you their...Mr Trinity took the generals hand and shook it 'till we meet again, we walked to where Portis was waiting with Fairy Nough to carry us to our next destination the domain of King Gandelin and his people. We reached Portis and said our goodbyes once again to General Giedroyc and his wife Indasa. We mounted Portis once again who ran along the flat hard ground to pick up speed and suddenly we were in the air once more, she circled around the village a couple of times as if she was saying goodbye and then headed towards the bright morning sun. It was a beautiful day not a cloud in the sky we had been quite lucky with the weather up to now.

On we travelled no clouds just clear blue sky above us. We passed over lush green fields with the odd tree dotted about here and there; sometimes we saw the odd bird who came up alongside us to see who we were probably out of curiosity. The sun was high in the sky now beating down on us, the heat was becoming a lit bit unbearable but we had to keep on travelling. Mr Trinity said if we can travel all day then we should be at King Gandelin's at midday the next day, I was wondering if Portis could last all day in this heat. I was beginning to feel rather tired now as we had been flying most of the day and I was beginning to feel rather stiff having sat in this position on Portis's back most of the day. "Look down their John? 'There is the forest of no return a lump came into my throat I just hoped that Portis kept on flying I did not want to fall into that forest not with those creatures I just wished we could land

I was tired and hungry now and wanted to sleep. 'Won't be long now there's a small oasis's up ahead! 'We will camp there for the night. Just as Mr Trinity had finished speaking the oasis's came into view, as we got nearer I could see a few trees dotted around a small pool, a few large boulders lay at the edge of the pool. Fairy Nough got Portis to circle the tree tops a couple of times just to make sure everything was all right, then brought Portis down to land in the clearing beside the trees. We dismounted and she led Portis to the circle of large boulders beside the pool. Mr Trinity spoke "this will make a good campsite for the night! "Come John we will gather some branches and get a fire going for our food to keep us warm for the night! I gathered a few branches for the fire and placed them in the centre of the circle of boulders, but I did not know how we were going to light the fire as we had no matches or as General Dylantos called them fire sticks. I need not have worried Fairy Nough just moved her tiny hand across the top of the fire, and suddenly it burst into flames. Mr Trinity took the small piece of silk cloth that he kept in his cloak pocket, and laid it on the ground in front of him. He waved his hands over the cloth and suddenly it grew to the size of a couple of double bed sheets. He did not say anything he just waved his bony hand over the cloth once more and it began to rise from the ground like some magic carpet he directed it over the circle of boulders till they were covered making them look like a solid piece of rock. I looked on fascinated at what Mr Trinity had done he certainly had some magic powers but he never used them this was only the third time I had seen the strange powers that he had.

We entered into the small opening that the cloth had left in the circle of boulders there was a small opening in the centre of the cloth just big enough for the smoke of the fire to go through. Everybody settled down it was a tight squeeze but there was still enough room to lie down. Mr Trinity took the food from the lunch bag that General Giedroyc had given us and placed it onto the open fire. It looked a strange piece of meat but the aroma coming from it smelt wonderful. I did not care what it was I felt hungry I just wanted it to be ready as my mouth was watering at the thought of that succulent meat touching my lips. Soon it was ready and Mr Trinity passed me a chunk of meat which I devoured as I was extremely hungry after the days flight. After we had eaten our meal Mr Trinity spoke up! "It looks like rain we arrived just in time! And just as the words had left his mouth the sky darkened and the rain began to fall like some great waterfall cascading down a mountain. 'We will rest now and start early in the morning to see King Gandelin; 'we should arrive by midday. I lay down on the ground my feet at the entrance of the shelter that Mr Trinity had made for us and watched as the rain came down the drops bouncing back off the hard ground. As the earth began to get wet, the rain made small puddles on the ground where the force of the downpour had left small holes dotted about on the ground outside. I watched until my eyes had become heavy with sleep and I soon nodded off to the sound of the rain bouncing off the roof of the shelter Mr Trinity had made.

The next morning I awoke to the sound of the fire crackling and the aroma of some more meat cooking over the fire. Mr Trinity had gathered some water from one of the rain puddles outside for me to wash in. "Get washed then come and have some food as we won't eat again till we reach King Gandelin's domain! I jumped up and stretched my body to relieve the aches and pains of me sleeping on the hard ground. Mr Trinity gave me a bowl of the cold rain water and told me to wash. Fairy Nough spoke up 'would you like me to wash behind your ears for you? 'She said mockingly as she flew up and down in front of me. 'Don't tease him Mr Trinity said; I just smiled because I knew she was only having a bit of fun and trying to lighten the day. After I had washed, I sat down beside the fire alongside Mr Trinity and Fairy Nough and ate my breakfast. Fairy Nough just nibbled on a small piece of meat she had in her tiny hands. I began to think selfish thoughts, I was glad she was small because if she had been the same size as me there would be less food to go round. I could see Mr Trinity looking at me with a smile on his face, he knew what I was thinking it was uncanny how he did read people's minds maybe one day I would find out and he could teach me.

The sun was beginning to come up over the horizon; it looked like it was going to be another lovely day in this world of Sofala. Mr Trinity put some damp earth on the fire to put it out. I stepped outside and watched the sun come over the horizon rising into the air like a yellow fireball making the ground dry out in front of me, leaving small round holes in the earth, which the rain had made the night before. I watched in awe as the puddles dried leaving white misty clouds like some ghostly army in front of me, until they disappeared into the sky to form a large white cloud that drifted away on the morning breeze. Mr Trinity brought me back to reality "It's time to leave now. I turned round and saw Portis was ready for our journey. Mr Trinity removed the silk cloth from over the boulders we had sheltered in, laid in down onto the ground and instantly it shrunk back to its normal size. He picked it up and put it back into the pocket of his cloak, he then put his arm around my shoulder and we headed to where Portis was waiting with Fairy Nough to carry on with our journey. We mounted Portis and off she set, running along the ground picking up speed. She flapped her great wings a few times; suddenly we were airborne heading into the sun. We were on our way to the lands of the Volsci peoples and King Gandelin. We flew on the morning sun beating down not a cloud in the sky; it was as if we were the only people in this world of Sofala. We must have been flying for about a couple of hours, when in the distance I could see a formation of birds coming towards us, nearer and nearer they came until I could make out in the distance that it was a flock of large birds. It was King Gandelin's Synisaurous. Portis began to panic slightly but Fairy

Nough calmed her down, as they got nearer. I could make out there great wings flapping up and down each bird in unison with each other. Closer and closer they got till I could make out a figure on the lead bird, he sat behind a large crossbow attached just behind the great birds head. As he got closer, I could recognize instantly it was General Travin the commander of King Gandelin's bird squadron, he smiled at Mr Trinity then waved his hand in a circular motion.

The great birds began to take up their positions around us in a diamond formation. General Travin pulled up alongside Portis and waved to Mr Trinity, who waved back. I was so glad that the General had recognized him, as we would have stood no chance what so ever. He shouted to Mr Trinity to follow him, he took the lead in front of Portis, and we headed for the Ipichtau mountains to the home of the Volsci people and King Gandelin. On we travelled until I could see the mountains, as they came into view we began to descend until we were just flying above the ground. By this time, all the other Synisaurous had left just leaving Portis and ourselves and General Travin flying along to the entrance of the Ipichtau Mountains. As we got nearer to the entrance of the Mountains, I could see the soldiers guarding the entrance to the pass on the parapets that jutted out from either side of the mountain. On each parapet, there was that great crossbow with their large harpoon arrows. A few more soldiers came from the doors that were cut into the mountain side. They were dressed in the same uniforms that I had seen on my first visit, each one was dressed in black with a black leather helmet, and each one carried a small crossbow and a sheath of arrows slung across his back and a short sword hung by his side. General Travin blew the horn which he had attached to his belt to signal the troops that we were coming. We flew low into the mountain pass past the parapets and along the river below us with those lush green fields. As we flew along the people came out of their houses which were carved into the side of the mountain and stood on their balconies just as they did the last time we were here. On we flew past house after house hundreds of them carved out of the side of each mountain one on top of the other till we came to the great lake in front of King Gandelin's palace protruding from the side of the mountain in front of us. It was just as I remembered, its large pinnacles topped with gold and silver. The whole palace painted white to contrast against the dark mountain, the battlements were painted white with gold and silver flecks to catch the morning sun, which gave off different colours as the palace battlements shone in the bright morning sunlight. We flew over the lake to a small beach in front of the palace. General Travin had taken the bird squadron back to their nests high up on the side of one of the mountains to our left. Portis came down just skimming the top of the lake and landed on the soft sand...Mr Trinity and I along with Fairy Nough dismounted Portis and stood on the sandy beach. In front of us was that large wooden door that slowly opened creaking on its great black hinges, the door opened wide and out stepped General Rol he walked towards us the bright red plume on his helmet blowing in the afternoon breeze. He stood in front of Mr Trinity removed his helmet and bowed slightly and said, "so nice to see you again' 'King Gandelin sends his regards would you like to follow me please! Mr Trinity nodded his head General Rol turned round and beckoned to us to follow him. We walked behind the General apart from Fairy Nough who just flew alongside. We entered the through the door into the great hall, General Rol closed the door behind us. It had not changed much since the last time I had been here. The walls still covered with all different kinds of weapons swords shields crossbows and some evil looking type lances with long barbs on the end. We walked past the great long oak table that stood in the centre of the great hall to a wooden door at the end. General Rol knocked a couple of times and waited for a response, which came from the other side of the door a deep booming voice came from the other side of the door, "enter! General Rol pushed open the door to reveal King Gandelin standing by the open fire in his long golden robe that just came over the top of his jewelled shoes. He walked towards Mr Trinity smiling through his thick bushy red beard and holding out his hand in front of him. When he reached Mr Trinity he grasped his hand in between his two hands and shook it up and down, at the same time telling him how pleased he was to see him and of course you as well Fairy Nough and not forgetting you young John! "Follow me the King said, and we walked towards a staircase at the other side of the room. We entered through a stone archway and began to climb the circular stairway each one of us behind the other. We reached the top and King Gandelin opened a small wooden door at the top of the staircase. We all entered it was just as I remembered the large marble fireplace at the end of the room its fire burning brightly in the hearth, giving off a welcome glow, windows along one side and a door which led to a balcony. The two large settees stood either side of the fireplace and the great oak table standing in the centre of the room, with its large candlestick standing in the centre of the table. King Gandelin ushered us to the large settees beside the fire and asked us to sit down. "You must be hungry after your journey? "I shall order some food and you can eat, and tell me why you have come here once again to my lands. As soon as I heard the word food I soon perked up, because if I remember rightly King Gandelin did himself proud last time we were here with all the food he had laid on.

Chapter Fourteen

King Gandelin picked up a bell which was lying at the side of the fire and gave it three loud rings. A door opened from the far side of the room and four servants entered the room each one carrying a large silver tray, which they put down on the oak table. They disappeared back through the door they had come from and returned again with four large flagons of drink. One of the servants approached the King bowed and said "will that be all, my King! King Gandelin replied yes and ushered him away with a wave of his hand. "Let's eat now I am feeling rather hungry, rubbing his portly belly which I think had grown since the last time that I had seen him. We sat down at the table Mr Trinity and me on one side the King the other Fairy Nough just sat on the edge of the table her legs crossed waiting for the King to remove the covers from the silver platters. King Gandelin stood up and removed the covers from the trays to reveal a large hot chicken, hot roast pork and a tray of vegetables there was also a tray of fruit on the table. I knew King Gandelin would not let us down, after all he did like his food just like me. Before we eat he turned to General Rol "could you summon General Travin to come and join us for a meal along with you General! General Rol left the room and quickly returned with General Travin. "Sit down and help yourselves plenty for everyone tuck in the king said, helping himself to a large leg of pork everyone began to help themselves to the food on the table. No one spoke all you could hear were the sound of everyone's mouth chomping on the food. King Gandelin let out a burp now and then between mouthfuls of food as he ate. His beard shining with the fat of the pork round his mouth I thought to myself for a king he did not have very good table manners. Fairy Nough just picked at the food not eating much as she was such a small person but I could see was not very pleased with King Gandelin at his table manners. After we had finished our meal we sat at the table our belly's full and quite content after our evening meal. The King spoke up "now tell me Mr Trinity why you have come? "I suppose this is not just a social call! Mr Trinity began to tell the king the story of Kaunn and how he was taking over where Dr Zaker had left off, because as you know he was only using Dr Zaker for his own ends. "So tell me how many men have you gathered together? Mr Trinity spoke well I have seen General Dylantos of the Gawen peoples; "and Alyconeus from the Scordisi tribe is crossing the mountains of Thodulf to meet General Dylantos at his village. "Master Remlin is on his way north to the ice people to ask for their help once again. The King sat for a few minutes looked across at Generals Rol and Travin and said to them 'well what do you think? The two Generals nodded their heads in unison and the King like some excited schoolchild clapped his hands together and said "goody goody a fight I like a good fight! Mr Trinity just smiled as he knew that he had the King in the palm of his hand. The King turned to General Rol and said 'get the men ready for we leave in the morning' 'and you General Travin I want a full bird squadron; 'and get my Migasaurous bird ready also for tomorrow we fly. The two Generals stood up, saluted the king, turned around, and left the room, leaving just Mr Trinity Fairy Nough and myself at the table. We sat in silence for a few minutes, and then Mr Trinity took the crystal globe from his cloak, placed it in the centre of the table, and rubbed his hands over the smooth surface of the crystal globe.

The lady began to rise out of the globe, until she stood in front of Mr Trinity. She was such a beautiful lady all dressed in white with long golden tresses of hair hanging down her back to her tiny waist. She grew until she was about a foot tall, I just looked on in amazement I had seen her a few times before but I had never seen her do that before. King Gandelin looked on in astonishment his eyes wide open looking on in amazement. Mr Trinity spoke "tell me lady of the crystal what news of Kaunn, the lady of the crystal globe spoke in a soft high pitched voice! "He has gathered quite a formidable force with him mainly the Troglodytes' 'and those evil creatures the Angasaurous. 'Beware when you cross the green mountains for that is the domain of the Troglodytes! 'that is all I can tell you till the next full moon, she began to shrink back to her original size and disappeared back into the crystal globe her voice still echoing around the room "beware beware Mr Trinity. Then there was silence no one spoke King Gandelin came back to reality and said! "Well at least she has warned us about the green mountains, but we will worry about that when we get there. Mr Trinity said 'I think we should all get some rest now, 'looks like we have busy day tomorrow! The King nodded his head you can sleep on the two settees beside the fire, it will keep you warm during the night. I am sorry but I do not have any spare bedrooms, just my room for Queen Lindas and myself 'but you will be fine! The King rang the bell again and a servant appeared 'yes my King! "Bring some blankets for my guests will you please. The servant turned quickly on his heels and disappeared through the open door from which he had come. He had only been gone a couple of minutes when he returned with a pile of blankets in his arms and placed them onto the two settees. He then bowed once more to the King and went back through the open door he had come from and closed it behind him. "Sleep well long day tomorrow the King said! "I have ordered the servants to have breakfast ready early in the morning so we can get a good start to the day. 'Goodnight to you all! "We all replied in unison good night the King smiled and headed for his bedroom at the far end of the room to leave the three of us with our own thoughts for the night. I settled down on the settee for the night, underneath the blanket along with Fairy Nough who lay at the other end of the settee. Mr Trinity settled down on the other one. No one spoke I just lay there and watched as the yellow flames of the fire danced in the hearth, casting ghostly shadows on the ceiling above me it was not long before I fell into a deep sleep.

The next morning I awoke to a wonderful aroma coming from the other side of the room. I got up stood in front of the warm fire and stretched my aching bones. Mr Trinity shouted from across the room "hurry John you will miss breakfast! I hurried across to my place at the table where Mr Trinity was sitting along With King Gandelin Fairy Nough and the two Generals Rol and Travin. The food looked as good as it smelt there was hot chunks of ham and the biggest eggs I had seen, huge chunks of bread and what looked like beans in a large bowl. "Help yourself the King said you will not get anything else to eat till we reach the flatlands of Sondron!

I loaded up my plate with everything until there was a small mound in the middle of my plate. I tucked in greedily until my little belly was full. I then proceeded to take two large pieces of bread from the table and put some of the hot ham and eggs in to make myself a large sandwich. "That is for the journey I said sheepishly to King Gandelin what you might call a belly buster I said rubbing my tummy. He just smiled and waved his hand and then spoke to Mr Trinity. "He likes his food doesn't he! "Can't understand why such a small person can eat so much?" Mr Trinity just smiled and said 'hollow legs I think, which left King Gandelin with a puzzled look on his face. As to whether it was true or not I do not think the penny had dropped as they say when all of a sudden he let out a booming laugh followed by the words "hollow legs very funny Mr Trinity very funny indeed! Everyone filled the room with laughter at the joke Mr Trinity had said. He just sat their smiling to himself as everyone else just kept on laughing. Mr Trinity held up his hand and spoke! And as he began to speak everyone stopped laughing and listened "are we ready to leave he said to King Gandelin! The King turned to the two Generals 'well are we ready he said in an excited voice "yes my King! "Good good! "Come Mr Trinity we all rose up from the table and headed to the balcony which protruded from the side of the mountain. King Gandelin opened the balcony door and we all stepped out onto the balcony. It was a bright sunny day, and there in front of me was an awesome sight. The sky was full of King Gandelin's Synisaurous birds along with their pilots sitting behind those huge crossbows attached just behind the head of each bird on their thick necks. They circled around above us blotting out the sunlight, there must have been at least two hundred of the creatures. I looked down far below me and there on the ground stood at least one hundred baskets. I knew each one carried at least fifty troops. I quickly did the sums in my head. I could not believe it that meant we would be taking along five thousand troops. King Gandelin explained to Mr Trinity he would be taking at least three quarters of his army with him! "This time he will not get away! "Come follow me! We headed for the stairs which would lead down to the beach in front of the lake. We quickly hurried down the stairs through the stone archway to the great wooden door that led outside to the beach. General Rol pushed open the door which creaked on its Hugh black hinges. The door opened wide to reveal all the troops running around getting everything ready for the journey to the flatlands of Sondron. A man came running towards General Rol "good morning sir everything is ready for the journey! 'Thank you sergeant back to your duties" the sergeant saluted and ran back to where the soldiers were waiting in line beside the baskets. General Rol took a small horn from his tunic and gave it one long blow, all the troops climbed into the baskets that lay one in front of the other. The Synisaurous flying up above us in a circle formation parted and began to descend. One by one, they came; some more of the Synisaurous except these were much bigger than the rest. They swooped down upon the waiting baskets and grabbed the long 'T' shaped poles which protruded from the front and rear of the baskets. As each one of the great Synisaurous swooped down, each bird grabbed a pole secured at the front and rear of the baskets two birds to each basket. A soldier at the front and rear of the baskets attached a hook to a chain tied to each of the great birds legs, the basket then began to roll along the ground its wooden wheels making a loud noise as they rolled over the hard sandy beach. One by one they took to the air it was a fantastic sight these great birds carrying those long baskets with all those soldiers aboard. Off into the distance they flew. General Rol took his horn from his tunic, gave it three long blasts, and out of the sky came one of the great Synisaurous that landed on the beach. General Rol saluted King Gandelin he turned and ran to the great bird that he mounted. The great bird flapped its Hugh wings ran along the beach and into the air. The General circled the great bird a couple of times and signalled for his squadron to follow him. I watched as they began to disappear into the distance just leaving Mr Trinity and me along with Fairy Nough Portis and King Gandelin. The beach was deserted except for one solitary basket and a couple of soldiers. 'Who is that basket for I asked the King? 'That he replied is for Portis and Fairy Nough as you know Portis has to stop along the way my great birds do not have to stop they can fly for days! Fairy Nough led Portis to the basket where she quickly jumped in and settled down on the floor of the basket. Fairy Nough covered her eyes and said something to her and instantly she fell asleep. King Gandelin signalled to the soldiers who jumped into the basket and waved a large piece of cloth above their heads, all of a sudden two of the Synisaurous came down with their pilots, grabbed the two poles of the basket and whisked it into the air leaving just the three of us standing on the beach. A couple of servants ran out and gave King Gandelin his leather suit of armour. One of the servants waved a cloth above his head and out of the clouds came King Gandelin's mighty Migasaurous with its pilot, it landed on the beach in front of us its great wings lying on the sand. We ran towards it, climbed into the small basket on its back, and settled into the seat ready for the journey.

King Gandelin waved to the pilot of the big bird it

Began to run along the hard sand its great wings flapping up and down. We gripped onto the sides of the small basket strapped onto the birds back, in case we were thrown out. As the great Migasaurous ran along the sand, she picked up speed, until all of a sudden we were airborne. We all got comfortable and settled back for our journey to the flatlands of Sondron and our meeting with Christinos queen of the Sondron tribe. We flew on for a few minutes, until I could see King Gandelin's great army just ahead of us. The great birds carrying all those soldiers, there great claws grasping the basket tightly as they flew. Just above them were the Synisaurous with their pilots flying along like some great black rain cloud, it was a fantastic sight. I could not help thinking to myself if any of Kaunn's army could see this now they would scatter back to where they had come from. We flew alongside Generals Rol and Travin who waved as we passed them to take the lead in front of this great armada. Fairy Nough left the basket which was carrying Portis and flew across and joined Mr Trinity me and King Gandelin in his basket. "I wonder, how Alyconeus, is getting along with his journey! Mr Trinity took the crystal globe from his cloak and placed it on his lap. He rubbed his hands over the smooth surface, and instantly the mist in the globe disappeared to reveal Alyconeus and Encaladeus his second in command standing on the ledge of the mountain of Thodulf. I watched as that craggy face appeared in the mountain and the stone tongue rolled out once more to form a bridge to the other mountain, just as it had done so the last time we all had to cross with Mr Trinity.

We all watched as Alyconeus and Encaladeus along with his soldiers marched across the bridge and disappeared into the open mouth of the mountain. The stone tongue rolled back into the opening and the face disappeared leaving once again just the flat side of the mountain. The crystal globe began to mist over once more and everything in the globe disappeared. Mr Trinity turned to King Gandelin and said "Looks like Alyconeus has crossed the mountains safely won't be long now till he meets General Dylantos. Mr Trinity spoke "I think Alyconeus has changed his mind" "he is passing through the mountain to the flatlands of Sondron. "How long before we reach the flatlands of Sondron Mr Trinity asked King Gandelin? 'We will fly all night and should be there by tomorrow lunchtime replied the King. Mr Trinity nodded his head "these are great birds you have how long can they stay in the air for? King Gandelin replied, "Oh if they did not have to carry all these troops they can stay in the air for days just gliding on the wind stream high above us, but with having to carry all this weight they can fly for about two days! I was quite impressed at what King Gandelin had said, it was beginning to get dark by now and Mr Trinity said to me. 'I think you should get some rest now and before you know it we will be there when you wake up. I lay back into the seat and got as comfortable as I could, and looked up at the stars, as they seemed to pass by with great speed. However, it was not the stars it was the great Synisaurous, as they flew onwards towards the mountains of Thodulf which we had to pass over to reach the flats of Sondron. I watched as they sped by until my eyes became heavy with sleep and I drifted off. I woke up feeling rather cold my hands and feet were like blocks of ice and my lips were blue with the cold. King Gandelin gave me a thick blanket to wrap myself in and keep me warm. We were about to pass over the mountains of Thodulf. I looked behind me at King Gandelin's great army, one of the baskets behind us was covered with a large piece of what looked like canvas it was stretched across from the front to the back and from side to side. I could just make out in the darkness tiny glows coming from each basket, like small yellow lights drifting through the night air. I turned to King Gandelin and asked him what they were! "Those he said are small fire lanterns to keep the troops warm they are quite safe. Mr Trinity said, "We are passing over the mountains of Thodulf now John he said 'so keep yourself well wrapped up. I sat there in the blanket all snug and warm but, Mr Trinity just sat there not feeling the cold he was such a strange man he looked extremely warm and comfortable while everyone else was feeling the cold. By this time dawn was beginning to break over the mountains I looked down in the early morning light and could just make out the snow topped tips of the mountains Thodulf. As we passed over the sunlight came up from behind one of the mountains and bathed everyone in its warm rays of sunshine. We flew on the sun getting higher in the sky and warmer and warmer till it was beating down on me warming my now aching body, after sitting in this basket for the past day and night. We flew on for most of the morning over the mountains nothing below us but snow. As it began to melt, small shrubs appeared where the snow had once been. The top of the mountain was flat and in the centre was a small frozen lake, surrounded by four large peaks that formed a circle. On one of the mountain peaks, a waterfall was clinging against the mountainside, as if frozen in time just waiting for the sun to melt it. And let its powerful force cascade down into the lake below. Mr Trinity told me it will soon be spring, on this part of the mountain and it will team with life. Animals will come out of their hibernation and feed on the lush green pastures that lay all around the base of the four mountain peaks. He also told me the lake was abundant with different species of fish. This world of Sofala it was dangerous but it also was a strange place filled with warm generous people and many strange creatures. We flew on over the tops of the mountains. When Mr Trinity shook me by the shoulder and pointed up ahead. "Look John there they are the flatlands of Sondron! We began to descend from the top of the mountains until we were just above the flatlands. Mr Trinity said 'won't be long now before we reach the village of Christinos and her people? 'She will be expecting us! Alyconeus will be here by now with his Scordisi giants, after about an hour's travel there in the distance appeared the village of Christinos. I was really looking forward to seeing her again, as I gathered Mr Trinity also would be pleased to see her. I knew he had a certain soft spot in his heart for Christinos. We headed for a large flat field about a mile from the edge of the village. King Gandelin landed his great Migasaurous at the edge of the field followed by Generals Rol and Travin on their Synisaurous. The two Generals dismounted there great birds ran to the edge of the field. They signalled for the rest of the Synisaurous to descend with the rest of the troops. One after the other they came, down in single file like a swarm of locusts. Each bird releasing their baskets to roll along the hard ground, the soldiers jumped out of each basket as it slowed down and pushed them to one side, until they were altogether in line, stretching from one side of the field to the other. The soldiers stood in front of the baskets in line, at least six abreast the full length of the field. It was an awesome sight five thousand soldiers standing abreast of each other their shiny leather helmets glinting in the morning sunlight, each one adorned with different coloured plumes to signify their rank within King Gandelin's army. As I looked down the line of soldiers every thirty feet or so a soldier stepped forward each one with a bright blue plume on his leather helmet "attention they shouted in unison, and like a great clap of thunder they stood to attention the sound of their boots echoing around the field.

Chapter Fifteen

General Travin signalled for his great Synisaurous to land on the other side of the field. Down they came one after the other and landed at the far end of the field, each great bird jockeying for his place on the field squawking and flapping their great wings until they found a place big enough for them to settle down and rest for the evening. The pilots who had flown with them hammered metal poles into the ground and attached each of the great bird's legs to them with a long chain. They then ran to towards two of the baskets at the other side of the field and began to push them towards the birds. When they were about twenty yards away, the pilots jumped onto the baskets pulled back the covers to reveal large mounds of meat. They jumped up and began to throw the large chunks to each bird that stretched their long necks to catch the meat in their great beaks and devour greedily, squawking when they had finished as if they were asking for more. The pilots of the Synisaurous kept on throwing the meat until every bird had been fed for the night.

The soldiers then pushed the baskets into line. King Gandelin was marching up and down inspecting his troops proud of his men; after all, they were a magnificent sight. Standing with their shields in front of them, each one with a different motif on for the different regiments that they belonged to, their drawn swords presented in front of them each sword blade glinting in the late afternoon sun. I turned around and their coming towards me from out of the distance was a large cloud of dust, nearer and nearer it got I felt a bit quite bit apprehensive, but I knew deep down that I had nothing to fear as it would be Christinos and Alyconeus come to greet us. I was right through the shimmering haze I could just make out Christinos with a few of her warriors, also Alyconeus along with Encaladeus running alongside them. As she got near, I could see her great white horse galloping at great speed towards us its long white mane blowing in the wind. As she arrived before the horse could come to a stop she jumped off and ran towards Mr Trinity her feet kicking up the ground as she ran making small dust clouds, she reached Mr Trinity panting slightly. She removed her helmet from her head and shook it and her blonde hair cascaded down onto her shoulders, she stood there in front of me her bosom heaving up and down trying to get her breath back before she spoke. She stood their petite lady warrior dressed in her knee length leather pants and short leather halter-top. She had on leather boots, which came to her knees with a short dagger tucked into each boot a short sword hung down the centre of her back, the hilt of the sword just over the top of her right shoulder. Mr Trinity shuffled his feet around on the ground and I looked at him, his face was quite flushed and I could understand why Christinos was the most beautiful lady I had ever seen. Mr Trinity held out his thin bony hand to shake Christinos's hand when she smiled and her blue eyes twinkled "Mr Trinity! Come now" she said in her soft voice 'that is no way to greet an old friend! No sooner had the words left her lips she strode forward and hugged Mr Trinity "so pleased to see you, once again!" as she stepped back from Mr Trinity I looked at him and I could swear he was blushing, he kept on shuffling his feet he replied his voice stammering as he did so 'you as well. She turned to me "Ah young John you are here as well? And with those words, she stepped forward and gave me a big hug, out of the corner of my eye I could see Mr Trinity smiling at my predicament. By this time King Gandelin along with Generals Rol and Travin had strolled up and Christinos greeted them not with a hug but with a firm shake of each of their hands, I think King Gandelin was a bit disappointed that he had never received one but that was probably just my childish way of thinking. Christinos spoke to the king "have you plenty of food for your men! General Rol spoke up "I have checked' "and we could do with a little bit more? 'Have you any to spare? Christinos replied "I will send some food out to you? 'We have plenty that is one thing we are never short of is food" "it will not be much' 'but there will enough for your men tonight! "You can stay with me tonight she said to King Gandelin and the two generals! "Settle your men for the night we will leave in an hour it is about a fifteen minutes' walk to my village. Generals Rol and Travin hurried away to the sergeants of each platoon and told them to build their campfires and settle down till morning. The sergeants of each platoon stood down their men and told them to go about their duties for the night. Some of the men scurried away to a small clump of trees and bushes to collect firewood to build their campfires for the evening while the rest of us began to walk towards Christinos's village of Sondron.

On we walked towards the village and as we neared the edge of the village, I turned round and looked at all the campfires burning in the distance, lighting up the whole of the now darkening night sky as if the whole horizon was on fire. When we reached the village two manservants of Christinos strode forward and bowed, she told them to get six wagons of food ready and take them to King Gandelin's men at their camp. The servants scurried to do what Christinos had said when you are finished she shouted! "Come for me I want to make sure you have taken enough food there are five thousand soldiers out there so hurry" 'They will be hungry after their long journey! We walked towards Christinos's house in the centre of the village; I could see the firelight flickering through the open window. I just wanted to sit by that fire and warm my aching body after our long journey. Alyconeus and Encaladeus bade us all good night, as they were too tall to spend the night in Christinos home, besides they had to look after their soldiers and make sure they were well fed and comfortable for the night. Just as we were about to enter the house a man servant came running up to Christinos and said the wagons of food was ready for her to inspect. 'Follow me gentlemen she said, and we followed her to a large looking warehouse at the edge of the village. Outside stood four large wagons over flowing with food and flagons of drink. One of the wagons was full to over flowing with what looked like some sort of deer, also it held a few small creatures to what looked like rabbits to me. However, I did not ask what they were just in case I was getting one for my evening meal best not to know I thought to myself. Christinos inspected the wagons of food and turned to King Gandelin "will that be enough food do you think? The King nodded his head and replied, "Oh yes I would think so' 'after all we did bring along some food as well! "Good Good said Christinos she turned to the servant "gather some men together and take this food out to King Gandelin's camp! The servant bowed and hurried away to get some more men for the journey to King Gandelin's camp. Christinos turned to us and said, "we will eat now and talk about the last time we met and your plans for tomorrow, Alyconeus has told me briefly about Kaunn?' "But still not to worry we can discuss our plans in the morning with Alyconeus! We all headed back to the house in the centre of the village for our evening meal. By this time I was feeling rather hungry, as I had eaten nothing all night and most of today. Just a piece of bread Mr Trinity had given me just before we had landed outside the village of Christinos. We reached the house and Christinos pushed open the door to reveal a fire burning in the hearth, over the fire a small animal was roasting which looked like a small pig to me but whatever it was I was going to eat it anyway as I was extremely hungry after our long journey. I stepped into the house it was just as I remembered it. The fire burning brightly in the centre of the roundhouse, the straw beds that we had slept on before lay at one side of the room, and a table at the other side underneath a small round window. Two of Christinos servants were hastily filling the table with food and drink, another two were carving the small animal which was roasting over the open fire. "Sit down please and we will have our evening meal! I did not need to be asked twice my mouth was watering looking at all that food being placed onto the table. We all sat down and two of the servants brought over a large oval metal plate with the carved animal piled up on it, the aroma was really something. They brought long loaves of bread and fruit also drink, which was that green liquid which tasted like strawberry's it seemed to be quite a poplar drink in this world of Sofala. The table by this time was overflowing with all kinds of food. "Eat, eat" said Christinos you must be hungry after your long journey? She did not have to ask me twice, my hands reached out and I filled my small metal plate with everything I could get on until the food was hanging over the edge of the plate. I started to devour it stuffing my mouth until I could get no more in. "Take your time Mr Trinity said 'we don't want you ill for the rest of the journey tomorrow do we young man! I could not speak I just nodded my head as my mouth was filled with food. I began to take my time to everyone's amazement they all knew I was quick at eating my food. Everyone just sat there in silence as they ate. Fairy Nough just picked at the odd bit of food like she always did, King Gandelin stuffed large chunks of meat into his mouth, the juices shining on his red beard. The two generals were not eating much, just the odd piece of meat and bread, they seemed to be enjoying the wine the most, which the servants had brought them instead of the food. Christinos and Mr Trinity were talking with low voices between mouthfuls of food, and now and again, they laughed at each other. I watched I may have still been a child in their eyes but I knew they both had a soft spot for each other in their hearts. After we had all eaten our evening meal, Mr Trinity took the crystal globe from his cloak and placed it on the table in front of him. Everyone stopped eating and watched as Mr Trinity rubbed his hands over the globe. The mist began to clear and their standing on a large rock that jutted out from a small hillside stood Kaunn. As the mist cleared, you could make out those evil Angasaurous creatures, which we had hidden from on our journey to meet King Gandelin. They stood on a surrounding hillside squawking the bloodshot eyes in their half bird half human head looking all around, as the mist in the globe cleared further still down in a small valley stood the Troglodytes' and King Todec with some of his warriors. They were an evil looking bunch of men, some were adorned with facial tattoos most had long straggly hair; each one carried a sword and shield. They were dressed in long cloth like trousers with leather boots, with leather laces wrapped around the lower part of each leg tied just below the knee. They were also dressed in sleeveless fur waistcoats held together with a thick leather belt around their waists. I looked closer at them, and realised they just looked like the barbarians I had seen in my schoolbooks it was uncanny how this world of Sofala resembled the world of earth in centuries long past.

The mist in the globe began to reappear until you could see no more of Kaunn and His evil army but I gathered that was not all of Kaunn's evil army. We all looked at each other nobody saying a word then King Gandelin spoke up "we have to make sure that Kaunn does not get away this time! 'I quite agree Christinos replied. "We cannot let these people take over our peaceful world; 'it has taken us centuries to have the peace we have today! Everyone nodded in agreement. Mr Trinity spoke 'as you know I am not a violent man' 'even though Kaunn is one of the Uteve people? 'We cannot let him live' 'this has to be the final solution' 'so we can all live in peace once again and not worry about sleeping peacefully in our beds. Everyone agreed as to what Mr Trinity had said. Christinos replied, "I think we should try and rest now? 'For tomorrow will be a busy day. We all left the table and headed for the beds at the other side of the room, 'you will have to share tonight! 'I will share with Judithos she turned round and left the house.

Chapter Sixteen

The next morning I awoke I could see Mr Trinity sitting at the table along with King Gandelin Fairy Nough and Generals Rol and Travin. I jumped out of bed and just as I did so in walked Christinos with Judithos her second in command, as soon as she saw me she walked across picked me up and crushed me to her bosom, she was squeezing me that tight I could not breathe. She put me down and ruffled my hair like some small puppy dog and said "good to see you' my favourite little man smiling. She really had changed from the last time I had visited here. Everybody just smiled and then Christinos spoke up "come sit at the table young man and have breakfast for we have a busy day ahead. I sat at the table, Christinos clapped her hands, and four servants came into the room carrying four large metal platters and placed them on the table. They then proceeded to remove the oval shaped covers from the platters to reveal large pieces of what looked ham, there were eggs and those strange blue beans, I had eaten the last time I was here which actually tasted just like the tinned baked beans I used to get at home. The four servants left the room and soon returned carrying three large flagons of the green drink which tasted like strawberries and two platters filled with warm bread. "Tuck in and enjoy Christinos said! Every one began to eat and now and again between mouthfuls, they discussed Kaunn. Mr Trinity raised his hand and said "I think we should wait till we meet General Dylantos and General Giedroyc before we discuss any plans? 'After all, we are a long way off from meeting Kaunn and his army; many things could change before we have to engage him in battle! Every looked at Mr Trinity and after a few seconds nodded their heads in agreement. Mr Trinity turned to Christinos and asked how many of her troops could she muster for the journey to meet General Dylantos. She thought for a while and then spoke up, "all I can take are fifteen hundred troops and four wagons of food! I am sorry but that is all I can muster Mr Trinity.

Not to worry Mr Trinity said I know you would give us more if you could! "King Gandelin spoke "I have seen your soldiers fight Christinos? "And I know that your fifteen hundred warriors will fight like three thousand. "Thank you your majesty! King Gandelin waved his hand and said sheepishly "oh come now call me Gandy" "all my friends do, he said in a soft voice, which he then raised higher "apart from my Generals they call me sir as he looked at them across the table. Generals Rol and Travin just looked at the king and smiled, and I sniggered under my breath Gandy I thought to myself surely he could have thought of a better nickname than that.

After we had eaten, our fill of food Christinos rose up from the table and said to Judithos to go and get the soldiers ready and the four wagons of food for the journey we leave in a hour. Judithos got up from the table and left the room to do what Christinos had said. We sat there no one talking till Judithos returned and said to Christinos "the troops are ready for us to leave. "Come Mr Trinity it's time to leave and we all headed outside to where Christinos's soldiers were waiting for her. It was a magnificent sight all those soldiers mounted on their different coloured horse's their silver helmets glinting in the bright morning sunlight. Each soldier had a small round shield attached to the saddle at the rear of the horse. Some had long lances others had crossbows slung over their shoulders, with a pouch of small arrows slung over their right shoulder. However, the most fearsome weapon each one carried was a thick broadsword sharp as a razor. It could sever a man in two with one mighty blow. Christinos walked to her great white horse and mounted. "Time to say goodbye? We will meet you at General Dylantos's in two days' time have a safe journey." And with those final words, she led her soldiers out of the village towards the quaking grounds, which they had to pass through to reach the lands of General Dylantos.

We all watched for a while until they began to disappear over the horizon leaving just a few soldiers behind to guard the village until she returned Mr Trinity said "time to leave young man? We descended the steps of the roundhouse and began our journey towards where King Gandelin's troops were waiting.

We all walked back no one saying a word, each person with his own thoughts as we marched towards the camp. After about a fifteen-minute walk we reached King Gandelin's troops who by this time were already for the journey. All the troops were standing beside each basket waiting for the order to leave. Fairy Nough flew to where Portis was waiting and began to stroke her long neck. Portis began to make a cooing noise as if to say she was pleased to see her. Fairy Nough got Portis to fly into the spare basket and she settled her down once more for the journey to the lands of the Gawen people and General Dylantos.

King Gandelin shouted out his orders and all his troops climbed into the baskets and settled in for the day's journey to the land of Gawen. The soldiers waited then King Gandelin gave the order for the Synisaurous to descend down and pick up their basket. I looked up into the blue sky and watched as the great birds circled up above me. They circled in to layers one above each other high in the sky. King Gandelin's other Synisaurous birds with their pilots flew on the outskirts of the circle guarding the Synisaurous who were going to carry the baskets with the troops in. General Travin signalled for his bird to come down it landed a few feet away from him he quickly mounted the great bird and instantly flew into the air. General Rol ran to the first basket at the front of the line and climbed in, King Gandelin gave the signal once more and the great birds began to descend towards the baskets that held the waiting soldiers. Down they came one after the other their great wings beating the air making the dust on the ground swirl around just inches off the ground. Down they came two by two and grabbed the long poles that protruded up from the front and rear of each basket.

The soldiers at the front and rear of each basket hooked the chains onto the great bird's legs again and each basket began to roll along the ground until suddenly they were in the air one after the other. I looked up at the sky it was like one great big black cloud blocking out the sun above me. King Gandelin Mr Trinity and I ran towards King Gandelin's great Migasaurous we jumped into the basket attached to its back and King Gandelin gave the signal and the great Migasaurous began to run along the field its great wings beating the air, making a loud whistling noise with every flap of its great wings. On it ran along the field we all hung on to the sides of the basket as we were buffeted from side to side inside the basket. All of a sudden we were in the air the great bird circled a couple of times and headed for the other convoy of birds which had left just before us that morning. "How long is it to the lands of the Gawen Mr Trinity? "We should be there before nightfall King Gandelin said before Mr Trinity could say anything! "I just nodded my head and did not say anything. I looked up ahead and there in front of me was King Gandelin's great army flying in front of us the baskets which the Synisaurous were carrying swaying gently in the morning breeze!

I thought to myself how exciting this was, and wished my best friend Sutherland was here with me to witness this great armada flying through the clear blue sky, it was an awesome sight and a fearsome one. We took the lead in front of King Gandelin's troops who by this time had taken an arrow formation in the sky, the sun beamed down on to us casting a long shadow on the ground below. Mr Trinity nudged me in the shoulder "look down below," I looked down and could see Christinos with her troops nearing the edge of the quaking grounds. King Gandelin signalled to his pilot to take his Migasaurous down a little closer to the ground. The great bird fell from the sky and then suddenly levelled out just above the ground a short distance from Christinos "Good luck Mr Trinity shouted see you at the lands of Gawen waving his skeletal like hand! "You to Mr Trinity see you there," King Gandelin gave the signal to the pilot once again and instantly we began to climb once more till we were now at the head of King Gandelin's army. On we flew over the quaking grounds I looked down and watched as the grounds below moved and bobbled up and down. Now and again, the quaking grounds would throw up the debris of its last victims, who had panicked and strayed from the only path that led through the quaking grounds. To lie, there for a few, seconds and then disappear once again into the moving ground. I could not see Alyconeus and Encaladeus. However, I need not have worried because as we neared the edge of the quaking grounds, I could see Alyconeus with his Scordisi giants along with the Sondron men setting up camp for the arrival of Christinos and her soldiers. As we past overhead I waved down at Alyconeus, I also noticed that he had brought the two giant dogs with him I had never seen them at the Sondron village. Alyconeus must have left the dogs with his men at their campsite on the other side of the village, "after all they would frighten anybody, they were defiantly scary looking creatures with those long fangs that protruded from their mouths hanging down over their bottom jawbone. However, I was glad Alyconeus had brought them along; you were quite safe if you had them by your side. "Mr Trinity I thought Alyconeus was going to go straight to see General Dylantos? "Oh, he changed his plans at the last minute and decided to visit Christinos he thought he would be more helpful if he went their first! I just nodded my head and looked back into the distance as Alyconeus and his men got smaller and smaller until they disappeared over the horizon behind us.

On we flew for the rest of the day passing over fields of green and tall trees swaying in the breeze, a few animals grazed on the lush grass. As we past, overhead they began to scatter at the noisy flapping of the Synisaurous's great wings beating up and down making a slight whistling noise as they flew through the air. I was beginning to feel rather tired after being cooped up in this basket all day. We had left the green fields and tall trees behind us and we were now flying over a large desert plain nothing below us but the flat barren landscape disappearing into the distance. The sun was by this time beginning sink low on the horizon and night was beginning to set in. I just hoped we would reach General Dylantos before it got to dark. A loud piercing noise filled the air it was General Rol trying to attract the attention of King Gandelin. Who looked across at him General Rol pointed ahead to a large hill in front of us I recognized that hill over the other side were the lands of the Gawen people and General Dylantos, I was quite relieved at least we would be there just before it got dark. The hill got closer and closer till we past overhead and their down below me was the valley and the lands of the Gawen people. It was just as I remembered the tall conifer trees and the fields of golden corn shimmering in the evening sunlight. The river wound its way through the valley and disappeared into the distance towards a snow-capped mountain. A waterfall cascaded down the mountainside into the river that ran along the base of the mountain. The deer on the banks of the river began to scatter and head for the trees at the edge of the forest of Parek. As we circled above General Dylantos village it looked even more beautiful from up here in the sky as we flew around in a large circle waiting to land. The volcanic geysers that lay in the lake at the edge of the village spurted their warm water into the air, in the distance I could see Fairy Nough's home the island Siphonos jutting out from the lake. I could have stayed up in the air forever just taking in the beautiful sight that lay below me.

Mr Trinity brought me back to reality. "We are about to land? "Hold on tight' by this time darkness was beginning to set in, and in the distance at the far end of the village General Dylantos's men had lit two lines of small fires to show us where to land. King Gandelin's great Migasaurous landed first and we all jumped out of the basket. We were followed by Generals Rol and Travin who after they had landed left their birds and began to signal the other birds to land with their baskets of men. Down they came, dark shadows in the moonlight landing between the fires of the landing strip. The soldiers at the front and rear of each basket unhooked the chains from the Synisaurous legs, the great birds then released the basket which then began to rumble over the hard ground. As each one landed the soldiers pushed it to one side ready for the next one to land. I looked at the field in front of me, it did not seem very large how would all these men and King Gandelin's Synisaurous birds get into this field it did not seem big enough, but they all landed safely, even King Gandelin's Synisaurous air force much to my surprise all landed safely on the small field. The pilots of the great Synisaurous settled their birds down for the night and fed them, there squawking filling the night air echoing all around the village. Generals Rol and Travin also settled their troops for the night, small fires began to be lit all over the field dotted about like stars in the sky. General Dylantos had come out to meet us along with Poppy one and two. Poppy one picked me up and put me on his broad shoulders "so glad you're back young John?" "Likewise" said poppy two I felt special in this world of Sofala, everyone was so kind to me I just wish I could stay in this world forever, because I did not like where I was back at the school in my world.

"So glad you have had a safe journey and a successful one I see!" "Did you manage to see Alyconeus of the Scordisi tribe and Christinos of the Sondron people? "Yes replied Mr Trinity they are on their way here as we speak 'they should arrive sometime in the morning! "Good replied General Dylantos" "King Gandelin spoke about General Giedroyc" "I thought he would have been here by now? Mr Trinity replied 'I would not worry if says he is coming he will come! Everyone nodded their heads in unison and General Dylantos spoke up "come on everybody we will retire to my house and partake of an evening meal! "Good I thought to myself! "Some hot food at last and General Dylantos did put a good variety of food on and plenty of it; my mouth was beginning to water with the thought of all that lovely food. We walked towards the rickety bridge and crossed over the small moat that surrounded the village. We walked past the square houses each one with their small square windows and straw roofs and with their own little garden where they grew some of their crops for eating. As we past, some of the houses had their front doors open. I could see people laughing and joking while they cooked their evening meal over the open fire. Some of General Dylantos's men were sitting at the front of their houses sharpening their weapons ready I guessed for the battle we were to have with Kaunn and his army when we finally met. We past house after house dotted about the village until we reached the house of General Dylantos. As we neared the house I could see the flames of the fire flickering in the windows, the smoke rising out of the large chimney that protruded through the straw roof, the smoke drifted up into the bright starlit sky and disappeared on the breeze like some grey ghostly apparition. We reached the front door and General Dylantos pushed it open to reveal a big log fire burning in the fireplace, at one end of the room. At one side of the room was that great big bed that we had all slept in the last time we had visited the General. I looked around at my surroundings nothing had changed still the same old battered furniture. A wonderful aroma began to drift under my nose and I sniffed the air and turned my head to where it was coming from, and there in front of me was the most wonderful sight. A long table stood at the other side of the room, filled with food. There were all different kinds of meat chicken; a large pig lay in the middle of the table. Flagons of drink and large plates of bread sat alongside bowls of fruit along the entire length of the table. Mr Trinity spoke up jokingly "Are you expecting an army tonight? "as he looked at all the food on the table in front of him! The General said, "We always eat well" "you never know when you might get your next meal! Mr Trinity just nodded and smiled. "Come Gentleman and you my lady Fairy Nough! "We will eat now "we can worry about Kaunn in the morning" "when Alyconeus and Christinos arrive along with General Giedroyc! We all sat down at the table and General Dylantos said "Eat Eat plenty there for everyone? I did not need to be asked again I began to tuck in greedily tearing bits of hot flesh and crackling from the pig in the centre of the table. I ate and ate and tried almost everything that lay in front of me. After I was full I lay back in my chair and relaxed rubbing my full stomach. General Dylantos just shook his head and said in his gruff voice "where does he put it all Mr Trinity bits of food falling from his large red beard as he spoke. Mr Trinity just looked at the General and shook his head and said, "I don't know can't understand where such a small person can store so much food! Poppy one spoke he must have two stomachs that must be the answer. Everyone just laughed at his meagre attempt to be funny. After we had eaten our meal, General Dylantos shouted for two of his servants to clear away the table. A door at the far side of the room opened, and two women appeared dressed in long blue silken dresses, they had long black hair tied back in a ponytail that hung down their back, until it reached their slim waists. They were quite pasty looking not much colour in their cheeks. I was quite surprised because they were the first ladies that I had seen in the village of General Dylantos, because last time I was here I did not see one female anywhere. General Dylantos did not introduce the two ladies to us he just waved his hand and told them to clear away the table in his deep gruff voice, which they hurriedly did so and then disappeared again back through the door from which they had come from. No one said anything as it was not our business to question the General, or ask about the two ladies we had seen, but the way the General had spoken to them it did seem clear to me that the woman in this world of General Dylantos were of no importance to him. Mr

Trinity broke the silence and said to everyone "shall we see how Alyconeus and Christinos are getting on with their journey here. Everyone just nodded in unison still surprised by the way, the general had spoken to the two women. Mr Trinity took the crystal globe from his cloak and placed it on the table in front of him. He rubbed his bony fingers over the globe until the mist in it began to clear to reveal Alyconeus and Christinos marching with their army's through the night. You could just make out dark figures, marching towards the lands of the Gawen people and General Dylantos. We watched for a while, and then suddenly out of the darkness appeared a mass of dark figures heading straight for Alyconeus and Christinos. Christinos and her troops dismounted and formed a circle with her soldiers around their horses and Alyconeus along with Encaladeus formed a circle in front of Christinos and her troops. The dark figures came on then I could make out it was those horrible Geynie creatures as they bounded towards Alyconeus and his troops you could see the saliva dripping from their fangs their scrawny see through bodies bounding and howling towards them in the darkness. On they came one after the other as they leapt towards Alyconeus and his giant warriors they let out such a piercing scream that filled the night air, the screams coming from the globe were ear piercing, I had to cover my ears to shut out the noise that was coming from the crystal globe. As the Geynie reached Alyconeus and his soldiers they leapt into the air, you could see every muscle and sinew in their scrawny bodies. I watched as Alyconeus and his soldiers swung their great clubs with those evil looking barbs at the end of each club, which caught the Geynie who let out an unearthly scream then fell instantly to the ground to be finished off with the giant's great broadswords. The Geynie that had managed to jump over Alyconeus and his soldiers were quickly dealt with by Christinos and her warriors. The two giant dogs tore into the now dying Geynie that were lying on the blood soaked ground sinking their great long fangs into the flesh tearing them to pieces. Some of Christinos's archers had let fly with the arrows from their crossbows, as some of the Geynie had leapt over the circle of the giant soldiers to try and reach Christinos and her warriors. However, they were cut to pieces screaming until their life was snuffed out by a final blow from the swords of Christinos and her warriors.

The whole battle was over quickly, Alyconeus and Christinos stood for a few minutes with their soldiers and surveyed the carnage that lay all around them. Christinos stood there the blood from her sword dripping onto the ground. They left their circle formation. Christinos and her soldiers mounted their horses and along with Alyconeus and his troops began the march towards the lands of the Gawen people and General Dylantos. As the crystal globe began to cloud over once you could just make out Alyconeus and Christinos marching off into the distance leaving the corpses of the bloody Geynie lying all around on the blood soaked earth for the scavengers of the night.

Chapter Seventeen

We all sat just there in silence after what we had just seen, General Dylantos spoke up "I think we should rest now and be up early to greet Christinos and Alyconeus when they arrive in the morning!. Fairy Nough replied, "If nobody minds I think I will take Portis and spend my last night at home with my father and mother! that is if nobody minds!" "You do that Mr Trinity said and we will see you tomorrow along with your father! "Thank you Mr Trinity? Poppy one went to the door and opened it for Fairy Nough who said goodnight and flew out the door to where Portis was waiting to take her home. General Dylantos spoke "time to retire 'we will all have to sleep on the same bed? 'Bit of a squeeze but we will be fine! King Gandelin spoke "I will along with Generals Rol and Travin spend the night with my men it will give you more room. Everyone nodded and said goodnight in unison, I was quite pleased more room for us in the bed tonight. King Gandelin and Generals Rol and Travin said their goodnights to everyone and left the room just leaving General Dylantos with Mr Trinity the two poppies and myself. General Dylantos extinguished the candles that hung from a small chandelier hanging from a crossbeam, which spanned across the entire room, leaving the whole room in darkness apart from the firelight. The flames of the fire flickered in the darkness casting shadows that danced across the ceiling making weird shapes. I lay there and watched as the shadows danced on the ceiling until I fell into a deep sleep. The next morning I awoke to one of the Poppy's I could not tell which one letting out a loud noise from the nether region of his pants. I did not mind because the aroma of the food coming from the table masked the smell from his pants. I thought to myself they were great friends but they did not have any manners to speak of, but they really looked after me so I did not mind that sometimes it could be quite funny. Mr Trinity was up and about he never slept much that is if he slept at all he was a strange man but a good one. "Come on John you will miss your breakfast, Christinos and Alyconeus will be here sometime this morning. I jumped out of bed and headed for the table where everyone was sitting, King Gandelin Generals Rol and Travin were already at the table tucking into their breakfast. I hurried to the table and took my seat and began to eat everything I could put my hands on. We all sat at the table eating our breakfast when one of General Dylantos's soldier came into the house. "Excuse me sir! "Yes? "Alyconeus and Christinos are coming over the hill with their troops sir! "Ah good good now we can start to make plans for our journey to the plains of Tongees he waved his hand at the soldier and said I will be along shortly! Mr Trinity spoke up "we are only waiting for General Giedroyc now and of course King Ronough and his Fairy people. We just looked at Mr Trinity and agreed with what he had said. We all rose up from the table and headed outside to greet Christinos and Alyconeus when they arrived. We walked to the edge of the village and waited for them to appear over the brow of the hill that lay at the end of the valley. We stood there for a few minutes looking into the distance, when this great giant of a man appeared followed by the other Scordisi giants. Bringing up the rear was Christinos with her Sondron warriors, their helmets shining in the morning sunlight. Mr Trinity shuffled a little bit as if he was doing a dance and he just stared into the distance. I knew he was pleased to see Christinos but he never showed his feelings to anyone, for such an intelligent and magical person he was a rather secretive man I just wish he would be more like everyone else and show his feelings and tell her how he felt. He just carried on shuffling his feet and clenching his bony fists waiting with anticipation for Christinos to arrive. I could not blame him for the way he felt after all she was a beautiful woman. Christinos and Alyconeus entered the village. Christinos dismounted from her magnificent white horse and walked towards Mr Trinity who held out his hand to greet her. Grab her and give her a cuddle I thought to myself even though I was a child in their eyes I knew she felt the same towards Mr Trinity as he did towards her, but she was a Queen and could never show her feelings in public.

All the other soldiers would think she was a weak and feeble woman 'Pleased to see you Mr Trinity her deep blue eyes staring into his. They just looked at each for a few seconds then she spoke once more. "We would have been here a lot earlier but we encountered some of those evil wolves the Geynie late last night! ' I know we all saw you in the crystal globe. 'But you are safe now and among friends. My troops need to rest now it has been a long journey and not an uneventful one. General Dylantos spoke "Forgive my manners you and Judithos can use my house! "There is food on the table and a bed to sleep in? 'My men will take your troops to the camp at the other side of the village! General Dylantos summoned two of his soldiers and told them to take Christinos soldiers to the campsite and make sure they were comfortable and well fed. "Ah Alyconeus my friend said King Gandelin. "I have laid on a wonderful spread for you and your men. 'You must be hungry and tired after your long journey? 'Follow me and away they walked King Gandelin's head just coming up to Alyconeus, s waist. King Gandelin looking up at Alyconeus talking as they walked. Of course, King Gandelin not looking where he was going tripped over a small stone that lay in his path, and fell face down in the mud. Everyone just burst out laughing. Alyconeus took hold of the King and pulled him out of the mud, slung him under his arm and carried on walking unceremoniously towards King Gandelin's camp.

We all stopped laughing and watched as Alyconeus and King Gandelin walked away the Kings legs kicking in the air. General Dylantos spoke up "we have a problem how do we get Alyconeus and his men to the plains of Tongees we have to cross the inland sea to reach them. "

We build ships replied Mr Trinity we need them his men can fight ten of them to our one! "You have carpenters? 'Large rafts will do. 'I have a plan 'I want you to go and see Hipictu of the cannibals, and ask if we can have some of his trees from the forest! "And in return we will bring back something for his pot! Mr Trinity could be quite callous in his way sometimes but this was war and you could not be sentimental after all.

General Dylantos agreed and called for his horse, which one of his soldiers brought him. He mounted it and rode towards the forest of Parek to Hipictu the cannibal leader. After about an hour General Dylantos rode back into camp dismounted his horse and walked towards Mr Trinity. "He said we can take as many as we want" "he did not argue' 'I think he saw the size of the army we have and decided not to ask for anything in advance, like the last time when we gave him the traitor Honitos for his supper. .Mr Trinity nodded his head and said "most satisfactory! "Oh I forgot the General said "he wants to come with us' 'just him and a few of his men just to make sure we keep our side of the bargain. "I will organise some of my men and they can go and start cutting the trees down ready for the carpenters! "Young John run and ask Alyconeus if we can borrow some of his giants to fell the trees that we need! I ran towards Alyconeus camp where Alyconeus was sitting around the fire with Encaladeus and a few of his men. I slowed down for their in front of me were those two giant dogs I walked slowly towards the fire when all of a sudden the two dogs leapt up and bounded towards me and knocked me down. ", Oh god I thought to myself they going to eat me. I lay there with my eyes tightly closed and waited for the first bite. When all of a sudden my face began to get soaking wet, I opened my eyes slowly and their above me was one of the giant dogs its large fangs dripping saliva and its Hugh tongue licking my face. Alyconeus shouted at the dogs to come to him I got to my feet and walked towards Alyconeus. "They never forget a friend he said! I told him Mr Trinity would like to see him.

He rose up from his seat at the campfire this Hugh giant of a man. He picked me up put me on his shoulders and we walked towards where Mr Trinity was waiting. When we arrived to where Mr Trinity was waiting he began to explain to Alyconeus that we had to cross the inland sea and we needed his men to fell some of the trees from the forest of Parek. Alyconeus listened intently to what Mr Trinity was saying just nodding his head now and then. "Not a problem how many trees will you require! "About a hundred we need to make some rafts for you and your men.

Alyconeus rose up from his seat and headed back to his camp to get some of his men. He quickly returned with about fifty of his men, each one carrying a large axe, which they kept strapped to their side with their broadsword, and evil looking club they carried. "Can I go with them? "I promise I won't get in the way! Mr Trinity looked at Alyconeus who said. "He will be fine he will come to no harm with me! Mr Trinity waved his arm in agreement and off we set towards the forest of Parek; there I was sitting on Alyconeus shoulders with all these giants marching alongside with their Hugh axe blades glinting in the morning sunlight. When you saw these giants, marching along they would put the fear of god into anyone who crossed their path. We reached the edge of the forest and Alyconeus sat me down on a boulder to watch them fell the mighty trees. By this time Hipictu and some of his pygmy warriors had come from the trees covered in the white chalky substance they had spread all over their bodies. Hipictu stood there in his feathered headdress, his gold bone through his nose and his neck adorned with the gold necklaces' he wore. He just looked over at me and licked his lips, his tongue running over his top and bottom lip he made a chewing noise from his mouth. He then smiled at me walked over towards me, took my hand in his and shook it. He sat down beside me his other warriors also came over and sat down alongside Hipictu. We all watched in awe as the giants began to fell the trees one two three four five chops of the axe I counted as it cut into the tree felling it instantly to the ground. Down they came like ninepins in a bowling alley, their branches breaking and snapping off as they hit the ground making it shake as each tree fell. I must have sat there for at least three hours alongside Hipictu and his men watching these giants fell those tall trees till everything became silent all around. Alyconeus strode forward and made some sign language to Hipictu who stood up and walked back to the forest and instantly disappeared back into the trees from whence they had come from. Alyconeus picked me up put me on his shoulder once more and walked back to where Mr Trinity was waiting.

Alyconeus put me down and said to Mr Trinity "All the trees are felled and I have told Hipictu that we will gather at first light in the morning! "That's fine now all we are waiting for is General Giedroyc and his Tyrocdils and King Ronough of course! General Dylantos spoke "I think we should rest for tonight and make plans for our journey tomorrow when everyone arrives in the morning. Mr Trinity agreed Alyconeus headed back to his camp along with Encaladeus. Mr Trinity General Dylantos the two Poppy twins and I went back to General Dylantos's house for the night. It was going to be a long night but at least we could rest and sleep for the next few days were going to be very busy for everyone. We sat and ate our evening meal no one saying a word just deep in thought with their own thoughts of the forth coming days. I decided to retire early and sleep for I was really tired after all the excitement of the day. I lay down on the bed and instantly fell asleep to the sound of everyone talking about the forthcoming journey to the plains of Tongees.

I awoke to the sound of laughter, the two poppy twins must be telling their jokes again they were not very good but they kept everyone's spirits up. I jumped out of bed and took my seat at the table for my breakfast, there was not much left but I tucked in anyway. After breakfast Mr Trinity said to General Dylantos "I think we should make a start and bring in those trees from the forest its going to be a long day! General Dylantos got up from his seat and went to the open door and shouted for one of his soldiers. "Will you go and ask the leaders of all the other tribes to meet here in ten minutes! The soldier stood to attention "Yes sir! He quickly turned round and headed for the large campsite at the far end of the village to summon all the leaders of each of the different tribes. It was not long before all the leaders of the tribes had gathered in front of General Dylantos's large round house. Everyone sat down in a circle to discuss the forth-coming journey when a great buzzing like noise began to get nearer and nearer. I looked up at the sky above me there was this great black looking cloud circling up above us except it was moving quickly around us in a large circle. Out of the cloud came a solitary figure and landed on the ground in front of Mr Trinity "Hope I am not too late Mr Trinity? It was General Giedroyc; he was dressed from head to toe in a black uniform that began to change to silver as it shone in the morning sunlight. The dark cloud up above flew over the village towards the campsite at the far end of the village. "Sorry I am late" he began to explain how he and his men had encountered those horrible creatures the Angasaurous on his journey here. "But not to worry Kaunn will be quite a few short now as they are all dead. He just smiled and sat down next to King Gandelin. While everyone talked I could see in the distance General Dylantos's men dragging the Hugh trees towards the edge of the river to build the rafts that were going to carry Alyconeus and his men across the inland sea to the plains of Tongees. "How many rafts do you think we will need? King Gandelin said! "Well we have a hundred trees that will be enough to build twenty five rafts! "I and my giants will need twenty that leaves five for Christinos and her warriors still not enough I think! "King Gandelin spoke up I have two hundred Synisaurous with me which is my air force! "Besides the pilots they can also carry an extra four people that makes eight hundred! "How many troops have you brought with you General Dylantos said? "I have fifteen hundred troops altogether Christinos said! "that's all right we have the spare food wagons" "five I believe they can take two hundred and fifty soldiers that will leave the five rafts for your horses and the rest of your soldiers! "That just leaves you General Dylantos "I have a few small ships lying idol but they will need some repairs if we can repair them they will do. "I think we will be able to manage. Mr Trinity said? "I have my two ships lying at anchor we can take some more of General Dylantos's troops along on my ships, "It will be a tight squeeze but we will manage I'm sure. Everyone agreed "well let's get to work and see if we can get everything prepared today so we can leave at first light tomorrow morning said Mr Trinity. We all rose up from our seats and headed to where all the carpenters were waiting for their instructions' to build the rafts.

The whole side of the river bank became a hive of activity. The Giant soldiers chopping at the Hugh trees, cutting them in half and ready for General Dylantos, s carpenter's to marry the sections together to form the base of the raft. It was fascinating to watch as they strapped the Hugh logs together with rope. On the top of the logs, the carpenters had attached long pieces of wood, about ten inches wide, and four inches thick to form the deck of the raft. These were then nailed to the logs with long iron spikes. After that was completed the carpenters', then built up the sides of the raft to about six feet to form a square. I was quite in awe, watching all these men work everyone working in unison it was unbelievable. They were like a swarm of bees around a beehive, as they worked only stopping for a drink now and then. King Gandelin had a plan on how to get the rafts quickly across the ocean we had just crossed to reach the plains of Tongee's. To save wood and canvas there was to be no masts or sails on the rafts, as it would take too long to cross the ocean. King Gandelin had suggested two metal rings attached to either side of the front of each raft, along with two long ropes. King Gandelin's plan was for one of his great Synisaurous to be attached to each raft at the front and tow them across the ocean to the plains of Tongees. Mr Trinity spoke up "Will your birds be able to do that after all they are carrying Christinos and her troops as well! "King Gandelin replied, "My birds are very powerful Mr Trinity" "what they can do is quite extraordinary! "Wait and see" "all we have to do is get those rafts down the river to the ocean and I will take it from their! Mr Trinity replied "Well we have nothing to lose we can only try! Mr Trinity sent for Jemima who had been left aboard Mr Trinity's ships along with Captains Raza and Rogas and Captain Thor Black. Mr Trinity introduced Jemima to everyone, her big yellow eyes wide with astonishment at seeing all those Giant soldiers working away on the rafts. Mr Trinity told her to take as many of the supplies off the ships we had come on and give them to General Dylantos's servants to prepare a large banquet for tonight, when everyone had finished building the rafts.

On they worked all day hundreds of men building and hundreds of men fetching and carrying everything the Carpenters needed to finish the rafts. No one stopped until at last the last raft was finished. It was now midnight and all the rafts lay alongside at the edge of the river, all complete and ready for the journey down the river tomorrow. Alyconeus and Encaladeus along with Christinos Generals Rol and Travin and King Gandelin walked towards Mr Trinity "Well we are all finished now time to relax eat and drink to celebrate our finishing of the rafts said King Gandelin! "I could not agree more replied Mr Trinity "Come let's eat!"

We all headed for the large campsite in the field at the edge of General Dylantos's village. Small campfires were dotted about all over the field like stars in the sky. Right in the centre of the field stood six great fires burning away, on each one a large oxen type creature was roasting over the open fire the juices from each carcass running down into the fire and making a spitting noise as they fell into the open flames. Twenty great barrels lay around the edge of the camp which everyone was dipping into with large drinking vessels. "Help yourself John Mr Trinity said it is not alcoholic just that green liquid that tastes like strawberries! What do you call it? No one has ever told me! "Don't you know Mr Trinity said" "It's called strawberry ours is green and yours are red he said smiling, Poppy one and two just laughed and shook their heads, everyone began to cut large chunks of meat from the carcasses' and took a large loaf of bread from a wagon that was lying to one side. "I see your servants have been busy today General Dylantos quite a good spread you have laid on for the troops! "Yes King Gandelin we must eat our fill tonight for when we reach the plains of Tongees we will have to hunt for food we need all your baskets and Mr Trinity's supply ship to carry as many soldiers as we can! You are right King Gandelin replied. General Giedroyc spoke "you need not worry my Tyrocdils will get the food we need and so can King Ronough's fairy soldiers hunt as well after all we can all fly, much easier for us than you so don't worry about finding food we can!

Mr Trinity nodded his head and smiled at King Gandelin who smiled back and said "let us enjoy ourselves tonight and forget about our troubles till tomorrow! "Have you any musicians amongst your soldiers General Dylantos said Christinos? "Oh we have a few tell me why? "I just thought we could have a dance tonight! General Dylantos summoned one of his soldiers and told him to gather the musicians that were in his army and report back to him. "Yes Sir, the soldier turned round and disappeared into a crowd of soldiers who were standing by one of the campfires laughing and joking amongst themselves. They quickly dispersed and came back to the General with some strange looking instruments, a couple of soldiers carried what looked like flutes, one soldier had a small round drum and three other soldiers carried what looked like a square box with strings that ran vertically and horizontally across each other to form small squares which if you plucked them each one gave off a different note. The soldiers began to play and Christinos looked at Mr Trinity and said "Dance Mr Trinity? However, before he could reply she took hold of his thin bony hand in hers and walked him into the centre of the campsite where she placed her other arm on his shoulder, she put Mr Trinity's arm on her shoulder and his other arm round her tiny waist and they began to dance. I watched as they moved slowly around the campsite Mr Trinity looking all around him trying to look inconspicuous, he glided around his long monk like garment just touching the ground leaving small round swirl marks on the dry dusty earth. Poppy one nudged me in the shoulder and said "I told you that they would make a lovely couple did I not young John! I just smiled because I knew he was right they did make a lovely couple but a strange one, what with Mr Trinity being a thin pale skeletal figure and Christinos a small petite lady beautiful and perfectly formed in every way. But who was I to judge for being just a small boy I still felt a pang of jealousy watching them glide around the campsite dancing. "Never mind Poppy two said jokingly one day you might meet someone just like Christinos and then you can dance around the campfire young John smiling as he spoke.

He was right I was still a bit too young and did not understand really what everything was all about. Everyone began to dance, some soldiers danced with some of Christinos's lady warriors. Some soldiers danced together jokingly like Christinos and Mr Trinity, while King Gandelin and General Dylantos did some kind of jig together round one of the campfires. Alyconeus the giant Scordisi leader was not going to be outdone; he had grabbed Judithos the second in command of the Sondron warriors. She balanced on his Hugh feet, his big hands gripping her gently by the shoulders. He began to move around the campsite it was really comical to see, not to be out done Poppy one and Two jumped up and began to do a jig singing as they danced Zaker is gone Zaker is dead, 'we will catch Kaunn and boil his head, repeating the words over and over again as they danced. I sat there watching everybody dance and enjoying themselves, but I could not help but think of home, wondering what everyone would be doing right now at this minute. I sat there for a few minutes deep in thought when Mr Trinity and Christinos walked towards me, Mr Trinity spoke 'a penny for your thoughts young John! "Oh I replied just thinking what everyone would be doing at home right now and I began to sob uncontrollably. Mr Trinity put his arm around my shoulder and said 'well shall we see! He took the crystal globe from his cloak and placed it on the log I was sitting on. He rubbed his hand over the globe. The mist began to clear and there was my mother cleaning the house. She walked towards a long sideboard, which stood against the wall, and began to polish it. She moved her hand along the sideboard with the duster until she reached the centre, and their sitting all by itself was a picture frame. I looked closer and there it was a picture of me all dressed in my sailor suit which my grandfather had bought me at the market before he had died. She picked up the picture and dusted it; she looked at the picture for a few seconds gave it a kiss and placed it back onto the sideboard. Christinos came over and sat down beside me and said "See no one has forgotten you have they' she pulled a small piece of cloth from her tunic 'here dry your eyes and have a dance with me!" The crystal globe began to mist over and my mother disappeared from view. Mr Trinity picked up the globe and put it back into his cloak. "Now go and have a dance with Christinos and enjoy yourself! Christinos took hold of my hand and led me to the centre of the camp where everyone was dancing. I began to cheer up straight away one because I was dancing with Christinos, and two I had not been forgotten at home so I was happy once again. Everyone danced and laughed well into the night, eating and drinking it was so good to see all these different peoples getting along so well, and I thought to myself this is how it should be, not like my world where everyone is fighting all the time. Eventually everyone drifted off back to their particular campsite, to settle down for the evening, as we were about to leave in the morning for the plains of Tongees. Mr Trinity along with General Dylantos, Poppy one and two and myself headed back to General Dylantos's house to rest and sleep, for tomorrow was going to be a very busy day. We entered the house and General Dylantos summoned one of his lady servants and told her to bring us all a hot drink before we settled down for the night. She left the room and quickly returned carrying a large flagon and five metal mugs and placed them in the centre of the table. General Dylantos said she could retire for the evening but told her to tell the other servant to have breakfast ready early in the morning as we had to leave at midday. She bowed and said "Yes General she said in a soft squeaky voice and retired back through a small door at the far end of the roundhouse! General Dylantos poured the steaming hot liquid from the flagon into the metal cups, "What is that I asked as the thick hot brown liquid fell into the metal cup. "That young John is chocolate we have it here in our world as well as yours you know! Strange how many things in this World of Sofala were similar to my world of earth? I knew Mr Trinity could come and go as he pleased along with Master Remlin but how many other people could do the same. Mr Trinity knew what I was thinking, so I drank my chocolate and went to bed and fell instantly into a deep sleep dreaming of what adventures lay ahead of me in the morning.

Chapter Eighteen

The following morning I awoke to the sound of voices coming from the table at the far end of the room. I jumped out of bed stretched my body and rubbed the sleep out of my eyes and headed for the table for my breakfast. I reached the table pulled out the chair and sat down everyone round the table said 'good morning young John? I just mumbled my reply and began to tuck into the food, laid out in front of me eating greedily, stuffing in my mouth everything I could get my hands on. I knew what everyone was thinking as I ate my breakfast, where was I putting all this food. They just watched me as I devoured my breakfast. .Mr Trinity had given me a small bag that I filled with scraps of food from the table, stuffing as much as I could get in. "For the journey I said 'just in case I get hungry on our journey to the plains of Tongees! Mr Trinity spoke to me "You don't have to worry' 'General Giedroyc and his soldiers will find us plenty of food when we get to the plains! "But you can take it with you as I know you are a very hungry boy. General Dylantos spoke up "It is time to leave now we will meet everyone else at the campsite! "Alyconeus left early this morning and taken the rafts down river to the edge of the ocean they will meet us there! Everybody got up from the table General Dylantos opened the door and we all stepped out into the bright sunlight and walked towards the camp where everyone was waiting for us. We all walked to the campsite no one talking just silence, everybody thinking their own thoughts about the forth coming journey. We reached the campsite and everything was ready the baskets were laid out in line with all the soldiers in them. Christinos and some of her soldiers were in the spare baskets, and the rest of her warriors were sitting on the great Synisaurous birds behind their pilots. But where was King Ronough and his daughter Fairy Nough and their soldiers, that was not my concern that was Mr Trinity's and there was still no sign of Hipictu and his men, he had wanted to come along after all, so where was he, all talk probably? Everyone was ready and settled in their place King Gandelin gave the signal and the great Synisaurous birds took to the sky circled a couple of times and came down two at a time to each of the baskets with the soldiers on board. The great birds picked up each basket in turn, as they picked up the baskets the soldiers stationed at the front and rear of each basket fixed the chains to the great bird's legs. One by one, they rumbled along the ground causing small dust clouds as the wheels sped along the dusty ground until suddenly they were airborne. They were soon followed by King Gandelin's air force of Synisaurous birds with the rest of Christinos's warriors four on each bird sitting behind the pilot of each bird, King Gandelin was right these birds could carry a lot of weight. Everyone was safely in the air and on their way to the plains of Tongees now it was our time to leave. King Gandelin signalled for his great Migasaurous bird. Mr Trinity along with the two poppy twins King Gandelin and me climbed aboard the bird and settled down into the basket. The King gave the pilot the signal and the great bird ran along the field flapping her great wings. We hung onto the sides of the basket as the great bird ran along the field until suddenly we were in the air, and heading for the rest of the Synisaurous that were flying in front of us.

I looked down and could see Mr Trinity's two ships along with some of General Dylantos's boats crammed with his men on board. "Don't worry Mr Trinity my Synisaurous will come back for them and tow them the rest of the way after we have reached the plains of Tongees! "But it took us three days to get here I stammered not wanting to put the cat amongst the pigeons so they say. King Gandelin spoke and said "These birds can fly five times more faster than Mr Trinity's ships can sail! "Therefore we will be there just before daybreak tomorrow! I was really in awe of these great birds that the king had in his service. We took the lead of this great armada flying in the sky, what a sight all these great birds flying behind us carrying their troops to our next destination. Up ahead I could make out the island of Siphonos the domain of King Ronough and his fairy warriors they might only be small but they could fight. As we neared the island, I looked and up ahead a great black cloud appeared to rise up from the top of the island. A loud buzzing noise, which sounded like a swarm of bees it, was so large it blocked out the sun momentarily the noise got louder and louder until it was right above us. Two figures came out of the swarm and landed in the basket were we all sat, it was King Ronough and his daughter Fairy Nough. "Good morning to you all! Did you think I would not arrive?" King Ronough said jokingly? "I knew you would not let me down said Mr Trinity! King Ronough settled down in the basket along with his daughter. I looked around me at this great armada of warriors and thought to myself how exciting this was.

Mr Trinity told me to look down, and there below me moving down the river was Hipictu in the largest canoe I had ever seen. It looked a bit more like a Viking ship with its central mast with some kind of strange beast carved on the front of the great canoe. Hipictu stood at the front of the canoe his bright yellow headdress blowing in the breeze, the canoe filled with his warriors, some of his warriors stood on a board that went the full length on either side of the canoe each one carried a Hugh paddle, which they constantly dipped into the water, and they did not stop Hipictu's warriors kept on changing places with each other as they paddled down the river to the ocean. "How many men do you think he has with him Mr Trinity said King Gandelin! "On a canoe that large I would say about two hundred at least' 'that is one mighty canoe I am quite impressed! We past Hipictu and in the distance I could see Alyconeus and Encaladeus lying at the mouth of the river with their rafts in an extended line. King Gandelin gave the signal and down came the twenty-five spare Synisaurous. One by one, they flew along the river just skimming the top, until each one was just above their raft. Alyconeus and his men had fitted two long poles either side of the raft, which lay at a forty-five degree angle at the front of the raft. Another pole had been secured with ropes across the front of the two forty-five degree poles. Two Giant warriors sat at the front of each raft waiting for the giant Synisaurous bird to come and take hold of their raft. The Synisaurous flew down low over the rafts that were waiting in line for them, until the first, one reached its raft, it then gripped the horizontal pole across the front of the raft and the raft began to skim across the surface of the ocean just like a hovercraft, it was travelling at an incredible speed. One after the other the Synisaurous birds swooped down and took hold of their raft for the journey across the ocean. It was a fantastic sight the rafts skimming across the top of the ocean and the great armada flying across the sky like some great big black rain cloud. King Ronough's Fairy warriors and General Giedroyc's soldiers their wings making a loud humming noise as they flew up above us. The great Synisaurous birds wings beating the air as they flew. And every time they flapped their wings, it sounded like a thousand wooden twigs snapping all at once, quite an eerie sound I thought to myself as we travelled on. We were now crossing the ocean, nothing below us but the deep blue calm sea, and the twenty-five rafts below being towed by King Gandelin's Synisaurous. We had left Hipictu and his great canoe with his warriors far behind us now. King Gandelin said he would send a couple of his birds back for them when we reached the plains of Tongees. We flew along no one saying a word just admiring this fantastic sight flying through the blue sky. .Mr Trinity spoke "How long do you think it will take for us to reach the plains of Tongees King Gandelin? "We will be there by tomorrow' 'around about midday I should think the King replied. "So quick said Mr Trinity these birds of yours really can fly at such speeds! King Gandelin said these birds can fly for days without landing, "Before we captured the first birds and we began to breed them, they used to fly to their breeding grounds far to the north of Sofala! 'Which is about two thousand miles over the mountains where the ice people live, "We have trained them to breed in our own land of the Volsci' 'but they have not lost their capability of flying long distances, 'and their sense of direction is second to none! 'They really are quite a fantastic bird the King replied 'I can see you are quite impressed?

I knew Mr Trinity was impressed by King Gandelin's great Synisaurous birds, but he did not show any emotion but then again that was Mr Trinity. We had left Mr Trinity's ships far behind along with General Dylantos and his few small boats. The sun began to settle down over the horizon like a great red fireball making the sky bright red. I watched as it slowly disappeared down over the horizon plunging us into entire darkness. There was a full moon but it just peeped now and then from behind the clouds that moved slowly across the night sky. Every time the moon showed, it cast a shadow of our great armada onto the sea below. I watched in awe as the shadow moved across the ocean below, like some great giant bird. Because that is what it looked like, as every one of King Gandelin's Synisaurous was flying in a tight formation with their wings about four feet apart. Up above them flew General Giedroyc's men and King Ronough's fairy soldiers, who I noticed took turns to land on each of the great Synisaurous, s backs for a rest, as they could not fly all that distance without one. I opened the bag I had brought with me and took out the food I had packed that morning at breakfast, it wasn't much but I offered it round to everyone but they all declined. Mr Trinity said, "You eat it we can get some food tomorrow, 'General Giedroyc will get what we need when we arrive! King Gandelin spoke "Don't worry I have told Generals Rol and Travin to make sure that each of my soldiers packed enough food away in there packs for two people" "That should sustain us till General Giedroyc can hunt for some food! I ate some of my food and put the small amount that was left back into my bag to save for my breakfast in the morning. It was beginning to get rather cold by now so I snuggled in between the two poppy twins and fell instantly asleep to the sound of the great Migasaurous's wings beating in the air. I dreamt of my home and the school and what Sutherland my best friend would be doing now. I probably would not be missed as I wasn't missed the last time I was in this world of Sofala, but that could have been down to Mr Trinity and his extraordinary powers of thought over everything and everyone that he met. He had an uncanny sense of reading everyone's thoughts but he never showed anyone, he just kept his secrets to himself. I hoped he would teach me how to do it one day or did you have to be born with the gift, maybe I would find out the longer I stayed with Mr Trinity. I awoke to the morning sun warming my aching body after being curled up in the small basket all night. "Good morning young John Mr Trinity said! "Did you enjoy your sleep? "Yes I replied and looked around me. The two Poppy twins along with King Gandelin were still sound asleep, all snoring their heads off when I suddenly smelt a horrible aroma drifting under my nose. I think it was coming from the nether regions of Poppy one's trousers, I put my hand over my mouth and waited for a few seconds, and then another aroma drifted under my nose this time from Poppy two. I knew they were identical twins but did they have to do that together like they did everything else. Mr Trinity just smiled he had known these twins a long time, and besides they really looked after me so I could not complain.

King Gandelin awoke coughing through his thick red beard and kicked the two Poppy twins until they were awake; they mumbled a few nondescript words and scratched themselves between their legs. "Good morning they said in unison not noticing the smell that hung around the basket, until it began to drift away on the morning breeze leaving nothing but the fresh morning air. The sun was high in the sky now, "We should arrive at the plains of Tongees in a couple of hours King Gandelin said! "Yes, I will be glad to do so it is quite uncomfortable sitting here all night said the two Poppy twins! Mr Trinity was not at all fazed by this; nothing seemed to affect him in anyway. We all sat there each one with our thoughts till King Gandelin spoke "Over there can you see them in the distance the plains of Tongees! I shielded my eyes from the morning sun and looked into the distance, and through the haze, I could just make out the edge of the ocean the waves breaking onto the flat desert plain. I looked down below; I could make out the rafts with Alyconeus, and his Giant Scordisi warriors moving at great speed towards the beach at the edge of the plains of Tongees. One by one, they landed on the edge of the beach. The great Synisaurous birds released the rafts, and flew back into the air and joined King Gandelin's other Synisaurous, who by this time were circling around high above the beach with Christinos and her warriors. Alyconeus and Encaladeus along with his giants jumped out of the rafts and pulled them onto the beach. King Ronough's Fairy warriors had landed along with General Giedroyc and his Tyrocdil soldiers on the beach and joined Alyconeus. Mr Trinity pointed ahead of me. "Look John the green mountains! I looked into the distance, and there on the horizon I could make out the shape of the mountains reaching up the tops disappearing into the clouds far on the horizon. King Gandelin gave the orders for everyone to land the great Synisaurous who were carrying King Gandelin's troops in the baskets began to land first, each Synisaurous released their baskets, which rumbled forward a few feet and then came to rest in the soft sand. I watched as everyone landed safely onto the beach. We were the only ones left circling up above in King Gandelin's great Migasaurous bird. We circled a few times and as we did so I looked down and watched as the troops below took the baskets that, they had journeyed in and formed them into one long line a few hundred feet inland from the beach. Now it was our turn,

King Gandelin gave his pilot orders to land. The great bird began to circle round getting lower and lower. She did so until we were just a few feet above the ground. She then headed for a space that had been made for her on the beach. She landed with a slight bump onto the soft sand. Mr Trinity myself, along with the two poppy twins, and King Gandelin headed towards where the rest of the other leaders of each tribe were waiting. King Gandelin called General Travin to him and told him to take some of his Synisaurous and go back to General Dylantos, who at this time was sailing towards us in the few ships they had mustered together. General Travin acknowledged King Gandelin and headed for the Synisaurous birds that along with their pilots were resting on the soft sand. He gave the orders to a few of the pilots General Travin mounted his great Synisaurous and gave the signal for his pilots, along with their birds to take off and head out towards General Dylantos and the ships. I watched as each bird ran along kicking up the sand leaving small dust clouds in the air. Suddenly they were in the air about fifty birds all in line heading out to sea towards General Dylantos and his ships. General Giedroyc spoke to Mr Trinity "I will take my men and forage for some food! "We should be able to find some from up above even though this is a desert there is still plenty of game roaming this plain! King Ronough spoke "I will take my men and scour the surface of the desert and see if we can pick any of those, small rabbit looking creatures that roam this flat desert plain! Mr Trinity agreed and General Giedroyc along with his Tyrocdil warriors took to the sky's to search for food. I watched in awe as King Ronough and his men flew low over the open ground beyond the line of wagons searching the ground for any creature that moved. I watched and waited when all of a sudden from a mound of sand some rabbit looking creatures began to run over the desert plain. They must have been frightened by the sound of the Fairy's wings beating as they moved over the open ground searching for food. This was a fantastic sight all these creatures running around trying to bury themselves into the soft sand. However, it was too late King Ronough's Fairy soldiers began to fire there crossbows at the creatures, each arrow piercing their bodies instantly bringing them to the ground. They struggled for a couple of minutes in their death throes and then lay quite still on the flat desert plain. I could not believe my eyes there were to many to count, they just kept running out of the large mound of sand that King Ronough and his men had disturbed with the noise of their wings, as they did so King Ronough's Fairy's arrows cut them down. The desert plain covered with the small creatures. King Ronough returned with his men landed in front of Mr Trinity. "That is my job done? 'It is up to the other soldiers to gather them in! I did not need asking twice I ran to where all the rabbit like creatures were lying and began to gather them up King Gandelin told some of his soldiers to go and help to gather the creatures 'for our evening meal.

Everyone began to pick up the creatures and bring them back to camp. They placed them in a large mound at the edge of the beach. Alyconeus along with some of his giant warriors were fishing off the beach, and seemed to be doing quite well gathering fish in with some large nets they had brought along with the complements' of General Dylantos. They began to gather in the nets, their Hugh arms bulging as they strained to gather in the fish. One or two of the fish jumped over the net and swam away, only to be caught in one of the other nets that the giant warriors had stretched out. They began to haul in the nets till Alyconeus and his giants stood on the beach with their catch. There were hundreds of fish all wriggling about in the soft sand trying to get back to the water's edge. Well we seemed to have been lucky in finding so much food, we were only waiting for General Giedroyc to return and see what food he had found. We did not have to wait long, for in the distance I could General Giedroyc returning with his soldiers. I could not believe my eyes all the soldiers were carrying a net below them, they flew over the line of wagons and dropped the net onto the soft sand, there were a few small deer, and what looked like some turkey like creatures. General Giedroyc headed towards Mr Trinity and said, "I see you have done well to? Mr Trinity replied, "That is down to King Ronough and Alyconeus and his soldiers! I held up my hand and said "Excuse me General Sir 'but what are those birds you have in your net? "Ah, young John they are desert turkeys just like your turkeys where you come from! "Have you tasted one of our turkeys I stammered? "I have young John courtesy of Mr Trinity "Don't worry they taste exactly the same as your turkeys do! King Gandelin said "I think we should get our campfires ready for tonight and share out the food so everyone has an equal share! 'It will be a long march tomorrow to the green mountains' 'but we should have enough food left for our journey, if we just give out enough to each person for tonight! "Also we will have to keep some food for General Dylantos and his men!

Every one began to line up for their ration of food for the evening to take back to the small campfires that were scattered all over the beach Alyconeus and his soldiers had chopped three of the rafts up to make the campfires for the evening. "We will just have to manage with the rafts we have left to return back to the lands of the Gawen people Alyconeus had said. The giant Synisaurous had eaten some of the small rabbit like creatures, which there pilots had given them. The two giant dogs were eating one of the small deer that General Giedroyc had caught; everyone agreed that Alyconeus and his soldiers should take the other ones as well. With being such big men, they needed a lot of food.

Jemima had made a campfire for Mr Trinity, who had invited the leaders of all the different tribes to join us in our evening meal. Jemima had cooked what looked like some sort of stew in a large pot she had brought with her, my mouth was watering with the wonderful aroma that was coming from the pot cooking over the open fire. We all sat round the fire King Ronough his daughter Fairy Nough the two Poppy twins, General Giedroyc King Gandelin Alyconeus and Christinos who sat down next to Mr Trinity. All the other generals had gone with their soldiers back to their campfires to settle their warriors and give them their guard duties for the night. After all, there may be a vast desert out there but you could not be too careful as no one knew what lurked in the darkness. The stew did smell really wonderful she was a great cook was Jemima soon it was done. Jemima handed each one of us a small metal plate with the stew on and a small piece of bread along with a spoon. Mr Trinity spoke "Tuck in you will enjoy this Jemima can do wonders with any ingredients 'you give her! Everyone began to eat, "Mr Trinity your Jemima is a wonderful cook would she like to come and work for me King Gandelin said between mouthfuls of food. Jemima's bright yellow eyes got bigger with shock, but Mr Trinity spoke. "You will have to ask Master Remlin that question' 'Jemima is his cook, 'they have been together a long time 'in fact since she was a tiny baby, 'Master Remlin found her after she had been abandoned by her mother one day while out walking. I see said King Gandelin "Ah well one can only ask! Jemima smiled with relief and offered King Gandelin another plate of food, she said she was honoured that such a great King would consider such a lowly person as herself, but she was happy with Master Remlin and Mr Trinity but thank you, she replied. King Gandelin smiled and nodded his head and went back to eating his food. Everyone sat and ate their food not saying much, but out of the corner of my eye I could see Mr Trinity deep in conversation with Christinos their heads close together and in the flickering of the firelight I saw Christinos take hold of Mr Trinity's bony hand squeeze it gently and then let go. I could swear that by the flickering of the firelight Mr Trinity was blushing, for such a great and forceful man he was quite shy in certain ways. After everyone had finished there meal for the evening Jemima took out from her tunic a small flute about the size of a small penny whistle and began to play a haunting melody. The music filled the night air with a beautiful sound, which drifted away on the breeze to the other side of the camp. King Gandelin said to Mr Trinity "she certainly is a very talented creature; I can see why Master Remlin is so proud to have her! Mr Trinity spoke and changed the subject. "I think we should get some rest now' 'General Dylantos will be here in the morning and we have a long march to the green mountain's, everyone nodded in agreement, they all rose up from their seats by the fire and headed back to their troops at the different campsites.

I was left with Mr Trinity the two Poppy twins and Jemima who made a bed for us out of the skins of the rabbit like creatures we had eaten for dinner that night. I lay down beside the fire between Poppy one and two and snuggled in. I tried to fall asleep, I looked across at where Mr Trinity was sitting and saw him rise up from his seat by the fire and walk off into the distance and disappear into the darkness. I knew he would be wandering about somewhere in the desert with his own thoughts he never did seem to sleep much. I snuggled down and fell asleep to the sound of Jemima still sitting by the fire playing her small flute. She finished playing rose up from her seat and disappeared into the darkness.

Chapter Nineteen

I awoke the following morning it was a bright sunny day; I could smell the aroma of the food as Jemima cooked breakfast. "Good morning John did you sleep well? "Yes Mr Trinity I replied! "Good come and have your breakfast! "General Dylantos should be here shortly! "When you have finished your meal we will go down to the shores edge and wait for him! I nodded my head, as I could not say anything; my mouth was full of the delicious breakfast that Jemima had prepared for us. I was eating away when we heard a commotion coming from the shores edge. We all jumped up and ran to the where the commotion was coming from fearing the worst, had something happened between the different troops, after all tempers could flare up about the slightest disagreement. But we need not have worried. Many of the soldiers had gathered at the water's edge, Mr Trinity strode forward and everyone parted leaving a path for us to walk through. As we reached the water's edge, Mr Trinity pointed at the horizon I could just make out some dark shadows in the distance.

They began to get nearer I could see King Gandelin's great Synisaurous birds heading towards us, there great wings flapping and beating the air as they pulled along the ships of General Dylantos. Three of the great birds were towing along Hipictu's great canoe, it was an awesome sight these great birds towing these ships along over the sea. Nearer and nearer they came, as they did so I could make out that at least four of the Synisaurous had picked up four of the really small ships by their central mast. The great birds were carrying them in their great clawed feet it was unbelievable these birds were immensely strong but it was a fantastic sight, now we would have Mr Trinity's army altogether at last. The great birds got nearer and nearer and I could make out General Dylantos standing at the bow of his ship his long red hair blowing in the wind. The four birds that were carrying the small ships were now flying low just a few feet above the ocean, as they got to about a hundred feet from the edge of the beach they let go of the small ships they were carrying and dropped them onto the sea at the edge of the beach.

The four small ships rocked a couple of times as they dropped onto the sea; they then began to float the few feet left towards the edge of the beach. Alyconeus along with some of his Giant Scordisi warriors ran into the sea and began to pull the small ships to shore and drag them up onto the beach. By this time General Dylantos's ships along with Hipictu and his large canoe with his cannibals in were nearing the beach. The great Synisaourous birds released their grip from each ship and with their momentum they came up onto the beach and landed in the soft sand. The great Synisaourous flew on low over our heads to where the other Synisaourous were waiting for the next part of our journey to the green mountains.

General Dylantos jumped down from his ship along with his soldiers and walked towards Mr Trinity. "Welcome General Mr Trinity said did you have a safe journey? "Well we did have until we met a ship full of ugly looking pirates! "They picked on the wrong person when they picked on me grinning as he told Mr Trinity the tale. Mr Trinity asked the General were there any survivors. "Oh yes a few! "But where are they Mr Trinity asked. General Dylantos pointed towards Hipictu and his great canoe "On there Mr Trinity on there. I gulped and a funny feeling came over me but I need not have worried Mr Trinity would not let anything happen to me. I looked across at Hipictu standing proud at the front of his large canoe, dressed in all his finery. His headdress of different coloured birds feathers his gold bone through his nose the gold nipple rings and his neck adorned with a solid gold necklace. His body along with his other warriors covered in the white chalky substance; they brushed all over themselves to make them look fiercer. He stood there and looked at me with his piercing dark eyes, licked his lips and smiled which sent shivers down my spine. Mr Trinity put his arm around my shoulder and said to me, "don't worry he won't harm you' 'it's just his funny sense of humour! I was quite relieved to hear those words from Mr Trinity. Hipictu and some of his warriors lowered down a gangplank from the bow of his great canoe onto the sand below. He strode down the gangplank and stood in front of Mr Trinity.

Hipictu held out his hand, Mr Trinity took hold of Hipictu's hand and shook it and said welcome to him in sign language. Hipictu nodded to Mr Trinity turned round and walked back to his great canoe. When he reached the canoe he shouted to some of his warriors, a man appeared his head looking over the side of the great canoe, he too had on a feathered headdress and a bone through his nose. Hipictu gave him some sort of signal and the warrior began to descend the gangplank bringing behind about a dozen men their hands tied behind their backs. A long thick rope tied around their waists held them all together. I looked on as they descended the gangplank a straggly looking bunch of men I had ever seen and ugly to, dark skinned long matted hair and some of them covered in tattoos in different patterns all over their faces.

I watched as they shuffled down the gangplank with a look of horror on their faces not knowing what to expect. Hipictu walked up to one of the pirates and licked his lips and using sign language pretended to eat, he then pointed his finger to them all. The men started screaming some fell to the ground grovelling and kissing Hipictu's feet; Hipictu kicked them away to lie in the sand sobbing with fear. I tried to say something to Mr Trinity but he just put his hand to his lips as if to say quiet. Mr Trinity summoned General Dylantos to him and told him to take Hipictu to a place at the far side of the camp away from everyone else, as he did not want anybody to see what he was going to do with the men he had captured. General Dylantos signalled to Hipictu for him and his men to follow him to where they were going to set up their campfire for the day. I began to feel a little bit queasy with the thought of what Hipictu and his cannibal warriors were going to do to those poor unfortunate men. Poppy one came up to me put his arm around my shoulder and said. "Forget about those men' 'for if those pirates had caught you they would have had no hesitation than to kill you for whatever Possessions you would have happened to have on you! He gave my shoulder a squeeze and I instantly felt quite reassured by Poppy ones words. General Dylantos returned and told Mr Trinity that he had settled Hipictu at the far side of the camp away from everyone. "Good Mr Trinity replied 'I think that is for the best don't you! General Dylantos nodded his head. "Come we will get your men settled for the day you must all be hungry after your journey, but I will need you all to prepare for the long march in the morning as it's too late now! "Besides I would rather travel by day! "General Dylantos agreed, "I will settle my men and tell them to prepare their weapons for tomorrow 'I will join you later to discuss the plans for the march in the morning. With those final words General Dylantos turned round towards his troops told them to follow him; they all saluted in unison and headed along the far end of the beach to set up camp for the evening. Mr Trinity along with the two Poppy twins and me walked back to our small campfire beside the wagons that lay in line at the edge of the desert. We sat down, Jemima had prepared some food for us which I picked at not feeling very hungry thinking of one of those pirates cooking over Hipictu's campfire for their evening meal just thinking about it sent shivers down your spine.

Just as I was about to eat my supper an unearthly scream rang across the entire camp then another scream then silence. I knew deep down that Hipictu had killed two of the pirates for his evening meal; all of a sudden, I did not feel quite so hungry. We sat there not saying a word just looking at each other, Mr Trinity spoke "We can't do anything about it" " We need his men' 'as long as they don't do their unspeakable things in front of us then we will get along just fine! I picked up my plate again and began to eat my meal. Soon Christinos and Judithos, Alyconeus Encaladeus along with General Giedroyc King Gandelin General Dylantos King Ronough and his daughter Fairy Nough joined us. We were also joined by Generals Rol, and Travin. Mr Trinity had told Captains Raza, and Rogas and Thor Black along with his sailors to stay behind with the ships until we returned from our quest to defeat Kaunn. Mr Trinity offered everyone a drink and began to speak. "We have a day's March to the edge of the green mountains tomorrow! King Gandelin spoke up "I will use my Synisaurous to take us there in the baskets we can make a few trips to take the troops to the edge of the Green Mountains,' but I'm afraid you Alyconeus along with your men will have to march; you are too big and heavy for my birds to carry you. Mr Trinity spoke "I think we should at least try' 'even if you can only carry two at a time' 'Impossible the King said "It will take us to long' 'and my birds will not be able' 'they will get exhausted" 'we are going to need them if we meet any of those Angasaurous birds! "Besides, we have to consider Christinos and her soldiers do not forget she has horses with her!

Mr Trinity thought for a moment and said 'has anyone else any ideas how we can solve this problem? Everyone just sat there in silence looking at each other. I thought to myself these were great leaders surely they could come up with some sort of compromise. "Excuse me Mr Trinity but can I say something! "Yes go on I knew he was irritated by my interruption. "You know that King Gandelin's birds towed Alyconeus and his soldiers along with Christinos's horses over the sea! "Yes, "Well can we not tow them over the desert if we put wheels on them? Everyone gave a slow handclap 'and where do we get wheels from King Gandelin said sarcastically seeing that there is no forest for miles around! "Wait said Mr Trinity he's right why didn't we think of that we take some of the wheels from the baskets and attach them to the rafts! "After all Alyconeus and his soldiers can do that! "When your birds reach the edge of the green mountains they can bring back the rafts and we can attach the wheels to the baskets once again' 'what do you think? "To save time King Gandelin said I will take everyone's troops to the edge of the green mountains in the baskets' 'the same way that we got here' 'except we will have to make a few extra trips to compensate for General Dylantos and his troops along with Hipictu and his warriors! "It will take a day and my birds will be tired after all that work so they will have to be well fed! "We might have to sacrifice some of our food! 'Well if it has to be then so be it said Mr Trinity. "Come we will eat now and worry about tomorrow when it comes' 'I think young John there has solved our problem for us don't you think so? "We can only try said Christinos smiling at me. I felt really good in my self-knowing that I had contributed in some way to our dilemma. Alyconeus spoke "if you don't mind I will retire now for the evening as me and my soldiers have a busy day tomorrow! "Good night, everyone said in unison! Mr Trinity spoke "I think we should all take an early night after all we do have a busy day tomorrow! Everyone nodded and rose up from their seats by our campfire leaving Mr Trinity the two Poppy twins and me. I settled down by the fire on the bed Jemima had made for me, and watched the stars flickering in the heavens. The odd shooting star flew across the sky leaving a bright yellow flame behind it, I remembered what my mother had said when you see a shooting star make a wish, and I did so wishing for success in our forthcoming journey and the battle, which must eventually take place to bring this world of Sofala peace once more. I kept looking at the stars in the bright moonlight sky until my eyes became heavy with sleep until I nodded off to the sound of the fire crackling away next to me.

I awoke the next morning to the sound of everyone moving around in the camp. I looked around the whole camp was a hive of activity. I glanced across to where Mr Trinity was sitting his elbows resting on his knees and his thin skeletal face resting on the palms of his thin bony hands. "Good morning John he said quietly not moving a muscle! "Good morning, I replied. I could see he was deep in thought after all he did have the responsibility of all these soldiers and he knew that quite a majority of them would not be coming back. 'Have some breakfast' 'and then we will go and join the others' 'they have been up early this morning preparing for our journey. I jumped up and sat down beside Mr Trinity, Jemima passed me a plate of food which I quickly devoured as I was so excited about the forthcoming journey. After I had eaten my fill I got up with Mr Trinity and headed towards, where everyone was getting ready for the journey to the Green Mountains. The camp was a hive of activity, King Gandelin already had his baskets ready for the journey towards the green mountains, Hipictu had already gone on ahead as they could march for hours without food or drink. They had left some of the prisoners behind so as not to slow, them on their journey. General Dylantos told me that they had taken some of their food along with them the odd arm or leg and certain parts of the body which made me feel quite sick. He could be quite perverse sometimes, and I think he quite enjoyed being so. King Gandelin said to Mr Trinity "Christinos and her warriors have already gone! 'My birds have taken them to the edge of the green mountains and we are now on our way there to. "My baskets will come back for General Dylantos and his men to take them, when they return. Alyconeus can take the wheels off the wagons and prepare the rafts for himself and his soldiers! King Ronough came up to Mr Trinity along with General Giedroyc. "We will leave now we don't want to leave Christinos at the edge of those green mountains' 'we do not know what lurks in there yet? 'better to be safe than sorry said General Giedroyc! Mr Trinity agreed he did not want to leave Christinos there either even though she could take care of herself. See you soon Mr Trinity they both shook his hand took to the air and joined there soldiers who were just flying up ahead over the desert towards the

Green Mountains   We were joined by Fairy Nough who had stayed behind on her fathers' orders to travel along with Mr Trinity and King Gandelin the two Poppy twins and me. Fairy Nough hovered in front of Poppy one and began to stroke his big black beard smiling as she did so. "You know I think you would look nice with a pink beard then I could tell you apart from each other. Fairy Nough touched Poppy one's beard and it instantly turned a bright pink, everyone burst out laughing. Poppy one tried to chase Fairy Nough around the campsite, but with his crippled left leg, he could not run very fast he just kept on shouting wait until I get my hands on you I will make you sorry. We all kept on laughing filling the air with laughter. Poppy one dropped to the ground and began to laugh along with everyone; at last he began to see the funny side. Fairy Nough flew back in front of Poppy one and touched his beard which instantly turned to black again, she bent forward and gave him a kiss on the cheek and said "That was funny don't you think! "But don't tell my father I am not supposed to use magic for fun' 'only if we are in extreme danger '"You won't tell him will you? Poppy one smiled "No but you owe me a favour which I might call on you to do for me sometime. Everyone stopped laughing but at least it had brought a moment of frivolity into our lives, and it had taken the edge of what dangers lay ahead in those Green Mountains. King Gandelin stopped laughing and pointed across the desert, in the distance you could see his giant Synisaurous returning for General Dylantos and his men, they circled the camp and came in low and dropped their baskets into the soft sand. General Dylantos and his men ran towards them, and began to climb in. His soldiers settling down into the baskets ready for the great birds, to pick them up and take them to join the rest of the troops that had already gone on before.

The great birds flew down in twos, each of them picked up there baskets in their Hugh clawed feet and headed off across the desert towards the other soldiers. Mr Trinity wandered off towards the ships lying at the edge of the beach, to give Captains Raza and Rogas their orders until we returned from the quest we had to undertake. I sat on a boulder, which lay at the water's edge along with Fairy Nough and the two Poppy twins. We watched as Alyconeus and Encaladeus along with his soldiers turned over the rafts until all were upside down and ready to apply the wheels to the base of each raft when the Synisaurous returned with the empty baskets. After a couple of hours the great Synisaurous birds appeared on the horizon carrying their empty baskets. Nearer and nearer they came till they were flying above us in a circle the empty baskets swaying in the morning breeze. Eventually they flew down low and dropped their baskets once more onto the soft sand. Alyconeus along with his soldiers quickly overturned each basket, and began to remove the wheels and lash them to the base of each raft, eight wheels to each one. The great Synisaurous birds had landed at the edge of the beach to wait while Alyconeus and his soldiers got the rafts ready for the Synisaurous to tow them back across the desert. I watched in awe as Alyconeus and his soldiers removed the wheels from the baskets, and quickly attached them to the base of each raft.

They quickly turned them over and put them in an extended line ready for the Synisaurous birds to swoop down and take hold of each raft to take them across the dry desert plain, to where all the other troops were waiting. At last everything was ready Alyconeus along with Encaladeus and the giant soldiers jumped into the rafts. King Gandelin gave the signal to his Synisaurous pilots to come and pick up the rafts. Each bird rose up on their Hugh legs and began to run along the beach their great clawed feet kicking up the dry sand making small dust clouds as they ran, flapping their great wings till each one was in the air. Down they came each one behind the other heading for their individual raft. One after the other they came, each one gripping the horizontal pole that lay across the front of each raft. They began to tow the rafts across the desert the wheels rumbling over the dry desert plain until they disappeared, leaving nothing but a cloud of dust in their wake.

Chapter Twenty

King Gandelin turned to Mr Trinity and said, "Time for us to leave now; 'do you think your two captains will be all right looking after the ships! Mr Trinity replied "I do not think Kaunn will send any of his soldiers across the desert to attack the ships! "He will need all the men he can muster to try and defeat us! King Gandelin said "You're right they won't come this far they will try to ambush us in the green mountains! Mr Trinity nodded his head. 'But "I have one thing he does not have, and with those words he took the crystal globe from his cloak. "I have this and the lady of the globe, 'she will guide us through the green mountains! Mr Trinity put the crystal globe back into his cloak and said, "Shall we leave now time is short? King Gandelin nodded and we all started to walk towards where his great Migasaurous was waiting along with his pilot to carry us across the desert. We all got into the basket Mr Trinity Poppy one and two Fairy Nough and me. We settled down into the seat in the basket and King Gandelin gave his pilot the order to take off. The great bird began to run along the flat plain flapping its great wings; we hung on to the sides of the basket trying not to fall out as the great bird ran over the sand.

Suddenly we were in the air and heading across the desert to where all the other troops were waiting for us to arrive. We flew over the desert nothing below us except the dry desert plain, nothing stirred not even those rabbit like creatures that we had eaten a couple of days ago. All you could see was the shadow of the great Migasaurous cast by the sun on the desert below as she flew on towards the base of the green mountains. As we got nearer I could make out the Mountains rising up over the horizon their tips disappearing into the low lying morning clouds. Nearer and nearer we got. I began to make out Mr Trinity's army in the distance lying at the edge of the desert like a great swarm of ants busily going about their business. The Mountains began to get nearer; it was a fantastic sight, a deep green with red blue and purple horizontal stripes passing across the ridge of the mountains embedded into the rock face. The sun reflected off the different colours making strange patterns in the sky, a little bit like a rainbow after it had rained. "What do you think John Mr Trinity said 'they are beautiful are they not? 'but dangerous as well! "They are I replied but what are those different coloured rocks going through the Mountains I asked. "They are not rocks young man but semi-precious stones they just look like rocks as they are packed so tightly together! "Are they valuable I asked! "Maybe in your world, "who knows but here they are not worth much! "Besides everyone in this world of Sofala has what they want as you can see we all help each other to get along! "Your world is run by greed everyone out for what he can get! I could not disagree with Mr Trinity he was right after all. This world might not have all the comforts of home but I really enjoyed being amongst all these different people, maybe Mr Trinity would let me stay after we had defeated Kaunn. King Gandelin spoke. "We are about to land Mr Trinity, 'hang on to the side of the basket? 'I think this is going to be a bumpy landing! The Migasaurous circled around for a few minutes to look for a suitable landing sight amongst all the other birds, which had taken up quite a bit of space at the edge of the desert. She began to descend down onto the desert and as she did so some of the Synisaurous began to move out of the way squawking as they moved, probably not very happy at having to do so as the Migasaurous was twice the size of them. We landed with a bump and we all jumped out of the basket. We were greeted by General Dylantos and Christinos along with General Giedroyc and King Ronough. "So pleased you arrived safe said Christinos! "Come we have prepared some food for you; 'Jemima has done the cooking so you know it will be very tasty! We followed Christinos to a large campfire at the base of an overhanging rock that jutted out from the mountain side where Judithos was sitting along with Generals Rol and Travin, stuffing their faces with meat from a carcass that was turning on a spit hanging over the fire. We all sat down on some rocks that the soldiers had placed out in a circle round the fire, the meat did smell really good and my mouth was beginning to water, with the thought of all that succulent meat touching my lips I was really hungry. I looked around the camp to where all the other soldiers were camped; they all had a similar creature roasting over an open fire where did they get all this food. Then I took a closer look at the creature that was roasting over our fire it was an Angasaurous, you could just make out its half human half bird head, the flesh beginning to fall away from its bony head. King Gandelin drew his sword, with one swipe severed it from its body, and threw it towards his great Migasaurous who quickly picked it up in its Hugh beak threw back its head and quickly devoured it. "We don't want to look at that do we; 'while we eat our meal; and with those final words he pulled a large piece of meat from the carcass and began to eat. "I see you had a bit of bother when you got here Mr Trinity said waving his long bony hand around the camp in a circular motion! Yes-replied Christinos 'we encountered some of those Angasaurous? 'But General Giedroyc along with his Tyrocdils soon took care of them; 'Hence the wonderful meal you have before you she said smiling. General Dylantos spoke 'they may be ugly but they do not half taste nice don't they young John? I just nodded my head, as my mouth was full to bursting with the meat, I had stuffed into my mouth the juices running down my chin and dripping onto my shirt leaving greasy stains. 'How long will it be before Alyconeus and his giant Scordisi arrive General Dylantos said to Mr Trinity? "About another two hours then Hipictu should arrive about an hour behind them with his warriors! 'I think we should prepare our defensive positions when they arrive spoke King Gandelin! "We do not want to cross those mountains in the dark to dangerous; 'you're right said General Dylantos we will have to stay here the night! 'First, let us finish our meal and wait for Alyconeus and Hipictu! 'I agree said General Giedroyc we don't know if Kaunn has any of his soldiers scattered about in those mountains! "Do not worry said Mr Trinity I have the crystal globe and the lady of the crystal; 'she will help us; no need to worry! I was not quite so reassured but Mr Trinity had never let anyone down yet, he never worried or showed any emotion no matter what kind of situation he was in he really was an extraordinary man.

Everyone talked about the forth-coming journey through the mountains, and what awaited us on the other side, except Mr Trinity who just sat there in silence deep in thought. A shout from the edge of the desert quietened everybody. Mr Trinity rose up from his seat by the fire "That will be Alyconeus and his soldiers said Mr Trinity' 'come I think we should go and greet them! Everyone nodded in agreement we all got up from our seats and headed out to the edge of the desert to greet Alyconeus and his men. We arrived just in time to see Alyconeus along with Encaladeus and his men appear over the horizon the Hugh rafts rumbling over the desert plain, the great Synisaurous birds' wings beating the air as they flew towards us. I watched as the great birds began to get nearer and nearer, each one towing its raft the wheels of each raft making small dust clouds as they rumbled over the dry sandy plain. It was a magnificent sight these great birds flying towards us, each one pulling their large raft with their giant warriors on board, this would put the fear of god into anyone. It was a pity Kaunn could not see this he would probably have second thoughts about taking on such a Hugh force as the one we had gathered together. Closer and closer, they got until they were about a hundred yards from the edge of the desert. The great Synisaurous birds released the rafts from their Hugh clawed feet and I watched as the rafts came towards us their wheels rumbling over the hard sand until they came to a sudden stop in front of Mr Trinity. Alyconeus jumped out of the leading raft and walked towards Mr Trinity, 'Good afternoon Mr Trinity 'has everyone arrived safely? Mr Trinity spoke "We are only waiting for Hipictu and his cannibal warriors to arrive; 'Did you pass them on the way here? Alyconeus said 'yes we did we offered them to come with us but they declined our offer! "Ah not to worry, we can wait we are not going to cross the Green Mountains till first light tomorrow! 'Besides, you must be hungry after your journey across the desert. 'Christinos and her soldiers encountered some of those Angasaurous creatures when they arrived, but General Giedroyc took care of them. 'We have left a few for you and your men to eat; 'so set up your camp for the night and then join me and the other tribal leaders at my camp where we can discuss our plans for the morning! Mr Trinity and me turned round and headed back to our camp below the hanging rock to await Alyconeus and Encaladeus who would join us later that day. We sat by the fire and Poppy one and two were playing a sort of game with a few stones they had found by the fire. I could not understand it I just think they were making it up as they went along but it seemed to please them.

I watched with a smile on my face as Fairy Nough began to do magic tricks. First, she would make their noses bigger and give them small pointy ears turn their beards different colours of the rainbow and make their hair stand up straight. All this went on oblivious to what she was doing, as they were too engrossed in the game they were playing. Everyone was laughing and sniggering under their breath, Mr Trinity kicked Poppy ones ankle and gave him a small mirror that Jemima carried with her. Poppy one held the mirror up to his face and let out an almighty scream, Poppy Two took the mirror and looked in the mirror as well, he screamed then everyone just rolled about laughing at their predicament. Poppy one reached out to try and grab Fairy Nough but she was too quick for him she hovered just out of his reach so he could not grab her. King Ronough intervened to the frivolities that was taking place round the campfire and began to chastise Fairy Nough and tell her that she could only use her magic powers for good and not to make fun of anyone. 'Sorry father she said and proceeded to make good what she had done to the Two Poppy twins. Everyone was still laughing even Mr Trinity had loosened up a bit and began to laugh, the two Poppy Twins just looked at everyone in disbelief their faces contorted in anger, when all of a sudden they burst out laughing their loud laughter filling the night and echoing all around the camp.

Soon Alyconeus and Encaladeus joined us. 'Missed all the fun, have we?' Alyconeus said! "Oh it was just Fairy Nough playing her tricks again on the Poppy Twins. 'She loves them replied Mr Trinity smiling 'here sit down by me; 'Have you eaten? 'If not there is still plenty of food here if you want some! Alyconeus and Encaladeus picked up a Hugh boulder as if it was a pebble on the beach and placed it down next to Mr Trinity; each one lowered his Hugh muscular body and sat down on the rock. They were massive men fifteen feet tall with arms and legs as thick as the trunk of an oak tree. Alyconeus and his warriors were fierce looking men but really gentle when you got to know them, I was just glad they were on our side and not Kaunn's. Everyone sat there talking about the forth coming journey through the Green Mountains the next day, when Mr Trinity interrupted; 'Gentleman he said time to discuss our journey for tomorrow! He summoned Jemima to clear a space around the fire so everyone could see, Jemima cleared the space and brought a large flat round rock and placed it on the ground in front of Mr Trinity. Mr Trinity took the crystal globe from his cloak and placed it onto the flat rock in front of him. He passed his long bony fingers over the crystal and rubbed the globe. The mist in the crystal globe began to clear and the lady of the crystal appeared. She left the globe and stood next to Mr Trinity, she began to grow until she was about two feet tall 'you sent for me Mr Trinity? What can I do for you?

Chapter Twenty-one

Mr Trinity looked at the lady of the globe and said 'We need to know what awaits us in those narrow mountain passes! 'Do not worry Mr Trinity I will help you to find where all your enemies are in those Mountains; 'they lie waiting for you amongst the rocks' 'but I will show you where; 'then it is up to you, 'look into the globe and watch. With those final words she flew off into the Green Mountains. We all looked on intensely into the crystal globe. We watched her glide in and out of the rocks like a ghostly apparition, as she passed unbeknown to Kaunn's warriors. She had a small like wand in her left hand, which she passed over each one of Kaunn's warriors that she came across. In and out of the rocks, she flew leaving her mark on everyone she passed. We looked on Kaunn had quite a few men stationed in between those rocks. The Lady of the crystal Globe returned and stood in front of Mr Trinity once more. 'I have done my work now, 'I must retire to the crystal once more; 'when darkness falls look into the crystal and you will see my mark on every one of Kaunn's soldiers in those mountains, 'the rest is up to you and your soldiers. The Lady of the crystal shrunk back to her normal size and disappeared once more into the globe leaving everyone dumbfounded except Mr Trinity and me who had seen this happen before. 'We just have to wait for darkness now said General Dylantos; 'but how will we know where they are! 'Don't worry Mr Trinity replied 'the crystal will show us when night falls; 'In the meantime we will have our evening meal, 'and after our fill we can discuss our plans on the best way to attack Kaunn's men and leave the way clear for us to cross the Mountains tomorrow! Everyone agreed we all began to eat our evening meal waiting for night to fall. I just wished it would hurry up I was quite curious to see what mark the lady of the globe had placed on each one of Kaunn's soldiers. We ate our meal and soon the sun began to settle slowly down on the horizon leaving the camp in total darkness, apart the campfires of the soldiers flickering away around us the moon peeping through the passing clouds leaving ghostly shadows from the soldiers as they moved around the camp. Mr Trinity said to King Ronough 'I will need your men for this operation tonight; 'they are small and can manoeuvre around quickly' 'Kaunn's men will not see them coming till it's too late then it will be all over! Mr Trinity took the crystal globe from his cloak and placed it once again on the flat rock that was in front of him. He rubbed his hands over the globe and the mist in the globe began to clear and there in front of us was about a couple of hundred what looked like white dots glowing in the darkness. 'Those white dots said Mr Trinity are Kaunn's men' 'they do not know we are coming it will be a nice surprise for them tonight. 'Don't worry said King Ronough 'I won't let you down; 'I will go and get my men ready and we will leave in an hour! 'Thank you King Ronough; 'we will wait for your return and we will watch in the crystal. We sat and waited soon King Ronough returned with his men. 'We will leave now and with those final words King Ronough took off with his men into the mountains. We all crowded around the crystal and began to watch as ghostly shadows began to seek out Kaunn's men hidden amongst the rocks. King Ronough and his small soldiers picked each one of Kaunn's men off with their small crossbows the arrows piercing Kaunn's men. In and out of the rocks, Kings Ronough's men flew every time picking off Kaunn's men, their screams filled the night air sending shivers down your spine. Every time one of Kaunn's men was killed the bright mark that the lady of the Crystal Globe had placed on them was extinguished saying that King Ronough had been successful in snuffing out the life of one of Kaunn's soldiers. I watched as each bright white dot went out leaving nothing but darkness and silence. King Ronough returned with his men, 'It is safe to cross the mountains in the morning King Ronough said; 'Thank you Mr Trinity said after we have crossed the mountains we will have to pass through the forest of Paqoun 'we will have to be on our guard; 'that is another place that Kaunn will try to ambush our troops, 'but we will be ready for whatever he throws at us till we finally meet him on the plains of Modecica the lands of King Todec.

'We will retire for the night now Mr Trinity' 'my men will have to regain their strength for the journey tomorrow King Ronough said! 'Thank you once again Mr Trinity replied 'I will see you in the morning goodnight to you. King Ronough asked his daughter Fairy Nough to follow him, they turned round and took off and flew towards where Kings Ronough's men had bedded down for the night.

There was only Mr Trinity I the two poppy twins along with Jemima left sitting beside the campfire, all the other leaders of the peoples of Sofala had gone to their own campsites to prepare their soldiers ready for the journey across the Green Mountains in the morning. I settled down into my bedroll, which lay beside the fire and watched as the fires in the camp began to go out leaving the whole desert in total darkness, except when the moon peeped now and again from behind the clouds to reveal the shadowy figures of the guards patrolling around the edge of the camp. I just watched for a while until my eyes became heavy and I then drifted off into a deep sleep.

Mr Trinity awoke me the next morning 'Come John time to get up now and have your breakfast,' 'all the other tribal leaders will be here shortly to discuss our journey for the day! I jumped up and stretched my aching bones after lying all night on the hard ground, Jemima pushed a plate of cold meat that she had kept from the night before for my breakfast along with a drink of the green looking liquid that tasted like strawberry's. I had no sooner finished then we were joined by all the leaders of the other peoples of Sofala. 'Good,' morning Mr Trinity everyone said in unison; Mr Trinity just nodded in return and beckoned them to sit down beside him. 'As you know we have to pass through the forest of Paqoun, 'an ideal place for an ambush with thick dense trees. 'Any suggestions Mr Trinity said. General Dylantos said 'Simple,' 'we smoke them out or even burn them out of the forest; 'after all it's not that big of a forest! 'Alyconeus and his men can cut down a few trees at the edge of the forest, 'pile them up and set fire to them if the wind is in our favour' 'the smoke will drift through the forest and smoke them out' 'then I can pick them off with my archers General Dylantos said! 'It seems the best option' 'we can't afford to lose any men in that forest' 'we need everyone for the battle we will encounter on the plains of Modecica said Christinos! 'Well if no one has any more suggestions on what to do then so be it! General Giedroyc said 'I will fly just ahead of you with my troops over the Mountains; 'King Ronough and his men can fly in front of you just in case there is any of Kaunn's men left if that is agreeable with you King Ronough General Giedroyc said! 'My Synisaurous will patrol the skies just in case we come across those Angasaurous bird like creatures, 'my pilots with their great crossbows will soon take care of them King Gandelin said! 'If we leave now we should arrive at the forest of Paqoun before nightfall' 'you and young John along with the two Poppy Twins can fly with me in my Migasaurous across the mountains! 'Excuse me I said to King Gandelin can some of your great Synisaurous not take some of the troops across the Mountains in the baskets? 'I know you can't take them all I stammered! 'You know young man you're right; 'How long will it take you and your men to put the wheels back onto the baskets King Gandelin said to Alyconeus! 'Not long about a couple of hours he said; 'Good,' the King replied then do it; 'Christinos and her warriors will have to cross the Mountains as we cannot take her horses across in the baskets it will take too long! General Giedroyc spoke we will accompany Christinos and her warriors through the Mountains and I to said King Ronough! 'Well that is settled then I think you should leave now, 'Some of your troops will have to go with Christinos as well I'm afraid General Dylantos I can't take you all I have to think of my men first said King Gandelin. At that moment Hipictu walked up to General Dylantos and in sign language said he was leaving now to cross the Mountains, he never mixed with anyone he and his men just kept themselves to themselves but it was good to have them on our side they were really fierce looking warriors. He turned on his heels signalled to his men and headed for a small winding path which wound its way across the Mountains to the forest of Paqoun which lay about a mile from the edge of the Green Mountains Mr Trinity told me. Alyconeus and his men were hastily removing the wheels from the rafts they had attached two days before and began to assemble them back onto the baskets. Mr Trinity was deep in conversation with Christinos, he held both of her tiny hands in his long bony fingers, he must have thought no one was looking for he bent down and gave Christinos a goodbye kiss on her cheek. He stood back and blushed and stammered 'take care; 'and a safe journey. Poppy one turned to me and said; 'He really has it bad never seen him like this before! I just smiled at him and kept on watching the giant Scordisi warriors working away on the baskets. General Dylantos walked up to Mr Trinity who had returned to where the two Poppy Twins were standing along with King Gandelin and me. 'We are going now Mr Trinity' 'I will take care of Christinos for you; 'Besides you need not worry she is a strong and fierce warrior and can fight as any man in this army! Mr Trinity placed his hand on General Dylantos's shoulder 'You are a good friend; King Gandelin spoke, 'Leave some of your men behind' 'my great Synisaurous can carry some of them across the Mountain just like they carried Christinos across the open sea! 'Thank you,' 'but I think it would be best if my soldiers and me crossed the Mountains with Christinos and her soldiers' 'Safety in numbers as they say! General Dylantos signalled to his men who were already standing to attention in one long single file, their shields glinting in the early morning sun. General Dylantos walked to the path, which led over the Mountains followed by his men, with Christinos and her warriors on their horses bringing up the rear. I watched as One by one they marched towards the path and disappeared into the mountains, leaving Alyconeus and his soldiers along with King Gandelin his soldiers Mr Trinity the two Poppy twins myself with King Ronough's daughter Fairy Nough. General Giedroyc along with his Tyrocdils and King Ronough had left early that morning to make sure nothing else or anyone lay hidden in the Hugh boulders scattered about in the Mountains. Alyconeus walked up to Mr Trinity and said; 'Everything is ready for you now; 'my men will leave now' 'we will meet again at the forest of Paqoun! 'Thank you King Gandelin said to Alyconeus and held out his hand. Alyconeus took the Kings hand in his Hugh hand and shook it gently; being such a big man, he could be a very gentle person. Alyconeus returned to his giant warriors and along with his two dogs with Encaladeus behind him walked to the path, which led over the Mountains. One by one, they marched past Hugh giant men, each one carrying a great spiked club with their great broadswords slung over their shoulder hanging down in between their massive shoulder blades. Soon they had gone now it was time for us to leave and cross the Mountains to the forest of Paqoun.

King Gandelin gave the signal to Generals Rol and Travin to assemble the troops into the baskets ready for the great Synisaurous to carry them over the Mountains. The troops climbed into the baskets and General Travin gave the signal to the pilots of the Synisaurous to come and pick up the baskets. One by one, the great birds ran along the flat desert sand their great wings flapping until they were all in the air circling up above the baskets. I watched in awe as these great birds circled round each one squawking, their massive wings beating the air creating a small sand storm on the desert below. Then down they came in twos, each pair of birds grabbing their basket one at the front and one at the rear of each basket. The two soldiers who were stationed at the front and rear of each basket attached the chains to the great bird's legs as before as the basket began to rumble over the flat desert sand, soon each one was in the air and heading out over the Mountains and all too soon they too had disappeared into the low lying Mountain mist. Now it was our turn we walked towards King Gandelin's great Migasaurous and climbed into the basket attached to its great back. We settled into our seats and King Gandelin gave its pilot the orders to take off. We hung onto the sides of the basket as the great bird ran along the sand, its great wings flapping to pick up speed until suddenly we were in the air heading out over the Mountains towards the forest of Paqoun .

On we flew just below the low-lying clouds; I knew that just above us was flying Generals Rol and Travin, you could not see them as they were flying just above the clouds. I looked down and their below you could see our great column of soldiers marching along in single file over the small narrow mountain pass towards the forest of Paqoun. The weather had taken a turn for the worse snow had started to fall in these high mountain passes and I was beginning to get cold. I could imagine what it must be like for the soldiers walking over that small mountain pass with no shelter to speak of just the snow and wind rushing into their faces. Do not worry King Gandelin said to me; 'They will reach the top of the mountain in about an hour; 'When they start to descend they have to pass through a gorge where the walls of the mountain are solid flat rock, 'the walls form an arch and that will protect them from the snow! 'I think we should fly higher above the cloud and join my men don't you Mr Trinity? Mr Trinity nodded his head and King Gandelin gave the order for the pilot to take us higher above the clouds. The great Migasaurous began to climb higher until we were above the clouds, it was quite a lot warmer up above, it was still snowing hard but the sun was shining which warmed me slightly taking the chill off my body.

I turned round and looked behind me; Generals Rol and Travin were flying along with the great Synisaurous carrying their baskets full of soldiers. The soldiers had covered their baskets with the canvas tarpaulins 'to keep them dry from the snow. King Gandelin took out a small roll of tarpaulin that lay on the floor of the basket we unrolled it, we attached it to the sides of the basket, and stretched it from front to back to form a kind of shelter to keep us dry and protect us from the wind. I soon began to get a lot warmer as the sun began to warm up the tarpaulin my clothes, which were quite damp, began to dry out and make me a lot more comfortable then I had been. How long before we reach the forest of Paquon I asked King Gandelin;' 'we should be there just before nightfall young man he said! I wondered how all the other soldiers below us were getting on, they should be about half way now across the mountains, heading towards the path that, would lead them to the edge of the forest of Paquon. We began to descend, and King Gandelin removed the tarpaulin that covered the basket we were flying in. We descended down through the clouds followed by Generals Rol and Travin in their baskets, followed by King Gandelin's soldiers in there baskets. As we came down through the clouds the snow had stopped to reveal the Mountain tops in all their glory, their icy tips reaching up into the clouds and the sides of the Mountains covered in small trees and bushes dotted about here and there. I could see the semi-precious coloured stones that ran through the side of the Mountains, like colours of the rainbow. When the sun peeped through the passing clouds above, the sunlight reflected off the side of each Mountain dazzling your eyes, making you shield them from the bright colours of the semi-precious stones that lay embedded into the side of each Mountain.

Chapter Twenty-two

We flew lower until we were flying in between the mountains we were so close you could almost reach out and touch the side of each Mountain as we passed alongside. 'Look there? 'Up ahead Mr Trinity said; 'There is Alyconeus and the other soldiers; 'they are about to enter the gorge and the path down to the edge of the forest of Paquon. Mr Trinity looked quite relieved that they had reached the final part of their journey without any misfortune befalling them. 'They should be quite safe now King Gandelin said 'that gorge is too narrow for anyone to ambush you! 'They should be there just before nightfall. 'We will be there in a couple of hours where we can set up a welcome party for them. Mr Trinity spoke 'General Giedroyc and his Tyrocdils along with King Ronough should be there by now. 'Let's hope they did not have any bother when they arrived at the Paqoun forest! We must have flew on for what seemed like hours in and out of each Mountain we flew till at last a large opening appeared in front of us. In the distance, I could see the forest of Paqoun its tall trees reaching up as if their tips touched the sky above.

As we passed between the two Mountains down below I could see a large expanse of grass, I could see General Giedroyc along with King Ronough and their soldiers setting up camp for the night. As we descended down General Giedroyc's men had made what looked like a small landing strip for us to land on. Down we came King Gandelin's great Migasaurous gliding lower and lower until we touched the ground. The great bird running along the ground, until suddenly she came to a halt in front of General Giedroyc. Everyone jumped out from the basket, attached to the great Migasaurous, King Gandelin told his pilot to take the great bird and settle her down at the edge of the field. The pilot took hold of the rope that was attached to the birds Hugh beak and led away the great bird, waddling as she walked to where she would sleep for the night, along with all of King Gandelin's Synisaurous when they landed with their troops. 'Did you have a safe journey? 'Yes thank you General Mr Trinity replied 'a bit cold' 'but we are here now. 'Excuse me will you please said King Gandelin; 'I must see to my men they are waiting to land!' I looked up above me and watched as the great Synisaurous birds circled up above carrying their load of soldiers in each basket. King Gandelin gave the order. The great birds began to land releasing each of their baskets in turn, and then flying to where the great Migasaurous was lying at the far edge of the field. The baskets rumbled along over the makeshift landing strip, as each one came to a halt the troops jumped out and pushed them to form one long extended line at the edge of the field in front of the forest of Paqoun, which lay about a mile away over the field. 'That will give us some protection tonight; 'we have the mountains behind us and the line of baskets in front of us said King Gandelin!' 'Now we just have to wait for the rest of all the other soldiers coming out of that gorge behind us said Mr Trinity! Jemima who had travelled along with King Ronough and his soldiers came up to Mr Trinity. 'We are running short of food? 'Everybody just carried enough for the journey here! 'There will be food in the forest, deer and wild boar' 'plenty for everyone; King Gandelin said; 'I know said Mr Trinity 'but that is an ideal place for an ambush you know we have to be very careful we cannot afford to lose any of our soldiers; 'we don't know how many warriors' Kaunn has gathered together on the plains of Modecica!' 'Well we need food said King Gandelin 'this army cannot fight without it; 'and my birds will need feeding as well! Just as we were discussing the food situation Alyconeus along with Encaladeus and the two giant dogs began to appear walking across the open field followed by Christinos and her warriors with General Dylantos bringing up the rear, but there was no sign of

Hipictu and his cannibals. Alyconeus approached Mr Trinity 'I see you have arrived safely; 'You look a little bit concerned what seems to be the problem? King Gandelin said 'food is the problem,' 'we don't have any' he then went on to explain that there was plenty in the forest but everyone was concerned in case any of Kaunn's men were lying in wait to ambush Mr Trinity's soldiers. 'Well we need food so' 'I will go with my soldiers and the two dogs and bring food back with me! King Ronough spoke 'I will go to with my Fairy soldiers,' 'after all we are small and can hide in the treetops and pick off anyone who tries to ambush Alyconeus and his soldiers. General Giedroyc spoke 'I will help,' 'my Tyrocdils can fly above the treetops and watch for any movement on the forest floor! Not to be out done General Dylantos stood stroking his thick red beard 'I am not going to be left out of this I want to have some fun as well! I just looked at him in astonishment. Fun I thought to myself, he thought this was fun; people could be killed in that forest. After some more conversation everyone agreed on what they were about to do. Alyconeus pushed one of the large wooden baskets to one side and along with Encaladeus, the two dogs and his men began to walk across the open field towards the forest about half a mile away. General Dylantos took some of his men and followed Alyconeus and his soldiers. King Ronough took to the air with some of his men, their small crossbows at the ready and flew towards the trees. General Giedroyc with his Tyrocdils took to the air to patrol the skies above the forest just in case they encountered any of those Angasaurous half bird half man creatures, who was no match for General Giedroyc and his army of Tyrocdils. I watched as everyone started to walk towards the trees, when they were about twenty-five yards from the edge of the forest Alyconeus released the two giant dogs they bounded towards the forest and disappeared into the trees. We waited for a few minutes and then I heard the most awful sound it was someone screaming, the noise sent shivers down my spine. I kept on looking to where the screams were coming from. Then I saw one of the dogs dragging what looked like a human form from out of the trees, it was one of Kaunn's men. Alyconeus strode forward and took hold of the poor unfortunate man picked him up by his neck his feet about two feet from the ground. The man struggled for a while General Dylantos must have said something to Alyconeus for he put the man down. General Dylantos summoned two of his soldiers to bring the man back to Mr Trinity so Mr Trinity could question him. They ran back to where we were waiting dragging the unfortunate man back his legs dragging along the ground. The two soldiers threw him to the ground, the man lay their cowering with fear. He was a big man dressed in knee length pants; he wore fur boots and a sleeveless short waistcoat. His arms were covered in tattoo's, he was also tattooed with strange markings on his face he had straggly long shoulder length dark hair; he did not look very fierce now lying cowering on the ground. Mr Trinity walked towards the prostate man lying on the ground with his arms and legs kept down by four of General Dylantos's soldiers. Mr Trinity bent down over the man his eyes wide with fear as Mr Trinity bent closer to his face. The man tried to close his eyes but Mr Trinity put his long bony fingers onto the man's forward and pressed onto either side of the man's temple. 'You can leave go now' he said 'I will take over now. The four soldiers let go of the man, he just lay there on the ground as if he was dead. Mr Trinity looked into his eyes, his deep blue eyes piercing into the man's dark eyes. Mr Trinity looked into his eyes for a few minutes; the man lay there in some kind of trance. Mr Trinity then got up from the ground; 'I have all the information I need 'Come with me John' "We will go and give Alyconeus and General Dylantos the information I have taken from Kaunn's soldier. Mr Trinity turned to the two Poppy twins when Hipictu arrives give that creature there to them it is their supper for tonight! With those final words he turned on his heels and started to walk towards where Alyconeus was waiting with General Dylantos and the other soldiers I followed behind. King Ronough joined us and Mr Trinity told them. 'Kaunn has five hundred men lying in wait in that forest for us. 'He knows that we need food' 'He also knows that we could not travel this far bringing food with us; 'too much to carry! Mr Trinity signalled to General Giedroyc who was patrolling the sky's up above to come down and join him. He began to explain what he had told King Ronough Alyconeus and General Dylantos. 'I need you to fly over to the far side of the forest at the edge of the plains of Modecica and burn it. 'Wait till nightfall when everything is quiet' 'Kaunn will not suspect anything' 'He is hoping that we fall into his trap in the forest' 'his men will not leave the forest to attack us tonight; 'we are too many" 'and we have a good defensive position with the Green Mountains behind us! 'Also the animals in the forest will run towards us and we will have food for tomorrow! 'Ah I see said General Dylantos kill two birds with one stone as they say; 'We get our food and Kaunn loses five hundred men. I like it said General Dylantos stroking his thick red beard! He was a nice man but a bloodthirsty one.

'Let us return to camp, we started to walk back to our campsite for the night by this time the sun was beginning to get low on the horizon. I looked up at the sky and coming over the horizon was what looked like a large black cloud. I tugged on Mr Trinity's arm and pointed upwards. 'Angasaurous Mr Trinity shouted; General Giedroyc instantly took off with his men and head towards the Angasaurous to engage them in combat. I knew they would be no match for General Giedroyc and his Tyrocdils they were too big and cumbersome, where the General with his Tyrocdils were much too quick for them. We all ran back to the safety of the camp. I looked around and King Ronough had taken off and joined General Giedroyc and his Tyrocdils. Maybe this was a blessing in disguise, now we might not have to burn down that beautiful forest tonight, as it would not only kill Kaunn's men who hid in the forest but all the animals as well. In my eye that was not right, we only needed a few for food, General Giedroyc and his Tyrocdils with King Ronough and his fairy soldiers would take care of that.

We reached the safety of the camp; Alyconeus pushed the Hugh basket back into place to seal up the gap between the forest and our camp. I looked up at the now darkening sky and watched as General Giedroyc and his Tyrocdils and King Ronough with his soldiers began to engage the Angasaurous in combat. The Angasaurous were too big and cumbersome and soon killed by the Tyrocdils and the Fairy soldiers. The odd one got through and headed for our camp but they too were quickly dealt with by General Dylantos's archers, their big cumbersome body's falling to the ground with a sickening thud. They wriggled for a while in their death throes and became still, their large ugly bloodshot eyes staring blankly into the now dark sky. The screams from the battle got louder then as quickly it had started it ceased leaving nothing but silence over the field that lay in front of the forest. General Giedroyc returned along with King Ronough and their soldiers. 'We have food for tonight it just needs gathering in said General Dylantos. I looked at Mr Trinity and thought to myself, actually, we were no better than those evil creatures that had just killed but this was war. You could not be sentimental in war I had found out, they would have done the same to us without any hesitation if we had been defeated, we would have been ripped to pieces and soon be turning over on a spit on an open fire. The thought was too unbearable to think of and made my whole body shudder with the thought of it. Alyconeus strode up to Mr Trinity and said 'We will go and retrieve those evil creatures" and with those final few words he pulled back one of the baskets and along with Encaladeus and a few of his soldiers disappeared into the darkness to retrieve the Angasaurous from where they lay on the large open field of death.

Chapter Twenty-three

Alcoyneaus soon returned with his men dragging that evil Angasaurous creature behind him. I counted around a hundred of those horrible looking creatures. I did not feel any compassion for them. I was beginning to feel like everyone else now; it was just food in my eyes now. Whereas before I would have felt sick at the very thought of eating one of these creatures. Alyconeus and his men piled them up in the middle of the camp and summoned the soldiers from different tribes to take their share. King Gandelin spoke 'I will need twenty of those creatures to feed my birds tonight; 'They will not be able to fly if they do not get fed! Mr Trinity agreed with the King and told him to summon his soldiers and take the twenty Angasaurous and ten for his men for the night. 'There is plenty to go round at least our bellies will be full tonight said General Dylantos...Mr Trinity told Jemima to take one of the creatures away he also asked the two Poppy twins to help, as she could not manage on her own. I was in for a treat tonight Jemima was a wonderful cook she could make anything taste nice. All the tribes had taken what they needed for their meal that night and went back to their fires to cook the evening meal and probably talk about the event of the day, the defeat of the Angasaurous, which has made their bellies full that night.

General Dylantos said 'Look, here comes Hipictu with his warriors they should have been here a good few hours ago! Hipictu strode up to General Dylantos and in sign language explained why he had just arrived now, he shouted to three of his men and forward they came each one dragging a lifeless man behind them. General Dylantos told Mr Trinity that they had been ambushed in the Green Mountains by about twenty Troglodytes' who they defeated and that is why he has arrived late. 'Tell him I have a gift for him Mr Trinity said to General Dylantos! Mr Trinity asked King Gandelin if he would be so kind as to ask one of his men to bring forward the unfortunate man that we had captured earlier that day. King Gandelin summoned one of his soldiers and told him to bring the man back to him. The soldier ran away and quickly returned with the soldier from Kaunn's army and threw him onto the ground in front Hipictu. The man looked up his eyes wide with fear and he began to plead with Mr Trinity not to give him to Hipictu and his cannibals. He began to sob uncontrollably begging all the time for his life. I began to feel quite sick at this poor unfortunate man begging to Mr Trinity not to be given to Hipictu...Mr Trinity just looked at the man with his deep blue eyes piercing into his eyes; all of a sudden, the man became calm as if in a trance. Mr Trinity told Hipictu to take the man away; Hipictu picked up the man and led him away to the camp his warriors had made at the far end of the field away from everyone else. Mr Trinity turned to Christinos who had been watching all this going on. 'I am sorry you had to witness that; 'but we cannot afford to be sentimental; 'after all if' Kaunn had his way; 'we would all be suffering the same fate as that man 'except it would be the Angasaurous that would be tearing us to pieces! Christinos took hold of Mr Trinity's arm and looked into his blue eyes. 'You are right Mr Trinity.' 'I hold nothing against you; 'we have to do what we have to do.' 'It is sad; 'but if we need peace in our world of Sofala then it has to be done for the good of everyone! Mr Trinity smiled at Christinos, he probably felt a lot better knowing that she agreed with what he had done after all she was the one person he needed in his lonely life at this very moment in time. 'Would you like to join me for dinner tonight he said going back to his shy way every time Christinos was near him. Christinos smiled her blue eyes twinkling in the moonlight, 'I would be honoured she said !She took Mr Trinity's arm in hers and began to walk towards our campfire where Jemima was preparing our evening meal. I walked slowly behind keeping my distance. I might have been young but I knew when two people needed to be alone together. She was the one person that brought happiness to Mr Trinity out of all that was going on all around us in this world of Sofala. We reached the campfire where Jemima had prepared our evening meal. The Angasaurous was turning on a spit over the open fire, it smelt wonderful. Poppy one and two were already eating, the three of us sat down to eat our evening meal. I was really quite hungry having had nothing to eat all day, so I tucked in greedily tearing bits of flesh away from the Angasaurous that was roasting over the open fire. We must have sat there for about an hour just eating and talking amongst ourselves when we were joined by Kings Gandelin and Ronough along with his daughter Fairy Nough. Generals Dylantos and Giedroyc along with Generals Rol and Travin also joined us. Alyconeus Encaladeus and Christinos's second in command Judithos, was there, the only person who was missing was Hipictu but then again he did not mix with anyone he and his warriors just kept themselves to themselves.

'Mr Trinity General Dylantos said' 'I think we should attack Kaunn's troops in the forest at dawn tomorrow take them by surprise; 'then we have the forest for our protection. 'We will have food; 'and we can set up camp in the forest and prepare our troops ready to meet Kaunn on the plains of Modecica! 'King Ronough spoke up 'I and my fairy soldiers can fly into the treetops and pick off any of Kaunn's men from there. General Dylantos spoke, 'I will take my men and form a long extended line of soldiers behind their shields. Christinos replied 'We are the only troops here with horses; 'we will gallop through the forest and panic Kaunn's men. 'When they show King Ronough can pick them off with his archers. General Giedroyc interrupted. 'I will take my Tyrocdils to the other side of the forest and wait for anyone who comes out of the other side. Alyconeus spoke 'my troops will go ahead of General Dylantos along with my two dogs' 'they will flush out any of Kaunn's soldiers. 'We know there is a thousand of his men in there, 'and we can defeat them' 'they will be still half asleep they will not be expecting us! My

Synisaurous will patrol the skies above the plains of Modecica just in case Kaunn decides to attack said King Gandelin. Mr Trinity spoke 'is that what you all want to do? Everyone nodded his or her heads in agreement. 'Well if your adamant then so be it 'let's prepare our troops for early in the morning; 'about three o clock for that is when I know they will be still fast asleep' 'they will not be expecting us that is the best time. Everyone agreed they all left our campfire to ready their troops and try to get some rest before we left very early the next morning. Mr Trinity told me to try and sleep and not to worry about what tomorrow might bring. I lay down on my bedroll which Jemima had prepared for me and tried to sleep, but I just tossed and turned my heart was pounding at the thought of what tomorrow would bring. Through my broken sleep, I could see Mr Trinity just sitting by the fire. I wondered if he ever slept at all, only once did I ever see him lie down but then he had his back to me so I never knew if he had slept or not, he certainly was a very strange man but a good man.

I drifted in and out of sleep until finally Jemima awoke me, 'time to get up John; 'everyone is here! I jumped up out of my bedroll and sat next to Mr Trinity who was his calm usual self. General Giedroyc said 'I will leave now with my men to attack from the rear; 'can you give me about an hour before you set off? Mr Trinity nodded and General Giedroyc took to the air with his men and set off to the other side of the forest. I watched as they flew away into the distance. They formed into a formation, which looked like a dark rain cloud.

King Gandelin left us to give General Travin his orders for the great Synisaurous to take off and circle above the forest in case Kaunn had decided to send some more of his Angasaurous to attack our camp in the morning. King Ronough along with his daughter Fairy Nough was ready. She looked fierce dressed in her blue tunic, she had a small sword hanging from the left hand side of her tiny waist and a small bow in her right hand, slung over her back was a small pouch of arrows. She was only two feet tall but she was afraid of no one or anything. 'We will leave now said King Ronough to Mr Trinity and take to the trees in the forest! And with those final words they took off and headed for the forest. We all sat for an hour no one saying anything, then Mr Trinity said 'it's time to leave now; and with those words he rose up from his seat by the fire and took Christinos to one side. I could hear him say to her in a soft voice to take care and not to do anything stupid. She nodded her head, mounted her horse, and took to the front of her troops along with Judithos. It was quite a formidable sight, all the warrior women lined up alongside each other, their faces all blacked out so they did not reflect in the moonlight.

Alyconeus led the way along with Encaladeus and the two giant dogs, followed by his giant Scordisi warriors. General Dylantos brought up the rear with some of his troops as he had left some behind to guard the camp. Hipictu of course was nowhere to be seen, anyway he did his own thing but what he and his warriors did they always contributed to the outcome of the final battle, they were fierce warriors and were feared in battle I was so glad they were on our side so to speak.

Mr Trinity gave the signal, everyone set off in unison and silence, even the hooves of Christinos horse, and her soldiers were bandaged to keep down the noise as they walked towards the forest of Paqoun. We walked forward until we were about twenty-five yards from the edge of the forest; the moon peeped from behind the cloud casting ghostly shadows on the ground from the tops of the trees as they swayed gently back and forth in the slight breeze. We moved forward cautiously towards the edge of the forest, by this time the moon had once again disappeared behind the clouds. It was pitch dark nothing stirred as we walked slowly towards the forest no one uttering a word. Mr Trinity gave the signal and Alyconeus released the two giant dogs, they bounded towards the forest growling and snarling as they ran into the trees. Then all hell was let loose

Alyconeus and Encaladeus ran forward with their soldiers into the forest followed by Christinos and her soldiers on horseback General Dylantos brought up the rear with his soldiers' Mr Trinity and me ran after them into the darkness of the trees. We entered our way into the forest and through the undergrowth of small bushes, of which everyone could hide a potential enemy. On we travelled slowly picking our way through the dense undergrowth in every bush could be hidden one of Kaunn's men. We were deep in the forest by this time and still not one of Kaunn's men did we encounter everywhere there was a deathly silence we advanced slowly through the forest picking our way through the undergrowth. I was beginning to become quite afraid by this time walking through this dark forest just the odd twig snapping here and there, as we walked on deeper into the forest.

When would they attack I thought then as my eyes became more accustomed to the darkness a small figure came out of the darkness it was Hipictu or so I thought, closer and closer he walked towards Mr Trinity till he was only a few feet away. Then he made his move he withdrew a small dagger from his loincloth and lunged at Mr Trinity, but Mr Trinity was to quick he knew that it was not Hipictu that was walking towards him but a Troglodyte they could take on any human form that they wished. As he lunged forward Mr Trinity held up his hand and the Troglodyte stopped dead in his tracks frozen to the spot you could see the fear in his eyes knowing he could not move. Without any hesitation King Gandelin strode forward withdrew his sword, severed the Troglodytes head from his body with one swift blow, and sent it flying through the trees to land in the bushes. The Troglodytes body dropped to the ground and began to take on the shape of what they really looked like. The body lay their covered in its long shaggy fur its feet and hands just like a humans except it had six toes and fingers. I remember Mr Trinity telling me that is how you could tell it was a Troglodyte, it was the only bits of their body they could not change, and that was how you would know. We all stood in silence for a moment then a terrible scream erupted from the trees in front of us and out of the dense undergrowth came a hoard of screaming Troglodytes running towards us with their monkey like faces, their lips snarled back showing their black razor sharp teeth, each one was waving a sword above its head and screaming like a banshee as they advanced towards us through the forest. As they were about to take on the form of the person who they were going to engage in battle, out from the treetops a thousand arrows came down from through the trees like raindrops falling from the sky. Thud, Thud, was the sound of each arrow as it reached its target piercing the Troglodytes, some fell to the ground mortally wounded but others came on towards us. Christinos and her troops galloped into the throng of Troglodytes, some of the Troglodytes tried to take on the form of Christinos and her soldiers so in the battle no one would know who was who. Alyconeus and Encaladeus ran forward through the undergrowth towards the Troglodytes and began to chop with their Hugh broadswords and clubs, the spikes of their clubs sinking into their heads. Mr Trinity just stood there not looking concerned at all, as the battle raged on in front of him. Poppy one and two stood beside Mr Trinity and me their swords drawn ready for anyone who came towards us. The Troglodytes had taken on the human form of some of General Dylantos's soldiers but they were no match for them, they too were cut down where they stood. Dawn was beginning to come up over the horizon and Troglodyte body's littered the forest floor. The remainder of the Troglodytes began to run to the other end of the forest screaming as they ran, and dropping their weapons onto the forest floor. It was light by this time. The sun began to peep through the treetops, the battle had raged on for about two hours. As the Troglodytes ran towards the other end of the forest, they ran into some of General Dylantos's troops who quickly dispatched them to meet there maker. We all walked through the forest floor, which was littered, with the bodies of the Troglodytes, their monkey like faces contorted in death, their lips pulled back in a snarl. They lay their showing their razor sharp black rotten teeth. Mr Trinity gathered all the leaders of the tribes together and asked if they had lost any of their soldiers. Christinos had lost ten King Gandelin twenty along with General Dylantos who had also lost twenty men. Alyconeus had not lost any of his soldiers, as no one was a match for these giants. King Ronough flew down from the trees along with his daughter Fairy Nough, we were also joined by General Giedroyc and his Tyrocdils...Mr Trinity said 'We should bury our dead now and bury them deep' 'we do not want any of the animals of the forest to dig them up they fought bravely and they should lie in peace! King Ronough said 'we should move on now to the far edge of the forest and set up our new camp there in front of the plains of Modecica. Mr Trinity agreed; 'General Dylantos said 'I will go on with my men and begin to set up camp just inside the forest! Alyconeus spoke 'Encaladeus will take some of my men and help to clear away some of the undergrowth to make a clearing for the baskets; 'I have an idea how we can use them against Kaunn and his army.

'Fine we can discuss that later, 'time is short we want to have control of the forest before nightfall. 'Thank you Alyconeus' Mr Trinity replied' 'but first let us bury our dead and then move back to camp. Alyconeus gave some of his men orders to dig the mass grave for the soldiers who had fallen in battle, as it would not take his giant warriors very long to dig the grave. After the grave had been dug, every one of the fallen soldiers were placed neatly together, each one with their arms crossed over their chest, and their weapons neatly placed by their side. Christinos stood by the graveside and looked down into the mass grave. I could see her shed a tear as she stood looking down at her soldiers. Mr Trinity came across to her and put his long thin bony arm around her shoulders and led her away sobbing, that was the only time I would see Christinos shed a tear.

When all the soldiers had been placed in the grave King Gandelin's and General Dylantos's soldiers filled in the grave, they scattered leaves all over the top of the grave so you would not know if any grave was there at all. I borrowed a dagger from Poppy one and carved a small cross into the bark of the tree, which stood at the head of the grave. Mr Trinity knew what the symbol meant and he began to explain it to all the other soldiers, he then stood at the side of the grave and said a small prayer, he then made the sign of the cross across his chest while everyone looked bemused by his actions.

After Mr Trinity had done what he had to do, he turned back to Christinos and began to walk with her back to our camp below the Green Mountains, everyone followed behind them in silence. I knew deep down in my heart that there would be more deaths within the next few days.

Chapter Twenty-four

We arrived back at our camp, Hipictu joined us and began to explain to Mr Trinity why he had not come with us, some strange superstition he and his tribe had about being evil spirits that roamed the forest at night, anyway that was his excuse and Mr Trinity accepted it. Hipictu said he would make it up to Mr Trinity for not being there. He would show how brave he and his warriors were by being the first into battle...Mr Trinity placed his hand on Hipictu's shoulder nodded and smiled, with that reassurance from Mr Trinity he turned around and headed back to his men at the far side of the camp. King Gandelin's great Synisaurous by this time had landed in front of the field at the edge of the forest. General Travin leader of the Synisaurous squadron came up to King Gandelin and said everything was quiet on the plains of Modecica. Mr Trinity spoke 'We have ten spare horses now' 'they will come in very useful when we engage Kaunn's army' 'Alyconeus has to make chariots out of the baskets we have! 'Come time is short we have to dismantle our camp and set up another camp in the forest before nightfall. 'We do not want to give any of Kaunn's army the chance to ambush us in the forest again. Everyone began rushing about doing their duty and dismantling the camp. King Gandelin along with some of his soldiers would guard the camp. All the other soldiers began to push the large baskets towards the forest but it was quite a struggle, it was not long before they had to stop exhausted. Run and get Alyconeus Mr Trinity said to me, 'You will be fine; I ran as quickly as my little legs would carry me on through the forest not looking back or side to side. There was a deathly silence, just my little legs disturbing the undergrowth the odd twig snapping under my feet as I ran. Suddenly I was not alone I looked behind and their following me was a solitary Troglodyte. His

Monkey like face twisted in a snarling grin, his long black sharp teeth chattering, his long shaggy fur flowing in the breeze as he ran after me; he held a sword in his right hand. My heart was pounding like a drum and I was beginning to sweat with fear. I began to scream at the top of my voice, the sound echoing all around in the forest. He was not very far behind me. I turned and looked the Troglodyte began to take on my human form, it was as if an identical twin brother was chasing me, but this was no twin brother it was a Troglodyte and he wanted my blood. I mustered all the breath I could from my now aching lungs and shouted at the top of my voice. 'ALYCONEUS,' 'ALYCONEUS help me? A voice came out of the trees in front of me, 'fall to the ground? I did as the voice said, as I fell to the ground the Troglodyte was above me it was like looking at a mirror image of myself, but I was not looking in a mirror.

I lay on the ground looking up at the sky through the treetops; a dark shadow began to hover over me. The Troglodyte began to change back into the horrible looking monkey like creature. He raised his sword I was shaking with fear, I began to cry when all of a sudden from nowhere an arrow flew through the air and pierced the Troglodyte through his throat, a look of surprise came into his eyes and he fell dead at my side. I wiped the tears from my eyes and a Hugh hand picked me up from the ground. It was Alyconeus he held me to his Hugh chest and said you will be fine now; he walked back to where General Dylantos was along with King Ronough and his daughter Fairy Nough. General Giedroyc took to the air and began to scour the forest just in case there were any more Troglodytes that had survived the battle. I told Alyconeus that Mr Trinity was having problems getting the baskets through the forest; he needed him, and his soldiers to help. Alyconeus asked Encaladeus to take charge. Alyconeus gathered fifty of his men, he put me on his shoulders and we all set off towards where Mr Trinity was waiting.

We bounded through the forest animals scattered from

the advancing Giants till finally we came out into the open field at the edge of the forest. Alyconeus walked up to Mr Trinity and said 'what is the problem Mr Trinity; 'we need you to take the baskets through the forest; 'I know you want to make some chariots out of the baskets! Alyconeus gathered his fifty men and told them what Mr Trinity wanted them to do. 'We have ten spare horses from the warriors that Christinos had killed in the forest' 'that means we can only use five baskets' 'two horses to each basket! The advantage we have is that Kaunn has no horses all his troops are on foot said Mr Trinity! Everything was agreed. Alyconeus and his men began to pull the five baskets towards the forest, leaving the remaining baskets behind below the green mountains for our journey back if we were successful in beating Kaunn and his evil army. We all followed behind Alyconeus and his men towards the forest along with all the other soldiers who had guarded the camp. Suddenly Mr Trinity stopped in his tracks, he turned around, I turned with him and their behind us was Master Remlin coming out of the pass at the edge of the Green Mountains which Christinos and Alyconeus had come through with their troops a few days earlier. He sat there on his great white horse his blue robe hanging over his shoulders, his long white hair kept in place by the jewelled headband he always wore. He strode towards us I could see he was also dressed in black leather trousers and a black leather waistcoat he had trimmed his long white beard so it just hung below his chin. He dismounted and stood in front of Mr Trinity his long cape like robe coming to just above his knee length boots, around his waist was a thick leather belt which held two daggers each with a jewel encrusted handle. He looked at me with his piercing blue eyes. 'Good day young man; 'I hope you have behaved yourself for Mr Trinity; I stammered 'yes Sir Master Remlin. 'Good, Good,' he said as he ruffled my hair with his long bony fingers. 'And you Mr Trinity? 'Everything is fine Master Remlin. He began to tell Master Remlin everything that had happened up to date. 'Here John take my horse' 'I will walk with Mr Trinity to our final campsite.

I took the reins of Master Remlin's horse and followed behind Mr Trinity and Master Remlin who were talking, I presumed about Kaunn and the forthcoming battle with him and his army. I looked back at our last campsite just the smoke rising up into the morning sun from the now dying embers of the hundreds of campfires. King Gandelin's great Synisaurous lay against the side of the Green Mountains, waiting for his signal to join us when the battle with Kaunn and his army which was about to take place within the next two days. We had also left the remainder of the baskets there also; we would need them to get back home if our outcome was successful. We were now approaching the edge of the forest. Alyconeus and his men were pulling the five baskets through the trees towards our next campsite. At the other end of the forest the rest of General Dylantos's troops along with the remainder of King Gandelin's soldiers were setting up camp. Hipictu and his warriors were still nowhere to be seen. We walked through the forest Mr Trinity and Master Remlin still deep in conversation with each other. I tried to listen to what they were saying but they just spoke in a whisper, besides I would probably find out later on what they were discussing when we reached our final camp for the night. We finally reached our campsite, some of Alyconeus's men had been busy along with General Dylantos and his soldiers making a large clearing at the edge of the forest. They had made a semicircle barricade with the trees they had felled, about five feet tall also they had left a small opening in the centre for soldiers to pass through for we needed food for our evening meal for in the forest there was an abundance of different animals for us to feed on.

Everyone was going about their duties; some of the soldiers were hunting for food, some were making small campfires within the semicircle of trees, for the food to be cooked. Alyconeus and his men took no time at all converting the baskets into four wheeled chariots' I watched in awe as some of General Dylantos's men made ropes from the vines hanging down from some of the trees to attach the horses to the chariots the next day.

Chapter Twenty-five

The day had gone quickly and now night was beginning to set in. The food was cooked, everybody had eaten their fill and the guards posted all around the camp, it was pitch black in the forest, the trees placed so tightly together the moon did not peep through the tree canopies up above us. We only had the light from the small fires dotted about the campsite. All the leaders of the different peoples of Sofala was sitting around our campfire discussing tactics for the forthcoming battle with Kaunn and his army on the plains of Modecica. Master Remlin told Mr Trinity to take out the crystal globe for the last time so he could see the size of Kaunn's army. Mr Trinity removed the crystal globe from his cloak and placed it on a small piece of wood, which lay in front of him. He cast his thin bony hands over the crystal the mist in the globe began to clear to reveal Kaunn strutting up and down like a peacock in front of his army. 'How many do you estimate Mr Trinity King Gandelin said; before Mr Trinity could answer Master Remlin replied 'he has six thousand men plus five hundred of those evil Angasaurous bird like creatures! 'How many troops do you have with you Mr Trinity said Master Remlin? 'I believe we have five thousand Mr Trinity replied; 'Well we need for him to attack us first give him a bit of confidence' 'I know Kaunn' 'we have the advantage of the forest behind us. 'Tomorrow we will send just half of our men out and draw him towards the forest said Master Remlin! We all watched in the crystal globe for a few minutes till Kaunn and his army disappeared in the mist of the crystal globe. We will make our plans tonight to defeat Kaunn. 'Mr Trinity and I will take care of Kaunn our two powers together are to great for him! Master Remlin picked up a stick which had been lying on the ground and began to draw in the soft earth the plan which he wanted everyone to follow the next morning. I felt a bit sorry for Mr Trinity after all he had been in charge of this army of ours and he alone had brought us all here to this final battle with Kaunn. Then Master Remlin spoke 'that is just my plan Mr Trinity is in charge I am only here as you might say an observer; Mr Trinity spoke up; 'I think Master Remlin's plan is a good one after all he has more experience in matters of warfare then I do! 'Has any of you any more input into this plan' said Mr Trinity? King Gandelin spoke' 'I think I should send my Synisaurous birds along with their pilots and attack Kaunn's Angasaurous ugly creatures on the ground before they can take off.' That way it will leave General Giedroyc and his Tyrocdils free to attack Kaunn from the air along with King Ronough and his Fairy soldiers. 'Do you agree he said to General Giedroyc and King Ronough? General Giedroyc and King Ronough agreed with King Gandelin. Who said 'then I will attack early in the morning just before dawn and take them by surprise. 'This is the plan Mr Trinity said. 'I want your archers General Dylantos to take up their positions just behind the tree line out of sight? 'Can you Christinos' 'along with your warriors and your horses make a frontal assault. 'I do not want you to engage the enemy; 'I want you to draw them into the forest where General Dylantos and his archers will be waiting! When Christinos begins to draw Kaunn's army towards the forest' 'I want some of your soldiers King Gandelin to advance in the chariots in a flanking movement. 'As soon as they are about a hundred yards from the forest' 'they will be followed by the rest of your soldiers and General Dylantos's soldiers in a pincer like movement! General Dylantos has had a word with Hipictu 'and he will be waiting in the forest just in case any of Kaunn's men manage to get in behind us! I think you should all go and make preparations with your men for tomorrow' 'but first we should all partake of an evening meal tonight and wish everyone luck. Jemima began to give everyone a plate filled with the stew she had been cooking while everyone had been in deep conversation making the plans for the next day. Everyone tucked in as Jemima was a really good cook and the stew did really smell wonderful. We All sat their eating not saying a word just deep in thought thinking about the next day. After we had finished eating our evening meal King Gandelin asked me if I would like to join him aboard his great Migasaurous for the battle that was about to take place the next day. I looked at Mr Trinity and he said if I wanted to go with King Gandelin it would be alright to do so. I jumped at the chance it would be good to see the battle from the air I thought. Mr Trinity told me to get some rest, as I would have to leave early with King Gandelin to walk through the forest back to where his great Migasaurous would be waiting for him along with his great Synisaurous birds. I settled down into my bedroll by the fire my mind in turmoil thinking about what tomorrow might bring I fell to sleep. I don't think I had been asleep for very long when Jemima shook me by the shoulders and told me King Gandelin was ready to leave. I rubbed the sleep out of my eyes and sat for a couple of minutes to get used to the darkness all around me. The fires had gone out and I could just make out dark shadows moving about in the camp all the soldiers getting into their positions for the attack at dawn. Mr Trinity walked over to me his blue eyes shining brightly in the darkness. 'Are you ready King Gandelin is waiting for you to take you to his Migasaurous' 'it will be light in an hour no time to lose! 'Poppy one and two are going with you just to look after you in case anything should befall you! King Gandelin walked up to me 'are you ready young man? I nodded my head and he said 'come on then let's go! I jumped up brushed the leaves from my clothes and joined King Gandelin and the two Poppy twins for our walk through the forest to King Gandelin's great Migasaurous. As we walked through the forest, you could hear small dead branches falling from the trees onto the ground making you stare into the darkness, hoping you would not see anything or anyone you did not wish to see. It really was very eerie walking through that dark forest my eyes looking around and my heart thumping like a steam hammer. Eventually we left the forest and I began to calm down. We were nearing King Gandelin's great air force of Synisaurous birds along with his great Migasaurous. King Gandelin asked General Travin if everything was ready, to which the General replied 'Yes my King; 'Good said King Gandelin then let us be on our way before it gets to light. King Gandelin along with me and the two Poppy twins climbed into the basket attached to the great Migasaurous, King Gandelin gave the signal to General Travin for his great Synisaurous birds to take off and head over the forest to the plains of Modecica. The great birds ran along the field in front of the forest, one by one, they took off their great wings beating the air, causing a small draft from their wings as they flew just above our heads until they were high in the sky, circling above us waiting for King Gandelin and his great Migasaurous to join them. King Gandelin gave the pilot his orders to take off. The great bird ran along the field its great wings flapping up and down until suddenly we were in the air, and heading over the forest of Paqoun followed by King Gandelin's Synisaurous towards the plains of Modecica. On we flew over the forest; the sun was just beginning to appear on the horizon like a big red fireball. We were now over the plains of Modecica and down below in the distance I could make out Kaunn's camp. Just beyond that sat the Angasaurous tearing at bits of some animals with their great beaks they were squawking and tossing the meat into the air before they caught it and devoured each piece. We were high in the sky by this time, the great Synisaurous just gliding around making no sound, then King Gandelin gave the signal and the great Synisaurous descended out of the sky dropping like stones till they were about fifty feet above the ground. They flew on in an extended line their wings just a couple of feet apart. They had taken Kaunn's army by complete surprise. Kaunn's army were running about in panic. Kaunn was trying to summon his archers together to try to fire on the great

Synisaurous birds to bring them down. However, it was to late the Synisaurous were now upon the Angasaurous. Two hundred arrows the size of a small harpoon fired in unison, piercing the Angasaurous and pinning some of them to the ground. Others had tried to take to the air but they did not get far. The pilots on the Synisaurous had reloaded their crossbows once again and let fly with more arrows killing a few more of the Angasaurous. Some had managed to get airborne and fired on King Gandelin's great birds with their barbed arrows bringing down a few of the birds with their pilots. As they fell Kaunn's men quickly ran across, killed the pilots, and clubbed the great Synisaurous to death these were savage men. This incensed King Gandelin his face went as red as his beard. He gave the pilot the order to fly low over Kaunn's army. Down we went flying low along the ground, arrows were coming at us from all directions, some caught the Migasaurous but it did not seem to affect the great bird. By this time, we were over Kaunn's army the great Migasaurous grabbed one of Kaunn's soldiers between its great-clawed feet, the soldier was screaming and wriggling in the claws of the Migasaurous. King Gandelin who by this time had calmed down told the pilot to go up above out of the range of Kaunn's archers. We were high in the sky and I looked down at the chaos below me. King Gandelin told the pilot to release Kaunn's soldier from the grip of the Migasaurous. The pilot tugged on the reins attached to the great bird. Instantly the Migasaurous let go of Kaunn's soldier, down he fell screaming and waving his arms as if he was trying to fly. He fell into the middle of Kaunn's archers hitting the ground with a deep thud.

King Gandelin gave the signal for all of his Synisaurous to fly higher out of the range of Kaunn's archers. The Angasaurous had been dealt with they all lay on the ground dead or dying their screams filling the early morning air. General Travin blew on a horn that he kept by his side. Christinos emerged from the forest with her soldiers on horseback and began to charge Kaunn and his soldiers. By this time Kaunn had managed to gather his men in some kind of formation. His archers knelt down and released a volley of arrows towards Christinos and her soldiers, bringing down quite a few of her woman warriors. At a prearranged signal, she began to retreat towards the forest. Kaunn tried to take control of his army, who by this time were baying for blood, especially the troglodytes who were now jumping up and down their monkey faces contorted in an evil grin showing all their black rotten pointed teeth. Kaunn had lost control of his army they began to run forward chasing Christinos and the remainder of her soldiers. Some of Christinos's soldiers were trapped under their horses and helpless to the oncoming Troglodytes, who took great delight on taking on the form of its helpless victim and hacking her to death with his sword it was not a very pretty sight. By this time Christinos and her soldiers had reached the safety of the forest. The five chariots were ready with some of General Dylantos's archers on board. The horses reared up for a second and galloped out into the open taking Kaunn's men by surprise. The chariots proceeded to pick up speed down the right and left flanks of Kaunn's army. The archers released their arrows into the soldiers on either flank bringing them to the ground. General Dylantos gave the signal to the rest of his archers to release their arrows into the advancing King Todec and his warriors and the Troglodytes. A volley of arrows came out of the trees and fell into the advancing soldiers of King Todec and the Troglodytes.' I watched from up above as the rest of Mr Trinity's troops came bounding out of the forest and formed a pincer movement around Kaunn's army. Alyconeus and Encaladeus ran out of the forest with his giant Scordisi warriors the two giant dogs bounding ahead of them, it was an awesome sight these giant men running at Kaunn's army screaming and waving their swords and carrying those great spiked clubs in their right hands. Then everyone joined in the battle. King Ronough flew in and out of Kaunn's soldiers picking them off with their small swords. They were too quick and small for King Todec's soldiers as they flew in and out of the battle that was raging out on the battlefield on the plains of Modecica. Hipictu and his warriors were right in the centre of the battle stabbing with their short daggers. They had formed a circle in the centre of the battle that was raging all around they were also using their small blowpipes' with their poisoned arrows which did not kill you, they just paralysed so you could not move. After all they preferred their meat alive not dead it tasted much fresher alive then dead. The bodies were beginning to pile up on the battle field thousands of men on each side fighting for their lives. Mr Trinity signalled to General Travin up above in his Synisaurous to signal the troops to retreat back and form a large circle around the remainder of Kaunn's army. The general blew on the horn he kept by his side and Mr Trinity's troops fell back and formed a large circle around Kaunn's army. King Gandelin had landed his great Migasaurous on the field. King Gandelin the two Poppy twins and I joined Master Remlin and Mr Trinity. To avoid any more bloodshed Mr Trinity asked King Todec if he would like to surrender and go back to his homeland peacefully. The few remaining Troglodytes were dancing up and down screaming with rage and shouting for more blood, their monkey like faces contorted with hate. They began to run towards Mr Trinity and his soldiers but were quickly brought down with a volley of arrows from General Dylantos's archers. Mr Trinity asked King Todec once again if he would like to surrender. King Todec replied we do not surrender to anyone Mr Trinity.' I have waited a long time for this moment' 'you and your ancestors have made the lives of our once great people unbearable you and your Uteve people. 'Now is the time to finish what your ancestors started all those years ago.

King Todec let out a blood curdling scream he and his men began to run towards Mr Trinity and Master Remlin. They did not get far they were cut down by a volley of arrows from all the archers that surrounded them. Not everyone was killed the remainder of King Todec's troops laid down their weapons on the ground. A man strode forward his face etched with the scars from previous battles. He was a big man with long straggly grey hair matted with blood. He did not say a word he just pointed at King Todec. Mr Trinity nodded his head and the man picked up King Todec from the ground in his arms and said thank you. He then turned and walked away carrying King Todec; he was followed by what remained of King Todec's soldiers. They began to walk away back to Modecica their homeland past the bodies of their fallen soldiers. Kaunn had not escaped the battle unscathed he had been wounded and lay among the dead trying to hide from Master Remlin and Mr Trinity but that was to no avail. Master Remlin walked forward his blue eyes sparkling in the morning sun. He looked out across at all the dead lying on the battlefield from each of everyone's army, but there was no sign of Kaunn. Mr Trinity joined Master Remlin; they joined their thin bony hands together. They stood there for a few minutes looking out across the battlefield, then suddenly a body began to rise up from amongst the dead that lay strewn about the battlefield. It was Kaunn he floated towards us as if he was walking on air. He was dressed in his bright red cloak apart from a dark red patch of what looked like blood on his right shoulder. I looked on in amazement as I suppose everyone else did as well. He reached Master Remlin and Mr Trinity they lowered him to the ground so he stood in front of them. He was trying to resist but the powers of their minds together was too strong for Kaunn. 'What are we going to do with you Kaunn Master Remlin said' 'have you seen the outcome of your foolishness in trying to once again take over this world of Sofala! Kaunn just looked at Master Remlin his dark eyes peering into Master Remlin's blue eyes trying to regain some control over Master Remlin and Mr Trinity. Master Remlin and Mr Trinity did not take their eyes away from Kaunn's. 'WELL Master Remlin shouted making everyone around jump at the loudness of his voice. Kaunn spoke 'you have no right to be the ruler of Uteve that was my father's destiny' 'but you destroyed him' 'and I will destroy you! 'Your father was a traitor to the people of Uteve and you have followed in his footsteps? Master Remlin let go of Mr Trinity's hand and as he did so, Kaunn dropped to the ground and lunged towards Master Remlin producing a dagger from his cloak. But Master Remlin was too quick for him, the next thing I saw was a sword buried deep in Kaunn's chest, he fell to the ground blood oozing from the corner of his mouth, he struggled for a while and then he lay completely still all the time his bright red cloak getting darker with his blood. Master Remlin turned to all the troops and said 'it's over now we should cremate our dead and return to our homes this has been a sad occasion for everyone concerned, all through the greed of one man let us hope we can all live in peace again. Everyone turned away and began to search amongst the dead for their people. Everyone had lost quite a number of significant dead. Mr Trinity had suggested that having fought and died together that they should be cremated together. The battlefield was silent now; some of the soldiers began to remove their dead from the battlefield while others started to build a funeral pyre. Everyone had lost friends just like the last time at the battle to defeat Dr Zaker such a waste of good men. I began to shed a few tears at the sight of all the carnage that lay all around me. Christinos came up to me, put her arm around my shoulder, and squeezed it gently. 'Don't cry it's over now' 'I know it is sad,' 'but all these soldiers fought bravely and they are now with their loved ones who have gone on before them' 'they are together now. The Giant Scordisi soldiers had lain out the bodies of the soldiers who had been killed on top of the funeral pyre, side by side and head to toe, the funeral pyre was about fifty feet square. I watched as each leader of the different peoples of Sofala took a lighted torch and lit the funeral pyre, which slowly began to burn until it suddenly burst into flames. We all stood and watched as it burned the smoke from the burning pyre reaching up into the sky blocking out the sun. Master Remlin had asked some of General Dylantos's men if they would dig a grave for Kaunn which they obliged him by doing so. They pushed Kaunn's body into the open grave, Kaunn fell into the grave on his back his lifeless black eyes staring blankly into the morning sky. Master Remlin threw a small piece of cloth over his face and told the soldiers to fill in the grave. 'I do not want any marker on that grave; 'he does not deserve one; 'twice he has nearly plunged our world into darkness; 'no marker he said. He turned and walked away. He joined Mr Trinity and the rest of all the other leaders and soldiers around the funeral pyre. We stood there most of the day until the fire had gone out leaving nothing but the ashes of the soldiers. Master Remlin raised his hands and as if by magic, a great wind started to blow carrying the ashes of the dead soldiers across the plains of Modecica, casting them into the air for the wind to scatter the ashes across the world of Sofala. After a few minutes the wind subsided, all that was left was a pile of blackened timbers where the funeral pyre had been. We all turned and headed back to the forest to break camp and begin our long journey home.

Chapter Twenty-six

We entered the forest, we walked through it was as if nothing had happened, animals were grazing on the small bits of foliage scattered about the forest and birds were singing in the trees. On we walked till we reached the edge of the Green Mountains. This was where everyone was about to say goodbye and go their separate ways. We reached the base of the Green Mountains and King Gandelin said to Mr Trinity would you like to travel back with me. Mr Trinity declined his offer and said he wished to travel back with Christinos and her soldiers. King Gandelin winked at Mr Trinity and said I understand. He also asked if anyone else would like to travel back with him, but everyone wanted to stay together. King Gandelin went round shaking everyone's hand and said his goodbyes along with Generals Rol and Travin. He got into his great Migasaurous with Generals Rol and Travin and gave the signal to his great Synisaurous to swoop down and pick up the baskets with his soldiers on board to take them back to the lands of Volsci. The great birds swooped down, picked up the baskets with King Gandelin's soldiers in, and took off into the afternoon sun. King Gandelin's great Migasaurous ran along the field and took to the air circled around a couple of times before heading to where the great Synisaurous were waiting for him to join them. As they began to fly over us to cross the green Mountains I could faintly hear King Gandelin shouting don't forget to visit' 'you will always be welcome in my home goodbye! We all watched as he disappeared over into the Green Mountains leaving the rest of us down below. Everyone started back to the ships and rafts, which were waiting for to take us home. It had been a long march to get here but a few more days and I would be back at school once again. We did not stop until we reached the plains of Tongees where all the rafts and ships were waiting at the water's edge. It was a great relief to be here at last and all in one piece I was quite relieved to be here. Much to my surprise Master Remlin had brought thirty ships with him to take us back to the lands of the Gawen peoples, which was General Dylantos's domain. Master Remlin had somehow brought the rafts back from the edge of the plains of Tongees where we had left them at the base of the green mountains. Master Remlin's plan was to tow the rafts back across the inland sea to General Dylantos's village, where everyone who was left would say their last goodbyes. How he had brought the rafts across the desert back to the inland sea I did not want to ask as he could do some strange things with the power of his mind but they were here and that is all that mattered.

Hipictu had arrived before us with his prisoners to take back to the forest of Parek as they preferred their meat fresh. He did not say anything he just boarded his great canoe and set sail for home. Master Remlin's sailors had everything ready the ships were lying at anchor with the rafts fixed behind them with long towropes. It was time to leave this desert behind us all the soldiers boarded the ships, Alyconeus and Encaladeus along with his soldiers boarded the rafts one ship was used for Christinos and her horses and some of her soldiers the rest were spread out onto the other ships along with General Dylantos and his soldiers. King Ronough and his Fairy soldiers did not take up much room as they were only small and General Giedroyc's Tyrocdils said they would fly on ahead of us to tell General Dylantos's people we were on our way back. General Dylantos had told General Giedroyc to tell them to prepare a feast for us when we arrived back. We set sail that evening it was a bright clear moonlit night with the heavens dotted with thousands of stars. I was so pleased to be going home and I wondered if I had been missed. The next two days passed by uneventfully the weather had been good I had actually been able to sunbathe without the thought of being attacked by those evil Angasaurous creatures. I was sitting enjoying the sun when the lookout shouted from the masthead, 'land ho and he pointed just of the starboard bow, it was the island of Siphonos the home of Fairy Nough. King Ronough joined Mr Trinity and Master Remlin along with his daughter Fairy Nough, to say their goodbyes to Master Remlin and Mr Trinity. Fairy Nough hovered in front of me and stroked my face then kissed me on the cheek. 'I hope we meet again one day John' 'you are a good friend and I will always remember you. She said her goodbyes to everyone and with her father and his soldiers; they flew off back to the island of Siphonos where their families were waiting to greet them.

The ships headed for General Dylantos's village and dropped anchor just at the edge of the village, everyone was out cheering General Dylantos and his returning soldiers. Master Remlin told the sailors of all the ships to lower their gangplanks into the water for the soldiers to disembark. No sooner had the gangplanks been lowered then the soldiers ran down the gangplank into the shallow sea and waded ashore to greet their loved ones, but I could not help thinking to myself there would be sadness as well as happiness in the village tonight. After everyone had left the ships and rafts, Master Remlin got the captains of his ships together and told them to sail back to Uteve and to leave just one ship behind which was the ship of Captain Rogas. He had told Captain Raza to take Captain Thor Black to his homeland and then go back to Uteve. That night a great feast was laid on to celebrate our victory over Kaunn and his army, even Hipictu was there with his men offering meat to some of General Dylantos's soldiers who took it from him not wanting to upset him in anyway whatsoever. But of course when he was not looking it suddenly disappeared into one of the fires that were dotted about the village. Everybody sang and danced into the early morn celebrating their return home. As dawn broke, Master Remlin said it was time to leave and to say my goodbyes to everyone. I went round and said my goodbyes, Christinos hugged me Alyconeus ruffled my hair and General Dylantos gave me a small leather waistcoat, which one of his men had made for him to give to me. Hipictu strode forward and presented me with a necklace made of what looked like teeth, but Mr Trinity said not to worry they were the tooth's of animals that roamed the forest of Parek. I was quite relieved they were not human teeth; Christinos also gave me a gold ring from her little finger for me to wear on my small little finger. 'That is for you to remember me by and the adventures you have had with us' 'wear it always it will bring you good fortune. It was now time to leave Master Remlin Mr Trinity and me along with the two Poppy twins and Jemima got into a small rowing boat, which General Dylantos had supplied to take us out to our ship. We walked up the gangplank and Master Remlin gave Captain Rogas the orders to set sail for the homelands of Uteve. I watched as our ship began to sail away all the time watching everybody waving at us from the water's edge until everyone disappeared on the horizon. I wondered if I would ever see any of my friends again. On we sailed until we saw the lands of Uteve, we sailed up the river past the houses with everybody standing on their balcony's waving at us as we passed by. It was good to be back but I missed the excitement of all the days that had gone by. We docked to a multitude of people on the quayside shouting waving flags and cheering. Master Remlin acknowledged everyone and along with Mr Trinity the two Poppy twins Jemima and me we descended the gangplank. We walked through the cheering crowd to the palace of Uteve where I was to rest for the night before I had to go back to the school, which I was not looking forward to at all. I had made so many goods friends and lost some as well, but this world of Sofala was much better then where I had come from.

Later that evening I settled down with Master Remlin along with Mr Trinity for my last meal before I would have to leave the next morning, in a way I was privileged to be going back with Mr Trinity, for this time he was going to show me the way back. After my meal we sat and talked for a while then Master Remlin said I should retire for the evening before my journey the next day. I really did not want to sleep but I retired to my bed and lay down on the soft pillows and wondered if I would ever come back to this world of Sofala again and meet all the friends I had made both times I had been here.

I fell asleep and the next thing I knew was Jemima waking me up saying it was time to go. I jumped out of bed and headed for the room where Mr Trinity was waiting with Master Remlin. 'Ah good morning young John did you sleep well; said Master Remlin' 'yes thank you I replied! 'Good,' then follow me. Mr Trinity and I followed Master Remlin into a small round darkened room with no windows; the only light in the room came from a small round opening in the roof. Mr Trinity said to me; 'hold my hand' I did as he said he began to recite some strange incantation, the light up above us that shone down from the opening at the top of the room began to dim, till we were in total darkness. I held on tight to Mr Trinity as we began to spin and rise up towards the dark opening up above us. My head was spinning I did not know where I was faster and faster I rose spinning around in circles. I thought my head was going to burst. Suddenly I saw a bright light closer and closer it got when all of a sudden we burst through the light. I was standing alongside Mr Trinity on the glass mirror that lay on the floor of his cottage back in the school grounds. We both stepped off the mirror and the carpet in the room that had covered the glass mirror, as if by magic moved from across the room and covered the mirror also the table went back to its original place over the carpet. Hurry back to your dormitory before you are missed. 'But tell me before I go I have been in your world for quite a while; 'so how come I have only been away for one night from my world! 'You have not' 'let's say it's all down to mind control said Mr Trinity but that is something I will teach you' 'now go before everyone wakes up and you are missed. I left Mr Trinity's cottage and headed back to the dormitory sliding the door gently so as not to wake anyone. Anyway they would not believe me if they had asked me where I had been so early in the morning. I gently closed the door and tiptoed to my bed. I removed my clothes put on my pyjamas and settled down into my bed, it really felt good wrapped in my blankets so cosy and warm, but there was still a lot of things I did not understand about Mr Trinity but I knew he would teach me everything I needed to know. The years went by seven years to be exact. Mr Trinity taught us everything we had to know about mind control, but I was the only one who knew how to travel between my world and the world of Sofala. Mr Trinity had taught me in secret away from all the other boys. I remember the day that Mr Trinity left, he gathered everyone into the classroom, and told us that the school was closing. We had learnt everything we needed to know and now we were all about to go home and put to good use what he had taught all of us boys. Everyone left the classroom feeling rather sad that Mr Trinity was leaving for the last time. As I got up from my seat Mr Trinity called me back, he put a key into my hand with a piece of parchment. 'This is the key and title deeds to my cottage and the surrounding gardens; 'I want you to have them it is a gift from me! Mr Trinity said; 'you have been a good pupil and I have no use for them anymore. I took the key and deeds from Mr Trinity and placed them in my pocket. It was with great sadness that he had to leave but he had come to do what he had to. We said our goodbyes Mr Trinity hugged me for the last time turned round and disappeared through the classroom door. As the years went by all of us boys that had been to the school went on to do great things, some became surgeon's judges and high ranking politicians, everyone went into professions that did good as Mr Trinity said we should do. 'And me; 'I became a mind reader showing off my skills that Mr Trinity had taught me to audiences throughout the world. I also helped the police with cases they could not solve! They could not understand how I was always successful in every one they gave me bringing evil people to justice. Mr Trinity had taught me well. The school was demolished, and I bought the surrounding land around it so I had privacy. When I had the spare time, I would often travel to the world of Sofala through the glass mirror and travel around meeting my old friends again. And one day I would disappear and everyone would wonder where I had gone, I would be in Sofala with my friends where I was happy and truly wanted to be. Mr Trinity had married Christinos at last and they had two fine sons, not at all like Mr Trinity, they took their looks from Christinos. I was glad Mr Trinity had found happiness at last. Sutherland and I remained good friends, but he still could not remember our first adventure together with Mr Trinity. He would help me in my detective work solving case after case, maybe one day I would take him to the world of Sofala and it might bring back to him that great adventure when Mr Trinity's great army defeated the evil Dr Zaker. 'And me one day I would pass my powers onto my son after I had finished my work with the police force so he could carry on the work I had started bringing criminals to justice. Then one day I would disappear to the world of Sofala but for now I was happy visiting my friends there. And when the time came for me to go only my family would know where I had gone everyone else would be left wondering where John Trinity had gone I would be in Sofala with my friends where I was truly happy and always wanted to be but until then I had other adventures, after all a detective's work is never done.

THE END

Lightning Source UK Ltd.
Milton Keynes UK
UKOW02f2304020615

252794UK00001B/4/P